For Vera & Lena,
God be with you,
Stephen
3/6/01

PLEROMA
PRESS

# SALE DAY

## A Novel

Stephen Sturlaugson

This is a work of fiction. Names, characters, places, and incidents are the product of the writer's imagination, or are used fictiticiously. Any resemblance to events or persons, living or dead, is entirely coincidental.

© 2001 by Stephen Sturlaugson

All right reserved. No part of this book may be reproduced or transmitted in any form or by any means, electronic or mechanical, including photocopying, recording, or by any information storage device and retrieval system, without permission in writing from the Publisher.

Pleroma Press and Publishing Service
5645 73rd St SW
Carson, ND 58529

http://www.pleromapress.com

ISBN: 0-9636834-1-1

First printing: February 2001

10 9 8 7 6 5 4 3 2 1

Printed in the United States of America
by United Printing Inc, Bismarck, North Dakota

To Wanda

and my children

# Contents

Part One ..... 1

One: Specifications ..... 3

Two: Design ..... 28

Three: Coding ..... 63

Four: Debugging ..... 96

Part Two ..... 123

Five: Testing ..... 125

Six: Documentation ..... 158

Seven: Rest ..... 211

You have been weighed on the scales.
—Daniel 5.27

# SALE DAY

## Part One

EVERY THURSDAY is sale day at the livestock auction in Littleton, South Dakota. Not absolutely every Thursday without exception, of course, Stan thought. It's every other Thursday in slow seasons, unless Thursday happens to fall on a holiday. Certain holidays, anyway.

He knew he gave the auction's schedule more thought than it deserved, but he was prone to examine patterns and exceptions to the patterns, and patterns that might emerge from the exceptions. He wrote computer software. He had written the software for the auction's computer network.

On this day, after a year of trips to Littleton, he knocked on the metal door of the main entrance to the auction and nobody answered. Wasn't anybody here? The door was locked and he didn't have the key. It's Thursday, isn't it, he thought. Nine o'clock in the morning, two hours past opening, and not even a dog in sight.

He had driven all the way from his farmstead in North Dakota for this.

He walked to his pickup, climbed in, and sat in morning light lying flat on the vacant parking lot. The words *Littleton Livestock* painted across the side of the building in bold black letters three feet high addressed nobody but him.

Then he realized it was the 4th of July.

He let his forehead rest on the steering wheel. The auction's commercials on radio, the free ball-point pens, the imprinted baseball caps and jackets the owner and his relatives wore, and the Hereford calendars they gave out as gifts at the end of the year—all said Thursday.

He looked up, then wiped aside a skin of dust on the inside of the windshield.

Once he was on the road home, buttes would rise, ashen and striped as any in the Badlands, and rivers would glisten as they did on the drive down, and he would endure the recriminations of Mike (and his own self-recrimination) for not even knowing what day it was, now that the holiday had hit him.

This was the day Rose, his infant daughter, was originally scheduled to be born.

Try to be cheerful, he told himself. You just glide through the return trip and greet your wife and sons and daughter, the family you abandoned in their sleep, because by now they are wide awake to Independence Day in North Dakota, wondering where you are.

Chapter One: Specifications

STAN SHIFTED in a chair in Mike's office, facing the desk, while Mike talked on the telephone. Stan had often waited like this, feeling intrusive, while Mike did business over the phone. Mike didn't seem to mind, and Stan felt it would be wrong to get up and leave.

On a corner of the desk, in a plastic frame, was a photo Stan hadn't seen before. Mike was stooping slightly, six foot six, in what looked like a crush of black-haired children, smiling, extending a hand. Stan picked up the picture. The children, on closer look, were Oriental executives in business suits. Mike, who usually wore blue jeans and a flannel shirt, also was in a suit. He had been photographed in the act of bowing.

Mike hung up and said, "So how's the Southwest's premier computer consultant?"

Stan tried to sound casual under the forty-gun salutes of Mike's flattery. "I'm fine."

"You should be. Listen, how would you like to install two more networks? I'm talking maintenance agreements, custom hardware possibly."

"Lumberyards?" Stan asked. He had installed a network for a friend of Mike's, a lumberyard owner in Bismarck, and certain hardware problems arose that had been resolved, though several remained.

"No, no, no," Mike said. "Auction markets. Livestock auction markets in South Dakota—Littleton and

Piper. I shipped them ten loads of calves last year, and the owner hasn't stopped talking about it yet. We're discussing my hogs now. He wants to automate his operation, and I told him I knew an expert who could put it together for him."

"Sure," Stan said. "What's his name?"

"Spare yourself the details at this point," Mike said, then added, "Owen Yuler."

"At what point?"

"Of our business plan. We're going to put this deal together. Little Mr. Yuler will buy whatever I tell him to."

Mike loved to talk business and Stan liked to listen. He had been stopping in at Mike's office whenever he came into Mandan for supplies. Both, each in his own way, worked with computers. Mike had been a financial officer for a Silicon-Valley computer-chip company that had managed to succeed on an initial investment of six million dollars, at a time when industry analysts thought such a venture would require a hundred million. This had established Mike's reputation. He left the company a rich man, and was earning most of his money now as a consultant, developing business plans for high-tech companies in Japan and Korea. Each plan, if successfully set in place, might make Mike millions. He also helped clients through bankruptcy. I make money coming and going, he had said.

Stan noticed smudges on the picture frame, and buffed it clean on his sleeve. He had taught computer science in a state college but decided to start his own business. Complicating this was a desire to live in the country. He had run ads in *The Bismarck Tribune* and *The Mandan News*, and approached businesses in both cities, but there didn't seem to be enough interest in computers, even among accounting firms, to support the

# SALE DAY

idea. He wondered how computer stores in the capital were making it. From the looks of it, many weren't. There was quite a turnover. He had tried filling toner cartridges for copying machines, a messy task, but that brought in even less, and at the moment he felt stalled.

He returned the picture to the corner of the desk.

"Mr. Big Westerner."

"Absolutely!" Mike smiled in appreciation of himself.

"So you line things up with Mr. Yuler, and I'll install the networks? Is that it?"

"Let's put it another way. I'll lure the bear into the cabin, you butcher it, and I'll sell the meat." He was grinning at this, teeth as perfect as new dentures, and Stan grinned back; he wasn't sure what it meant. "You're not uncomfortable with the arrangement, are you?"

"No, not as I hear it," Stan said.

"Go down to Littleton, and figure out their systems needs. Don't go down on a Thursday. There's a sale every Thursday. Get down there and find out what we can sell them. I'll call Yuler tonight. Can you go this week? How about tomorrow?"

"Tomorrow's not Thursday."

"Okay, tomorrow then. At eight o'clock?"

"How far is Littleton from here?"

"From here, eighty minutes." Mike was a native of North Dakota, but after years in California he still spoke of distances in terms of minutes, not miles. "Sixty in my Jimmy." He picked up a sheet of paper and gave it a quick look. "You drive a Jimmy, Stan."

"It's a Ramcharger. There's also a time change, isn't there, from Mountain to Central? For me, I mean."

"Huh?" Mike said, looking up from the paper. "A time change? Right."

Stan saw Mike's mind was obviously elsewhere. "Make it nine then," he said.

"Good, I'll tell him." Mike picked up the phone, then set it down. "Honey?" He called to his wife, Candy, who was sitting at a desk in an adjoining office, visible to Stan through a plate-glass divider built into the wall between their offices. She was leafing through papers, head down, face hidden behind blonde hair. "Honey," Mike repeated. "Get Amerigro on the phone. I want to talk to them about our siderolls."

Siderolls, Stan had learned from Mike's phone conversations, were essential to Mike's irrigation system along the Heart River. He irrigated corn, and alfalfa for hay. He said it took eighty gallons of water to produce an ear of corn. He was an accountant, a number cruncher, a bean (or corn) counter. He calculated billions of kernels of corn: so many kernels to an ear, so many ears to a plant, so many plants to a row, so many rows to an acre. He owned twenty sections of land, twenty square miles, over twelve thousand acres, and poured the profits of high technology into every square inch of it.

And I rent twenty acres, Stan thought. As work on the call to Amerigro continued, he got up and went to the door. He turned and saw Mike and Candy in their separate offices talking to each other on the phone, as if in prison visitation. Toodle-ooo, he thought of saying, as his wife Grace might say to the children, and then wondered if Mike and Candy slept in the same bed.

"DO YOU WANT to try this song again?" Grace said, clearing her sonorous throat. "Or another?"

She reached out to Stan beside her on the couch in their living room, and ran her fingers through his hair. Hers was like wire. He had failed to check his pickup's fuel gauge after leaving Mike's office, and had run out of gas south of Mandan. A stranger had stopped to help and now, well, now it was near sunset. Their sons—Vernon, the oldest, who was seven years old; Lee, who was five; and three-year-old Dale—had been tucked into bed before he arrived home. Why do things like this always happen to me, he wondered.

Stan thought of telling her, *Put me to sleep*, then thought better of it. His dad, a veterinarian, put dogs to sleep—a term for euthanasia. Grace disliked comments of this sort applied to people. So he said, "Tuck me in, Grace." A double-entendre he felt she wouldn't mind.

"Honey?" she said. She was a lyric soprano with pitch so near perfect her voice often reduced him to tears. She had an identical-twin sister, Jean, whose voice was similar, and there were times, as the sisters sang in unison, when their separate voices seemed to merge into one flawless voice with stereophonic overtones. In their senior year of college, she played the role of Suzanna in a production of *The Marriage of Figaro*. Stan was drawn to every performance. She said she sang the love songs for him. Her voice had a brilliance all her own, he thought, and had mellowed with age. "Please? Just one more time."

"Okay, but this goddamn guitar! The strings feel like knives! Look at these—" He was about to say pussy fingers, but thought better of that, too.

"I know. Here." She took his hand in hers and kissed each enflamed fingertip. "How's that?"

"Much better," he said, fingering the guitar. "So, one more time?"

"If you're game," she said, clearing her throat again.

"You mean 'gamy.'"

"I do not."

"As in 'monogamy,'" he said.

"Well *then*." She passed her hand through his hair again. "This is fun. It's been too long. Let's go over 'All my springs of joy are in you,' then take it from the top."

Giggles. Stan glanced up at an air register in the ceiling that opened into the older boys' bedroom. "I can see you," Dale, the three-year-old, said. Stan couldn't see him. Whispers, then giggles again.

"You silly guys. Get into bed," Stan said. A rumble of footsteps overhead indicated their swift response, and his sore mood lifted with it. "*And does it not seem hard to you, when all the sky is clear and blue.*" As he spoke, he heard his mother's voice speaking in his.

"*And I should like so much to play, to have to go to bed by day?*" Grace said, completing Stevenson's verse. "They missed your reading to them you tonight. I gave them a music lesson instead."

After supper, after the dishes were washed and put away, the family would gather in the living room until bedtime, and sing, or read the Bible, or Shakespeare, some parts of which they would enact. The mechanicals' play about Pyramus and Thisbe in *A Midsummer Night's Dream* was a favorite, especially Snout's part, which they all begged to play, hopping in excitement about Stan's knees:

> *In this same interlude it doth befall*
> *That I, one Snout by name, present a wall*

That a guy named Snout would play a wall, that a wall would talk and tell the audience he was named Snout and played a wall—none of this was lost on the boys. Each would represent a wall, standing rigid, arm outstretched, making an O with a hand, while the others waited for their favorite lines:

> *And such a wall as I would have you think*
> *That had in it a crannied hole or chink*

These they all had memorized, even Dale had. Vernon and Lee would glance at each other, breathless, then gaze at Dale, anticipating the moment when their brother would say *quannied*, then they would whoop, and Dale would finish by peering through his fingers, one eye closed tight:

> *Lew which the lovews Pywamus and Lisbe*
> *Did whispew, often, vewy secwétly.*

"Good night, boys! I love you," Stan shouted. Loud enough, he thought, for them to hear through the chink in the ceiling. Had he heard a reply? He couldn't be sure.

"Do we have any recent photographs of the boys and me?" he asked Grace.

"If we do, they're packed away in the basement. Why?"

"I thought it'd be nice to have one—the boys at this age."

"You're always the one taking the pictures, so I don't know if we do. None since we moved here, I know that."

"I'll have to remember to take one," Stan said.

"*I'll* have to remember," Grace said, before he corrected himself.

HE SAW HER dark hair above a counter when he entered the lobby and walked across the room to a reception window, but she didn't move. He stepped up, holding a briefcase, to a chest-high counter of a window identified above by a wooden plaque that read *SELLERS* in black. Over the window to the left another plaque read *BUYERS*. He had positioned himself as a seller.

Below him, the woman sat at a desk, bent over its white top, a blank ledger open before her. Was she thinking, perhaps sleeping? She didn't seem to realize he was watching her. "Excuse me." Stan's voice cracked as he spoke. "I'm here to talk to Mr. Yuler about computers."

The woman looked up, surprised, then stood, smoothing her blouse.

"I'm Stan Thorlofson. Mike Becker was supposed to have called to arrange it." A clock in the office read ten to nine.

"Yes, yes, he did," she said, blushing as if she'd been caught taking a nap. "But I'm afraid Owen's not here. He's out looking at cattle, sixty miles away. He told me to tell you to wait."

"I see." *Why*, he wondered, but didn't complete the thought. He set his briefcase down, turned from the window, and saw a sunken black leather couch in the lobby. After a restless night, fearing he would oversleep, he woke woozy at three and finally decided to get up. He turned back to the woman. "Is there anybody else I can talk to?"

"About computers? I suppose you can talk to me. I'm Sharon. Bookkeeper, office manager, all around slave—you name it, ha!" She held out her hand, which he shook through the window. "You'd make a good Indian. The way you sneak up."

"I'm sorry I startled you. I didn't mean to." He set the briefcase on the counter, opened it, and took out a tablet and a pen. "What I'd like to know to begin with," he began, "is what you produce, that is, what *documents* you produce, on the day of a sale." The word seemed to him pretentious in that setting.

"Me? I make out the market report."

"A market report would be one," he said, jotting it down. "I didn't mean you personally, of course, but the market as a whole, including any and all pieces of paper

## SALE DAY

that might go out of the office." *Pieces of paper* sounded stupid, he thought. Condescending. "I don't mean candy wrappers."

She stuck her tongue out and snapped the gum she was chewing. "Like settlements."

Only then did he notice wrapped sticks of gum and gum wrappers on the desk. "Settlements?" The word rattled out.

"Vouchers, or checks, to the sellers. We also issue invoices and recaps to the buyers. And, of course, there are market reports. Is that what you mean?"

"Sounds like it," he said, writing these down. "Checks, invoices, and—recaps?"

"Recapitulations or buyer summaries."

"Do you have anything I could look at? Used copies maybe."

"Sure. Why don't you come in and I'll show you."

He entered the office, feeling her invitation zipped away some wall separating them but resisted checking his fly. Luckily as he felt later, the phone rang, and Sharon picked it up. "Littleton Livestock. This is Sharon. How may I help you?" She placed a hand over the receiver. "It's Owen. He has a mobile unit in his pickup."

Whew, Stan thought, then Nice. His dad, the veterinarian, had a mobile unit in his pickup. Mike had one. So did Jack, the lumberyard's owner. Cellular? Stan couldn't justify the expense. He wasn't on the road that much. He'd end up calling Grace merely to establish a line over which lovers might whisper. A phone would be nice in the winter, though, he thought, if you had car trouble. When he arrived in Littleton that morning, he had driven to a gas station and filled up first thing.

"He's right here," Sharon said, handing the receiver to Stan. "He wants to talk to you."

"Hello Stan, how you doin', buddy?" the voice on the phone said. "Say, I'll be in in an hour. Will you wait for me? Wait for me, why don't you. I'll be in shortly, and we talk can about those computers. I'd like to get a new one for my home, too, and tap into the information in the office. Suppose I could do that?"

"Sure," Stan said. "Eventually."

"Good. Mike says you're an expert, is that true? How's Mike?"

"He's fine." Like Mike, Mr. Yuler rattled off more questions than Stan cared to answer. Like Grace, he thought. He made it a practice with her to answer one.

"Listen, would ya put Sharon back on?"

Stan turned the phone over to her.

"Yes," she said, glaring at Stan. "I'll tell him... Okay, I'll tell him... Sure, I'll call him... Don't worry... Okay. All right. Goodbye, Owen. Goodbye!" She slammed the phone down on its cradle.

"Tell me what?"

"Oh, nothing. I'm supposed to call a packer in Nebraska, a buyer in South Dakota, a seller in Montana, and scrape the shit off some trucker's boots when he pulls in this afternoon. Good God, Owen! God!" Quick as the fury appeared, it vanished. She wore cowboy boots, blue jeans, a light western-cut blouse, and didn't seem angry at all. "Here's a settlement voucher, an invoice," she said, collecting papers from the desk. "A check-in ticket, and a market report."

"It's a start," he said.

"I'll make you photocopies," she said, walking past him. "What am I thinking? You can have these." She turned at the door, and handed the papers to him.

A weight-ticket printer was in the office. "In for homemade repairs," she said. Dry, peeling duct tape held the thing together. "You slide the scale ticket in here," she said, placing a used ticket in the printer. "And the printer prints the time and date, the kind of animal—bull or whatever." She handed him the ticket, and pointed things out as she spoke. "The head, total weight, average weight, the money (by the head or hundredweight) and the total price." He saw that *cwt.* was short for hundredweight.

"A dozen keys enter all this information?" he said.

"Yup. The weight, of course, comes from the scale in the floor."

"And this handwriting?"

"The weigher writes down the seller's name, the buyer's, the buyer's pen number, his own initials, and sometimes a note like 'crippled' or whatever. That ticket is the legal proof of a sale."

The ticket was a four-part document, with parts for the buyer, the seller, the yardmen, and the auction.

"I see the printer comes from a company called Barskills," he said.

"It's junk. They never come out. And Robert Bar's an ass."

Her remark startled him, then he asked, "Who operates it?"

"The printer? A weigher."

"Does Owen?"

"Work the printer? Owen?" she asked, raising her voice. "Not on your life!"

"He's the auctioneer."

"Sometimes. He usually just stands around eating and telling jokes. We hire several auctioneers."

"Mike Becker says he sold a lot of calves here last year."

"The biggest single sale ever. There's a picture of Owen and Mike commemorating the day hanging over the couch in the lobby." Wouldn't you know, Stan thought. "And you're working with him," Sharon said. "Is Mike an old smoothie or what?"

He didn't answer. He didn't know what she meant. "What sort of photocopier to you have?" he asked instead, arranging the documents in his open briefcase.

"A piece of junk. One of those old thermal jobs. You can barely read what it puts out." Stan said nothing more. "Why?"

"I refill toner cartridges," he said, thinking Littleton Livestock was, in terms of its equipment, a generation behind. His dad had used a thermal copier. Stan could still see its curling, wax-paper-like output, and his nose twitched remembering its peculiar burnt smell.

"Are you going to Montrose?" Sharon asked him.

"Montrose?"

"Yeah. The auction in Montrose. They just got a computer, and the girls there think it's great. I can't wait to find out. It's about time we did something around here to spruce the place up." She drummed her fingers on the printer, entering a private realm of thought as far away as her demanding boss.

"Where were we?" she asked and turned to him, her eyes glazed.

A HALL outside the office led him through double swinging doors, past bleachers towering on both sides of him, to the painted metal bars and posts that traced out the perimeter of a rectangular pen six feet high—the auction block.

He opened a gate to the pen, and passed into the center of what felt like a cage. The gate closed on its own with an echoing clang. The clean-swept concrete floor was weight-sensitive; the platform of a balance scale wavered under his feet. The voluminous room felt cooler than the August outdoors and smelled of wood shavings and cattle. He looked up into a booth where a microphone lay on a ledge. The cattle yards out back were quiet. His memory of the sales ring was a boy's. As a boy, he would try to follow his dad, the vet, through a crowd of farmers on sale day, and would fall far behind and lose sight of him. His dad worked in the yards, and Stan would step with care along vacant alleyways slick with manure, peering through slats of pens higher than he could see over. The close face of a bewildered cow once startled him. He would locate his dad by his voice. *Whoa, girl,* he would hear him say. His dad would be pregnancy testing heifers or bangs vaccinating cows—a memory more of words than of acts, and Stan would assist in some small way, holding a syringe or a bottle. Of the activity out in the ring, the clearest memory he had was of sounds—the bellowing of cattle, the clang of gates, the ringing voices of men. He could still feel the ringing in his ears, he thought. His dad was "Doc", or the Doc, and he was Doc's boy.

Near the front of the booth in Littleton Livestock were levers connected to hydraulic hoses running along the wall to doors where cattle entered and exited the block. An electronic scoreboard hung over the booth, with the words *Head, Weight,* and *Average* printed above arrays of bulbs that displayed numerals when lit. Grace, who was a math whiz, insisted on speaking of numerals when numerals were in view. The number two is a concept, she'd say, whereas a numeral is the concept's representation, as in *two* or *2* or *II*. You can't see a concept, she'd say; you see a number's representation. Numerals were, in this sense, the only things *in view.* And on Littleton's scoreboard, at that moment unlit, there weren't any. He had been imagining them.

He turned toward the bleachers, where buyers and sellers would loom, and the rake of the seats and the unsettling floor brought on a sudden chill. On the block, behind metal bars, animals were caged, weighed, and appraised. He wasn't in the back with his dad anymore. Now there were computers and that was his baby. He realized that, while talking with Mike, he had imagined dollar signs glimmering red as if branded on the air. An old smoothie or what? Sharon had asked.

"Stan Thorlofson, please come to the office. Stan Thorlofson." It was her voice over the PA. Her summons startled him. There's a chink in the armor, he thought, and cursed.

A NEW HOUSE, three blocks south of the auction, had gray steel siding and an etched-glass storm door with brass hardware. Stan pressed the doorbell and waited. A dusty Chevy S-10 Blazer was parked in the driveway, the words *Littleton Livestock Auction* painted across the hood's plastic bug deflector. He shifted his scuffed briefcase from one hand to the other, and rang the bell again.

A boy opened the door and said, "Are you Stan?"

"Yes I am. You must Owen's son, or one of them." The boy looked about Vernon's age, seven.

"I'm Rick, and I only have a sister. But her and my mom are gone."

"Your mother and sister are gone?" he asked, wondering if the boy meant something dire.

"Yeah, they went over to Mobridge to see my aunt."

Stan stepped into the entry, a quadrant of linoleum where the door swung. The rooms within were covered with light-gray wall-to-wall carpeting. The interior of the house was split-level with a living room, dining room, and kitchen on a level with the entry. To the right, carpeted steps led up—to the bedrooms, he thought—and others dropped into the basement. The rooms were immaculate. The weather-beaten house he rented had floors of worn fir that sent splinters into your feet if you weren't careful. One splinter had gone so deep into the flesh of the foot of his oldest son that Stan had to use pliers to pull it out. The boy didn't even flinch. Their downstairs was carpeted with remnants, different colors in every room.

"Do you work with computers?" the boy asked.
"Yes I do. Do you?"
"We do at school, and my dad has one."
"Stan, is that you?" A shout from downstairs. "Rick, bring him on down like I told you."
"My dad's downstairs. Come on, I'll show you."

Stan followed Rick downstairs into a family room where the boy flopped into an easy chair and put his hand into a bag of potato chips. A television was on in one corner.

Through a doorway Stan saw Owen Yuler standing at a desk in another room, threading computer paper into a printer. Little Mr. Yuler, as Mike called him, was shorter than Stan had pictured (five feet?) and chubby. Stan entered the room. On a desk were an IBM XT, a green monochrome monitor, a printer, a phone, an external modem, and a baseball cap that read *Littleton Livestock. The Thursday Sale.*

"Is this a good printer?" Mr. Yuler asked him.

Stan glanced at it, surprised by Owen's disarming manner. "Sure, it's a good brand. I'm Stan Thorlofson."

"Scandahuvian?"

"No. Icelandic."

"Owen Yuler. Pleased to meet you," Owen said, extending a hand.

"Same here," Stan said, offering his, making first contact. "I hope—"

"Have you seen this trip software?" Owen said, interrupting him. "Pull up a chair, why don't you." He motioned to a chair. "I'll show you how it works." He typed in *Omaha* as a city of origin and *Littleton* as a destination, and the program displayed a route between Omaha and Littleton—highways, junctions, and mileage. Software of the sort was familiar to Stan. "Let's see if the printer works. Pretty nice, huh? Look at this," Owen said, pointing to the scrolling output. "Truckers call in and I can tell them which way to come. You seen Xtree?"

"Your XT has Xtree?"

"Huh?" Owen said, as if he hadn't expected Stan to joke with him. "So you know all about it."

"I used it at the college where I taught."

"You taught at a college? Why'd you quit?"

"It's a long story."

"Say, I bought this software. First Works it's called." Owen picked up a manual and held it out to him. "You know anything about that?"

"Yes, I use it myself," Stan said, taking the manual from Owen without much interest.

"I was setting up a database, you know, but I couldn't get the bugger to work. Wanna take a look?"

"About the auction software. You—"

"Oh! There are some papers here that will show you everything I want. Now where are they?" He opened and shut several drawers in the desk, then pulled out some papers and handed them to Stan. "You oughta go to Montrose. They just installed a system there—this very one," he said, pointing to the papers. "They think it's the greatest thing in the world. Of course, for forty thousand dollars—"

So that's what they're selling for, Stan thought. He was stunned.

"You wouldn't want forty grand now would you?"

"Mike and I haven't gotten that far, but I don't suppose—" Stan trailed off. Maybe I could get a new pickup, he thought. With a phone. "So you're working with Mike. That guy's into everything, isn't he?"

"Mike's managing the business side, and I'm handling the technical."

"Well, Mike's quite a guy to my way of thinking. You know he sold ten loads of calves here just last year. I've got a picture of him and me to prove it. Over two hundred thousand pounds. Calves were selling for ninety-four, ninety-five cents a pound at the time."

"And your commission?"

"Starts at one-and-a-half percent. Same as now."

Three thousand dollars, Stan estimated. No wonder he's impressed.

"I hear Mike invented a computer chip," Owen said. "And that's how he made all his money. Is that true?"

"No, he didn't invent a chip. He was on the financial end of things. Same as now."

Owen looked at his wristwatch. "Oh shoot! Excuse me, would ya? I gotta make a call." He left the room and said, "Turn that thing off and scoot! Rick, I said turn that thing *off!* And leave the chips here." The TV went dead. Muffled footsteps bounded up the carpeted stairs.

What would businessmen do without telephones, Stan wondered. He had suggested to Grace that they do without theirs—to save money—but she wanted a phone for emergencies. For business it seemed a necessity.

He located Owen's database. It included the names and phone numbers of buyers and sellers, the kind of cattle bought or sold, and the months of the year in which a client would buy or sell in Littleton. He saw the program's potential for linking buyers to sellers. He also noticed that Owen had mislabeled the names of the fields, and he corrected them. Charge him for this, he wondered. How could he? It had taken less than a minute to fix. He'd just met the guy! Stan typed in his own name and phone number. If I can sell the system, maybe I can buy some cattle, he thought. Grace and the boys were more interested in sheep. Their small size was a factor.

He started the trip software again and located Mandan and Littleton. A single road connected them, but the highway number changed at the border between the Dakotas. The number wasn't something you do math with, but a numeric label. Something to mention to the boys.

"Absolutely," he overheard Owen say, speaking through a mouthful of chips. "You don't have to tell me cattle prices are good! They've been good for five, six years now. I just know it's gotta break one of these days but I honestly don't think any day soon."

Stan put the papers Owen had given him into his briefcase, and went into the family room. Owen was in the easy chair, the phone's receiver cocked up to an ear, a hand in the bag of chips. Stan waved to him.

"Just a minute, okay?" Owen said, closing a hand over the receiver. "How you doin', buddy?"

"Your database is ready. I corrected the field names."

"Well I'll be. That's great."

"Sharon gave me several documents. She was a big help."

"She's one in a million. Don't tell her I said that," Owen said, extending the bag of chips. "Here take one. Take a handful."

"No thank you."

"Rick," Owen shouted. "Rick!" The boy appeared at the top of the stairs. "Rick, show the man out, would ya?" He saluted Stan, then returned to the phone. "Say, where are you comin' from?" A city of origin, Stan thought.

Rick showed him to the door. Just as Stan opened it, another door opened further inside the house. "Mom's home," Rick said, running to meet her. Stan paused for a moment. I can meet her some other time, he thought, impatient to be home.

LEE RAN OUT the front door of their house shouting, "Vernon! Dale! We get to paint the wagon!"

"Lee!" Stan yelled, but he had spoken too late. He looked out the door. Lee raced across the driveway toward a merry-go-round some distance from the house, his shadow stretching long ahead of him in the morning light. At five years old, Lee tended to run wherever he went. Stan had warned him not to dash through doorways. You might bump into somebody and hurt him, or get hurt yourself, he had said. Lee had collided with him several times and the pain he suffered sent his hand to his groin when he suspected Lee might rush past.

Five years ago, plastic mesh had been sewn inside him, below his belt, in an attempt to correct a double hernia, a humiliating trial. The worst of it, in many ways, was the beginning, when a series of physicians were trying to diagnose the source of his pain. One doctor suggested venereal disease and, when Stan said he didn't think so, because he was monogamous, the guy swore at him.

Just before Lee reached the merry-go-round he fell down and disappeared in the long grass, then sprang up. He was prone to fall in his haste. He was pigeon-toed, and his feet seemed to turn in more when he ran. His pants had holes in the knees, or knee patches. Vernon, the oldest, was giving his youngest brother, Dale, a ride on the merry-go-round. Lee waited until Dale was on the far side of him, then jumped on opposite him.

  A Mormon physician, in a crisp white lab coat that set off his meticulously groomed red hair, examined Stan once, then with tight-lipped restraint suggested he see somebody else. That somebody advised him to perhaps relieve himself, since obviously he wasn't getting enough by way of his wife. Another suggested they keep the rough horseplay down. We're not athletes, Stan told him. And one urologist who had his index finger encased in a latex glove, of course, inserted up Stan's rectum, checking his prostate, said, Do you really have a problem, or do you do this for kicks?

  Finally, a routine physical exam Stan took for the college's medical-insurance program discovered the source of his pain. Surgery patched him up, but certain veins had varicosed over the years and the area remained tender.

  The merry-go-round's wooden seats were fastened to a metal frame fastened to spokes that spun around a central metal post. It looked like a mushroom's skeleton. Vernon was pushing on a spoke, as if engaging the interior of a wheel, and his brothers rode round. Stan had warned him not to push too fast. "Dale might fly right off. He's only three," he had told him. Vernon claimed Dale always said, *Fastew, fastew.* Vernon liked to imitate his brother's manner of speech—his *R*s sounded like *U*s. Vernon was maintaining a safe pace, Stan saw, but Dale was leaning way back, holding on with only one hand, and reaching for long stems of grass with the other. What a monkey, Stan thought. Lee copied Dale's antics. Vernon kept his brothers circling.

# SALE DAY

"WE'EW TALLEW THAN YOU, DAD," Dale said. The three boys stood on the wagon's weatherworn edge, barefoot, three feet off the ground, and Dale, the shortest, was indeed taller than his father was. "Watch out for slivers," Stan said, handing out wooden stirring sticks.
"On guard," Vernon said, provoking his brothers to a mock swordplay's wooden clicks. "I got you," he said to Dale.
"No you didn't."
"*A hit, a very palpable hit,*" Stan said. "Don't break them now."
"*Out sword,*" Vernon said. "*And wound the pap of Pyramus. Ay, that left pap, where heart doth hop.*" He had jumped on that last phrase the first time he'd heard it, Stan remembered. Lee had asked what a pap was. Vernon pretended to stab himself in the chest with the stirring stick. "*Thus die I: thus, thus, thus.*" He crumpled to the wagon. "*Now I am dead...Now die, die, die, die, die.*" Lee and Dale copied his actions. Three small corpses lay on the gray flatbed.
"How about a picture?" Grace called from the door of the house. She came down the steps carrying a camera.
"Perfect timing," Stan called to her. "They're all dead!"
"Oh for dumb," she said. "Get up now, you guys, and let's get a nice picture."
The dead didn't move, but they giggled.
"Just take it," he said. "Then you'll have evidence that I work them too hard."

HE OPENED six cans of old paint, and placed each one on the wagon. A half-gallon of yellow interior semi-gloss wall paint, an equal amount of green interior semi-gloss trim, three smaller portions of exterior white, and a partial quart of green chalkboard paint. "Let's mix 'em up and see what we get." He gave each boy a can to stir, then they took turns pouring paint from one can to another.

Dale spilled on the wagon. "Don't worry," Stan said. "We can cover that later." This is great, he thought. It doesn't matter if they happen to slop. Grace was pleased he had thought of letting them paint.

The mixture came out a frosty green yellow.

"On an old wagon like this?" he asked.

"It'll look neat," Lee said.

Stan had found the wagon abandoned in a field, hidden in a wrap of weeds. Its wooden bed, twelve by sixteen, was rotten. The tongue had rotted away; a metal hitch lay detached in a weedy tangle. The running gear was a truck's. The tires were flat, but three held air. The fourth he repaired. He fashioned a new tongue from two-by-fours, hitched the wagon to his Ramcharger, and pulled it out of the weeds. A hundred of embraces gave way in a moment. He stripped off the rotted boards and reconstructed the flatbed with lumber he pulled off an old shed. The restoration was crude, but sturdy. The wagon could be used for hauling hay, he hoped, and paint would protect it.

He handed out paint rollers and pans, filled the pans with what looked to him like cake frosting, and demonstrated how to saturate the roller and apply it to the wood. "Spread it on in the shape of a W, then fill the W in," he said, repeating the words of a procedure his dad had first taught him.

Before long, the work became a race—Vernon down one side of the wagon, Lee down the other, Dale right down the middle. Soon Dale was ahead. "Look at Dale go!" Vernon said. "Hooh!"

"There's no need to hurry," Stan told them. "I want it done right. Dale, you're going too fast. You missed several spots. And it's a little too thin. Take it slower."

"This wood sure soaks it up," Vernon said.

"Vernon, you're doing well," Stan said. "So is Lee." Better than I expected, he thought. The warped wood was hard to cover. A second coat would be needed. So let him put it on thin, he thought. He refilled their pans when they ran out.

"My awm's getting tiued," Dale said. He set his roller down and let his arm hang limp as a sleeve. They had painted a third of the wagon.

"Well no wonder, you little monkey," Stan said.

"So then just use your other arm," Lee said. "That's what I do." He cocked his tongue to the side of his mouth when he worked. Like his mother, Stan thought.

"Look who's coming," Vernon said, standing up. "It's the pity-ya-ya man, Dale."

Dale scowled at him.

Lee crouched near his pan, set his roller down, then jumped, rocking the wagon, and cheered. "The UPS man!" The rocking upset Dale's balance. "Would you quit it?" he said. Annoyed at Vernon's teasing, Stan thought.

"I wasn't expecting a package," he said.

The van drove up the driveway and slowed to a stop, the driver got out, greeted them with a crisp "Good morning," and walked to the rear. Dale stepped to the edge of the wagon and, when Stan set him on the ground, stepped gingerly over the gravel, while his brothers jumped off and ran toward the van. The man came out from behind, carrying a package, and the boys stopped short.

"Dale used to call you the 'pity-ya-ya man'," Vernon told him.

"Would you stop it!" Dale said.

"You boys having fun?" the man asked.

"Are we ever," Lee said. "We're painting that wagon."

"That's a pretty pale green," the man said. "For a wagon." He handed the package to Stan, got into the van, and drove off.

"It's from grandpa and grandma T," Stan said.

"I wonder what's in it," Vernon said.

"Let's find out." Stan took the box to the wagon and opened it with a pocketknife. "There's a note on the top. It reads *For the boys. And the big boy. All our love, Sig & May.*" He took out a cloth work apron, then another, then a third.

"What are they?" Lee asked.

"Work aprons. See, you put nails or screws in these pockets, and there's a loop for a hammer on the side. One for each of you," he said, handing them out. "And they sent a beautiful leather work belt for me."

"Just what we need," Lee said.

"To do painting?" Vernon asked.

"No, to do other stuff. Dad, would you tie mine on me?"

"Me too," Dale said.

Stan tied a bow in the strings at Lee's back and Lee put his hands in the apron's pockets and raised them, as if admiring tooled leather holsters for six guns.

"It'll go two times around Dale," Vernon said.

"It will not," Dale answered.

"Would you knock it off, Vern. We just got some gifts," Stan said, wrapping Dale's apron around him. Its corners met in the small of Dale's back, so Stan brought the strings around his son's trunk and tied a bow at his belly.

"Lank you," Dale said, patting the bow.

"You're welcome," Stan said. "Vernon?"

"No. I don't want to get paint on mine."

"Let's get back to work," Stan said. "When you're done with the wagon, if there's enough paint left over, I want you to paint the seats on the merry-go-round."

"Oh, that'll be fun," Lee said.

"Then tomorrow we'll have to paint everything all over again," Stan said.

"That'll be funnew," Dale said.

"More fun," Vernon corrected him.

Dale's shoulders and knees went limp, shaking his head as if he'd never grow to the mature age of seven. Tears emerged on his lower eyelids but he blinked them away. Stan knew Vernon adored his little brother, just as Dale looked up to Vern.

"Come on, Dale," Vernon said. "Do your happy-and-sad face."

"Yeah, come on, do it," Lee said.

Dale could switch his face fast from a grin to a frown, but this time he said, "No."

Like a clown, Stan thought, he can appear the most happy, and the next moment the most sad. "Children. Love one another. We just got new work clothes. Let's work on it."

## Chapter Two: Design

A WEDNESDAY SALE, and the seats in the Montrose Auction were filled to the furthest row near a two-story ceiling. Men in cowboy hats and baseball caps and overalls, women in jeans and quilted coats, girls with their hair in ponytails sitting beside their fathers, boys in the upper rows horsing around, laughing and punching and shoving one another—as his sons might do, Stan thought—a gathering of the regional family.

Stan found a comfortable fold-down seat of molded plastic in the second row, behind a lean-faced young man who wore a black cowboy hat decorated on one side with small brown feathers. Stan was from northeast North Dakota, the lower Red River Valley, where he had rarely seen cowboy hats. He'd tried on several after moving west of the Missouri, but felt his head had wings when he wore one, and looked like a duck in a baseball cap, he felt, so he went bareheaded. Lee and Dale wanted cowboy hats to match their boots. As he settled into the seat, he realized it was the first time in his life he would be witnessing a livestock auction as a spectator.

Cattle entered the block through doors to the left, and were auctioned and driven out the opposite side. An auctioneer in a booth spoke in a relaxed sort of way, his mouth right up to a mike, in a style of DJs on FM radio. He wore a bulky red sweater and no hat. He didn't look like a cowboy, and sounded like Garrison Keillor. A

# SALE DAY

younger woman sat at a computer monitor on the other end of the booth, facing the auctioneer, and from her looks she might have been his daughter. Above her hung a scoreboard, sleek and new, that displayed bright red numerals. Littleton Livestock would eventually replace theirs with one like this, Stan thought. The woman's computer controlled the scoreboard, and occasionally she couldn't clear the board after a sale. A couple of times after clearing it, she couldn't get it to light up again. The auctioneer paused until she did. Her computer and the scoreboard seemed to get out of sync, Stan thought. A problem of feedback, a flaw in the software, or hardware, but the woman didn't get flustered.

Once, the scoreboard displayed $1.40 per pound, instead of $1.04, and the crowd hooted and cheered. The cowboy in the feathered black hat emitted an ear-piercing whistle of a kind Stan could never do. The auctioneer went along with the joke, then explained the error to the woman in his casual way. She corrected it and smiled at the crowd's mock moans and laughter. Like the cattle, she was on display, Stan thought. She had to perform. A sale was entertainment.

A slim cowboy appeared in the booth from time to time. He would come through a door near the woman, take paper from her—a sister, perhaps; there was a family resemblance—then he would disappear through the door, and reappeared later. Stan didn't realize at first there were two different men. One wore a brown shirt; the other wore green. They looked like identical twins.

Two yardmen entered the entrance doors to the left and parted. Calves approached and, as they squeezed through the doors, the men counted them. Motes of dust glinted over the calves. The yardmen finished the count, the doors closed, and the scoreboard read 50 head. The men snapped slender whips, prodding the animals along. The calves inched forward, lowing in a mass of bodies and heads. Calf heads poked up this way and that, over the backs of the seemingly headless. Tan, buff, gray, cream—they were beautiful.

"Now here are some top-quality calves for you," the auctioneer said. "From the Ron Johnson Ranch. Ron, are you here? Give us a wave if you're out there." A man in a middle row raised a hand. In a gray cowboy hat and matching jacket, he looked tall, even when seated, trim and prosperous. "Buyers, it's time to fill those orders. Five full truck loads of the finest calves this side of the river. Uniform-size Charolais-cross calves just the way you like them. We're going to weigh them all, then sell them all together. Buyers, this is what you've been waiting for."

Stan knew that Charolais was a French breed. Cattlemen were crossing whitish Charolais bulls with what his dad called English Isle breeds—Angus and Hereford—or with a Hereford-Angus cross called black baldy. The crossings produced stunning offspring, he thought.

The calves were weighed and released. The scoreboard registered 22,000 total pounds, 440 pounds per calf on the average. A second group was driven in, then a third, a fourth, and a fifth, each containing 50 head. The crowd grew excited, talking louder than before, but Mr. Johnson sat silent and still.

"Fine spring calves. I've never seen better. They're milk-fed and pasture-grown, and have never seen a day in a feedlot. Ron, am I right?"

Mr. Johnson confirmed this.

"Absolutely," the auctioneer said.

These absolutes! Stan thought. Philosophers might say that absolutes are nil, but they kept popping up in exclamations of businessmen.

The scoreboard finally read 250 head. 110,250 pounds. An average weight of 441 pounds per calf. The woman at the computer leaned back in her chair. "Who'll give me a dollar twenty?" the auctioneer said. Somebody in the crowd said, "Ninety." He wore a straw cowboy hat and an insulated vest over an enormous belly like a keg of beer about to burst. Bidding began.

Stan didn't follow it. He was puzzling over the problem of merging the data from five groups of calves into one containing the data on all of them. The Montrose software had done this. The math was no problem, he thought. It was mere addition. The trick lay in crafting a good data structure.

The money, displayed in red on the scoreboard, stopped at $1.07. The buyer, identified as Stu, the keg who had offered ninety cents to begin with, was now given the opportunity to buy all, or some, of the calves. The crowd grew quieter. "I'll take them all," he said. Cheers and shouting, and another piercing whistle from the guy in front of Stan. Men behind Stu slapped him on the back, and knocked his hat off. He put it back on, turned to them, said something, and they laughed.

The purchase totaled $118,000, Stan estimated. The market's commission was about $1770. Mike had sold twice as many calves at Littleton Livestock. The amounts were staggering to Stan. Perhaps, he thought, forty thousand for a computer system is next to nothing. He was glad he hadn't said anything specific to Owen on that score. Money was Mike's job, he told himself.

"Thank you, Ron," the auctioneer said. "Hope to see you again this time next year." Mr. Johnson tipped the brim of his hat.

"Buyers, sit tight," the auctioneer said. "We've got lots more good calves coming your way."

IN THE MONTROSE OFFICE, two women stood behind a counter, each at a monitor and keyboard. Behind them, a dot-matrix printer on a floor stand printed a line, stopped, and then ejected a length of paper on top of a heaping tangle bunched up in a basket behind. Neither of the women seemed bothered by the buildup. A good way to jam the printer, Stan thought. A cable ran along the floor to a smaller room.

"Excuse me. I'm a computer consultant, and I understand you have a new computer."

"Yes we do," one of the women said.

"Do you mind if I take look?" he said, pointing to the small room.

"Why no. You go right ahead. We were expecting you."

"You were?"

"Sharon, from Littleton Livestock, said you'd be by."

"Is she ever excited," the other woman said.

He went into the computer room, thinking that Sharon and these two were already networked. The computer was a Texas Instruments minicomputer, a "box" slightly smaller than a washing machine. The monitors and keyboards at the counter were mere keyboards and screens, he realized, dumb terminals incapable of local processing. He stepped out of the room just as the printer ejected more paper—white data-processing labels, he saw, the kind that would peel off and stick. "What are these?"

"Weight tickets," the first woman said.

Why were they being printed in the office, and being ignored, he wondered. He lifted and studied them—abbreviations and numbers, but nothing resembling names. "How does the system identify a buyer or seller?"

# SALE DAY

"Each seller has a number, and each buyer has several."

"Where are their names?"

"Jim or John tell us that."

"The guys running in and out of the booth?"

"Uh huh. The twins get the names that go with the numbers from Betty, our operator."

So they are twins, Stan thought, then said, "The system assigns the number, and Betty, your operator, pairs it with a name at the time of a sale?"

"That's right. The twins bring us the names and numbers, we type the names in, and the computer writes out the check."

"Or the invoice," the other woman said.

"How do you like the system?"

"We love it," they said together.

Stan had been educated on mainframes and minicomputers like the TI, and he was familiar with primitive microcomputer networks. He realized now, however, that he had been expecting more from Montrose Livestock Auction, something state-of-the-art, something— Well, a local-area network running on IBM PS/2s. He thought the auction's hardware was obsolete.

And the software! It was outrageous. The critical links, which paired a person's name to a number, were handwritten lists, delivered on foot by twins. The lists did an end-run around all the automation, where there should have been a single, seamless software solution. Forty thousand dollars for a system requiring gofers was too painful to contemplate. A piece of paper for God's sake. Jeez, a gum wrapper would do.

Yet the system worked, he had to admit.

The women were happy.

WEST OF MOBRIDGE (west of Montrose), a bridge spanning the Missouri sliced through sky that appeared to swoop down on wings to the river, then open wide on both sides of the hovering highway. The bridge was the only crossing within sixty miles; Bismarck to the north boasted several. Mountain Time began halfway across the bridge, as a road sign informed him. The moment he passed the sign, the sun's sunset elevation felt right to him, growing accustomed, as he was, to life on the eastern edge of a time zone, as if time leaped younger there.

His dad's first veterinary office had occupied a room at the front of their house on Main Street when Stan was a boy. His dad performed surgery on small animals on a stainless-steel tilting table at the other end of the house, in the basement. Stan and his brother and sisters would sit on the basement steps and watch him spay cats and dogs. Once, when his dad was preparing to castrate a dog, one of his brother's playmates said from the steps, What are you doing? And his dad said, I'm about to take out this dog's tonsils. Can I watch? the boy asked. I'm gonna get my tonsils out tomorrow.

"Oops!" his dad would say in conclusion, whenever he told the story.

The basement also held cages for small animals—cats and dogs, a goose or a chicken. His dad eventually built a clinic on the west end of town, and his mother reclaimed and carpeted the front room, where she installed a baby grand piano purchased for his youngest sister, now a nurse. The maturing family never again woke to a rooster crowing in the basement.

Stan often accompanied his father on farm calls, and farmers would ask him, What are you going to be when you grow up, young man? And he would say, A veterinarian.

West of the bridge, the highway curved southwest up the riverbank and, near the top of the slope, a sign advertised Sitting Bull's monument. The Missouri was the eastern border of Standing Rock Indian Reservation, comprised of Corson County in South Dakota and Sioux County in North Dakota—the chief's final domain. Stan felt he had, indeed, entered a singular territory. The land formed a unique habitat, more rugged than where he grew up—broad pastures, coulees and steep ravines, rising hills, and buttes with tips like nipples. Cattle looked like colored dots grazing miles away. Only the highway's right of way appeared to be fenced. Nobody seemed to work in the fields along the road. He seldom met or passed another car, but when he did, it always seemed to happen on a narrow bridge or sharp curve as if, in the distances of the plain, people were appointed to meet.

In high school he started saying, Biologist, then Biochemist, to questions about his vocation. He worked at the vet clinic until he left for college, where he majored in pre-med for a year. The following year, he switched to psychology, then as a junior changed again to philosophy, specializing in epistemology (the theory of knowledge) and logic. His brother became a physician, his sister a nurse. His other sister was a secretary to his mother, an insurance agent. None followed his father into veterinary medicine. None would inherit the practice.

Owen's father, so Stan learned, had started the Littleton and Piper auctions, and still operated another a hundred miles south of Littleton.

There were also stories of Mike and his brothers, but their business partnerships (and there were several, it was said) faltered largely because of Mike, according to the rumors he had heard.

Mike, well, Mike was a loner, he felt.

He wondered what life would have been like if he had stuck to his guns, as his mother would say, and become a veterinarian. Now, here he was, driving through the least populated counties in the Dakotas, with more scribbling on a tablet than money in the bank, a loner himself, picturing the auctioneer, his daughter, and twin sons in Montrose together, and recalling a time when he was Doc's boy.

One of his dad's teachers in vet school had said that the average veterinary practice would grow over the first five years, level off for ten, then suffer decline. His dad's was now in its thirtieth season and, over that period, business had increased every year. Four veterinarians were added and the supporting staff grew to seven. The business was getting to be too much for his dad to handle. So much for academic projections, Stan thought.

Another bridge crossed the Grand, a tributary of the Missouri, between Mobridge and Littleton. The river coursed around a congregation of cottonwood trees that lifted naked branches to the sky. Without bark, their bone-gray trunks had the look of bleached stakes driven into the bottomland. The Grand River flowed into Lake Oahe, a reservoir that swelled a portion of the Missouri from Sioux County in the north to the Oahe Dam near Pierre, South Dakota's capital, for a hundred and twenty miles. The river must have backed up, once or more, and submerged those trees on the river bottom, he thought. Then came the drought of the '80s, the flood receded, and the trees were left dead in sunlight and wind.

He liked working for his dad, even the repetitious chore of cleaning, and appreciated the income he made in his high-school years, but his dad cursed the late nights, the cold, the dumb animals, the weird predicaments, the people; and these curses assailed Stan's memory with the force of a stinging whip. *Get along,* he imagined his dad saying. *Git!* And somehow it hadn't been appointed for Stan to remain.

Dead trees reminded him of fields ripe with sunflowers—the stalks shriveled and dry, the heavy heads hung as if in shame. He once called his wife's attention to their appearance. "Yes in shame," Grace had said. "A moment before mercy." He came to love that rebuke, and loved her for it. In one moment, she altered his bleak outlook on sunflowers for good. His dad always said love for animals wasn't enough. Maybe, but Stan was feeling an inexpressible stirring. He crossed the invisible border from one state to the next, and in the reflection of the headlights a sign read *North Dakota: Discover the Spirit!* None too soon, he thought.

The land felt lonely at twilight and, at moments, a lot like the Badlands, drained of life, but he was on his way home to Grace and his sons. What will become of them, he wondered, those boys who work and play and depend so much upon one another right now? His brother and he communicated only around holidays, but there was mutual regard between them, even love.

"HAPPY BIRTHDAY!" Stan said.

He stood in their bedroom, barefoot, toweling his hair in sunlight after a shower, in a brown velour robe Grace had given him for his birthday. She was in bed, flat on her stomach, her face in a pillow. She didn't answer, or even move under the covers, and he stepped to the foot of the bed. "Are you awake?"

"Yeth." A muffled voice, unlike her.

"Are you all right?"

She rose from the pillow, turned over on her back, and stared at the ceiling. "My birthday was yesterday."

"Yesterday? It's the eleventh, isn't it?"

"Today's the eleventh. My birthday's the tenth."

"Of course it is!" He was appalled. "I've done it again. I'm sorry."

"*Beloved, don't delay, the night is falling,*" she sang softly, a favorite line from *Figaro*.

His mnemonic for remembering her birthday was to think of '1' standing for Grace, and '0' for Jean: 10. Or was it the other way around? Twin ones, as in 11, kept intruding themselves into his mind's eye, for obvious reasons, and he kept remembering her birthday wrong. He was always getting binary contrasts mixed up—an odd fault in a programmer, he felt. He would say left for right, east for west, hay for straw. Or would be about to, before catching himself. He was afraid that one day he might mistake death for life. "What good is a mnemonic if I can't remember it right?"

"*Hasten while love's delight is sweetly calling,*" she sang sweetly and, sitting up in bed, reached out to him. "I forgive you." He went to her, sat on the bed beside her, laid the towel on the bed, and took her hands in his. "You missed a good meal last night," she said. "The beef roast I'd been saving, shredded potato casserole. I went ahead with the presents, and the cake and ice cream. The boys wanted to sing. I hope you don't mind."

"How could I mind? I'm the one who goofed up." The night before, he had arrived home late after working at the lumberyard. Not a single light had been left on for him, and there was no exterior yard light. The sky had been overcast, and in the dark he had stumbled up the front steps, wrenching his tender groin, and had tried several keys in the lock of the front door before he found the right one and let himself in. She didn't normally lock the door when he was out. Then again, he thought, she was usually awake, or woke up and greeted him, when he came home after dark. "How about I massage your shoulders, a late birthday present?"

"I have something to tell you," she said, kissing his hands.

"There are leftovers?"

"I hope you won't mind."

"What is it?"

"I think I'm pregnant again," she said, and looked up with eyes as bright as her voice.

He looked away and let her hands drop. "I thought you were keeping track of yourself." He stood. "I thought you knew the days of the month!" The pill gave her headaches and they had agreed she go off it. She told him she was so regular she could rely on a schedule.

"It's not an exact science, you know. Maybe I've changed."

"We haven't finished paying for the last one yet!"

"I know."

"You just got Dale out of diapers! I'm just starting this job. We can't afford this right now!"

"What can we do? The Lord will provide."

"Your dad, you know, is going to take to this like a—" He couldn't think of anything quite appropriate.

"I know," she said, speaking with a sympathy that annoyed him even more.

"It's goddamn humiliating." He hung his head and sighed. "I must look to him like some goddamn lecherous fool."

"Please don't talk in that way."

"Please don't talk that way," he repeated, stepping to the foot of the bed. He had told her he was going to try to stop cursing, especially around the children, but he felt too weak to resist, too depleted, too much like withered sunflowers before harvest. "Grace, this— This is the worst goddamn news." A moment before mercy, he thought.

Dale walked into the room just then, as if this coincidence, too, were ordained. He padded past Stan in feet pajamas, rubbing sleep from his eyes.

"You missed 'Happy Bootday,'" he said.

The boy went over to the bed, and climbed into his mother's lap. She put her lips to his fine blond curls and kissed his head.

"Then I guess we'll just have to sing it one more time," Stan said, glaring at his wife, and thought, A *fourth* time.

"You should tame youw tongue," Dale said.

He had heard.

"WHEN ARE YOU LEAVING?" Stan asked his father-in-law.

"We're leaving tomorrow," Henry said. He got a glass from a cupboard and set it on the kitchen counter. "If the weather holds out." The look he gave Stan from his hooded eyes seemed wary.

"It's supposed to," Stan said. He drew into a chair at the kitchen table of his in-laws' house, alone with Henry, wondering if he should tell him Grace was pregnant. Emma, his gracious mother-in-law, was out getting her hair done.

"Yes, it's supposed to," Henry said, as if both were stalling for time. "But these weathermen—" He removed a two-liter bottle of diet cola from the refrigerator.

Henry and Emma were planning their semi-annual visit to Minneapolis-St. Paul to see their son Wayne and his family. Emma had visited Stan's family in the country several times, but Henry never did. Stan didn't ask why; he thought the reasons were obvious. Henry had been the first in Bismarck to own a TV, and he couldn't understand why his daughter and son-in-law refused to buy one. He wouldn't know what to do with himself at our place, Stan thought.

"Did you figure out what was wrong with my program?" Henry asked. He unscrewed the cap on the bottle and let off air.

Why not just tell him, Stan thought.

Henry had taught himself the BASIC programming language in semi-retirement, and had written a payroll program for a dairy farm he had inherited from his stepfather. The program worked well ninety-nine percent of the time. Henry was particular and wanted everything just right, so he had asked Stan to look at it.

Stan admired the program's performance, but the text was another matter. It wasn't structured. There was a GOTO statement in the fifth line, for starters. There were GOTOs all over the program and no documentation. Henry himself couldn't explain portions of it.

It was a perfect example of spaghetti logic, and Stan found it impossible to follow the tangle for long.

"Nope, no I didn't," Stan said. *Now if Henry would pay me—* He buried the thought deep, in a blink.

"That Pascal language is what I'd like to learn," Henry said, rhyming the word with rascal. He poured himself a glass of the diet cola, nearly to the brim.

"The industry is leaning more towards C. Pascal," Stan said, accenting the second syllable, "is for teaching structured programming. You'd probably like it, though."

"I want you to take that TV," Henry said. "I want you to take it today, or I'm throwing it out." He replaced the cap on the bottle, then pumped a pump built into the cap to control the fizz of the carbonation with a briskness that suggested anger.

"All right. I've talked it over with Grace, and we've agreed to take it. I see it's in the garage."

"And as soon as I get that VCR good and clean, I'm giving you that. Think of it as a birthday present for Grace, if you can do that." Henry put the bottle in the refrigerator and took a bowl of ice cubes from the freezer.

"We want to thank you for the VCR, too. It's why we thought we'd accept the TV—to watch videos." Henry owned three videotape machines, besides the one he had offered to Stan. The VCRs ran day and night, recording the programs Henry wanted to watch when he wasn't watching them live, usually at night. He had a large satellite dish mounted to the side of the house, in addition to cable.

"Or as a gift to the boys," Henry said. "I don't want them growing up backward."

This is as good a day as any, Stan thought.

"I don't suppose the reception's worth a damn in the country." Henry dropped an ice cube into the glass, the cola foaming up, spilling onto the counter. "I've done it again. Damn it! This new refrigerator. The ice is so cold." He got a dishcloth from the sink and wiped up his spill.

"I think you're right about the reception," Stan said. "We have to use rabbit ears but, as I said, we're more interested in videos."

Henry carefully added more ice to the glass.

"Is Wayne still playing guitar on weekends?" Stan asked.

Henry lifted the glass, took a sip, and grimaced. "I don't know."

"Wayne has perfect pitch. Did you know that? Of course, I'm not into 'R & B with jazz infusion', as he calls it, but he's quite a guitar player."

"Right. A guitar player that carried out groceries. But now that he's a programmer, I'm not supposed to bring that up anymore." Henry took another sip, and made a face again. "Why don't things taste like they used to?"

"Music, algebra, and programming have certain affinities," Stan said.

"You sound like a professor. But you're not."

"No, I'm a guitar player and programmer like Wayne," Stan said, then took apart the punch of that by adding, "And not much of a guitarist anymore either."

"Are you making ends meet?"

This, it seemed to Stan, was sooner or later the question between them. "More or less. Things are looking up. There's this Littleton Livestock."

"What do you know about auctions?"

"Very little, but I'm learning."

"They're a rough crowd at auctions. Believe me, I know. You should've never left teaching—what you were trained for."

No, not today, Stan thought. Though if Emma were here—

"And Littleton. It's smack dab in the middle of the reservation, isn't it?" Henry said. "Damn Indians. They'd work for a week, then want an advance on their pay—which I like a fool would give them, at first—and you'd never see them again."

Henry had a degree in electrical engineering, but he had spent his life managing a dairy processing plant started by his stepfather and, after selling the plant to a larger producer, managing the dairy farm of his stepfather, who had loved a cow as a cow. Henry would admit he enjoyed the dairy plant's production facilities but still complained of having to deal with the public, the people.

Stan felt tempted to use this unhappy fact about his father-in-law to further justify his change of vocation. The opportunity presented itself often, as it did now, but Stan couldn't bear to bring it up. The dairy business had yielded certain comforts associated with money, but Henry had grown bitter over the years. Wasted on those damn cows, he once let Stan know. Stan didn't want to rub it in.

Henry was also one of the first in town to own a personal computer. The Apple II, which he still kept on a shelf beside an old reel-to-reel tape deck and short-wave radio, had a green monochrome monitor and two floppy-disk drives. On the desk in his office he now had an Apple Macintosh. Wayne owned a Mac, which formed a bond between father and son.

"Now that I've put everything away, I suppose I should've offered you a drink," Henry said.

"Not today," Stan said.

Henry turned his head and blinked at his son-in-law as a hawk might turn its head and blink.

"*No thank you*," Stan said.

"Wouldn't it be nice," Henry said, as he was leaving the room. "If you could just pull out a chip and erase all the bad memories."

LEE PINCHED his nose, while Stan led the boys to the upper deck of the bleachers—no fold-down seats here!—and peered over the heads and hats and backs of men involved in a sale already in progress. This Thursday sale in Littleton was moderately attended. Vernon and Dale started elbowing each other as they sat down. What is it about boys on heights, Stan wondered. He chose the spot for the view, and for the distance it put between him and the crowd. Nobody will assault my hearing here, he thought.

"You'll get used to it after a while," he told Lee, who released his grip, sniffed, then put the back of a hand to his nose, as if to shield his face from a wind.

# SALE DAY 45

Stan was sure Owen had recognized him, had even tipped the brim of his baseball cap to him. Owen stood in the booth, one hand on the levers that opened the doors, eating a hamburger, promoting beef on the spot.

A man in a black cowboy hat, sitting beside Owen and serving as the auctioneer, slurred words into a microphone. In Montrose the auctioneer seemed relaxed, this guy sounded downright lazy.

A weigher operated the weight-ticket printer. He would tear the top sheet off a ticket, fold the sheet in half, and drop it down a plastic tube at his elbow—the yardman's copy. The taped printer controlled Littleton's scoreboard. The numerals were readable, but several bulbs were burned out.

Owen's house and pickup were new, but Littleton Livestock was on the shabby side. I fit right in, he thought.

Three other men in the booth served as spotters. With each bid, the spotters pointed to rival buyers and, when a buyer upped the money, the spotters yelled *Yo!* Owen joined them from time to time, but he maintained, when he wasn't chewing, a constant banter with everybody—this buyer, that buyer (Stu with his belly and straw hat), a seller, the seller's wife or daughter, the spotters, the auctioneer, the weigher, the men prodding the cattle on the block, the yardmen coming in from outdoors, even the cattle. He also fidgeted with the levers, as if itching for the next thing to happen.

In Montrose, a man and his daughter did the work of Littleton's six. Not counting the twins, Stan thought.

Cows were selling one at a time. Stan timed several transactions and concluded *One cow a minute.* After the cows, came bulls, then several lots of yearling heifers, then steers. When the first group of calves entered the block, Owen turned his job over to a spotter and exchanged places with the lazy auctioneer. He let out a whistle that made Stan flinch, took up the mike, and yelled "Yeehaa," as if he were trying to start a stampede. "Let's get this sale *movin'*." His chant was rapid, his voice clear. His skill was a cut above any other auctioneer Stan had heard. He sounded joyful, even jolly, and every cent pitter-pattered into place. When he was interrupted—by a need for a recount, for example—he played to the crowd. In the element of calves, calves, and more calves, Owen revealed his craft. He was a comedian.

Often the bidding narrowed to two rival buyers (Stu was often one of them) batting the money between them, as if it were a tennis ball. The spotters would urge a buyer on and, when he bid, they would yell and turn to the rival, acting as cheerleaders of sorts. Owen joined in, tipping his hat as if counting time with his head, and the effect of these cattlemen bobbing in concert became so singsong that Stan's sons started swaying in their seats, side by side, then doubled over with laughter. It *was* funny. A rough crowd? It was a little operetta.

"Sit up, would ya?" Stan told them.

Whenever a group of calves moved in, a dark-skinned woman, accompanied by another with a single dark braid down her back, stepped through a door at the back of the booth and sat on a stool. When the calves were driven out, the women left, and reappeared as more calves were driven in. The yardmen were Indian women, Stan realized.

A lone calf was brought in weighing 170 pounds. Owen announced that the calf was going to be sold by the head, and suggested an opening bid of one hundred dollars.

Stu bid fifty.

Stan bid sixty.

"What are you doing?" Vernon said.

Stu bid seventy.

"Eighty," Stan said, bidding a second time in pure recklessness, endangerment, feeling flushed, as when dollar signs had burned before his eyes looking at Mike.

"How're we gonna to get it home?" Lee asked.

"I don't know," Stan said.

Stu bid ninety.

Owen looked to Stan.

"Maybe we could put it in the back of the Chawgew," Dale said.

"One hundred," Stan said with a certain finality that surprised him, hoping to put an end to a whirl affecting even his vision, as if he were on dizzying ride. Stu bid a hundred and ten. Over a hundred dollars! Stan didn't have that kind of money. Grace, Grace, Grace, he said to himself. What would she think? He shook his head and Owen looked away. Someone else picked up where he left off and, moments later, the calf was sold to Stu for two hundred dollars.

"That's it," Owen announced. The end of the sale.

Don't I fit right in, Stan thought.

MEN MINGLED in the auction's lobby. Sellers received their checks from Sharon at her window; buyers their invoices from a striking buyer-side girl. Several women at a table set up in the office worked with adding machines and filled out forms.

Stan's sons waited in line to get into the restroom (the men's read COWBOYS) to relieve the pressure of their jumpy sauce—one of Stan's terms. He was the jumpy one. The boys' turn came and, when they returned, emptied, they asked to split a diet cola. It would go straight through them—particularly through Vernon—in reaction to the artificial sweetener. On the way home, Stan would have to stop along the road and witness his three sons pee in a ditch at the precise moment that the only car within ten miles would drive past. He hadn't bought the calf, so he splurged on four pops, as they called them here, diet colas.

Stan located the picture of Owen and Mike above the couch in the lobby, an enlarged black-and-white photo in a weathered-pine frame, and observed with alarm how much younger Mike had looked just the year before. A white cowboy hat sat cocked on Mike's head, incongruous, as if it had been lent to him. Not quite the old smoothie, Stan thought.

Owen entered the lobby and walked right past him, his voice the loudest in the room as he moved among the men, shaking hands with one after another and making remarks.

When he made his way back to Stan, he said, "Are you looking for that kind of thing?"

"The calf, you mean?"

"What else would I mean?"

"Not exactly. It just seemed a good idea at the time."

"It *is* a good idea. Listen, I'm glad you came to the sale today. Come back, why don't you. Better luck next time!"

*Did* Owen recognize him, Stan wondered. He was about to mention the trip to Montrose, the auction software, the reason for his being there, when Owen turned to the boys. "You boys like pop? Here, they're on me." He pulled out of his wallet two dollar bills. Vernon took the money and said, "Thank you." Lee said the same. Dale muttered "Lank you." Owen turned away and started his auction chant there in the lobby, then stopped and said, "Sharon, oh Sharon, where's my market report?"

# SALE DAY

"What a slave driver!" she yelled through the window, and men in the lobby laughed.

"Sharon, you're one in million!" Owen said as he stepped into the office, then he walked out without the report. There were still men in line and Sharon was busy with them. "Don't tell her I said that!"

"Do we get to keep the money?" Vernon said.

"You'd better," Stan said. "I'd just spend it." The boys were happy to hear this; and he was unhappy that he had. "Please don't tell your mother what happened today."

"Where would we keep a calf?" Lee asked.

Mike had warned him: Don't go on a Thursday.

STAN CALLED Barskills, the supplier of the auction's weight-ticket printer. A company technician told him that Barskills sold a complete auction system, hardware and software. Stan learned, however, that the operating system, called OS/9, ran only on Motorola hardware.

Stan wanted IBM-compatibility, software designed to run on an 80386—Intel's newest chip. The lumberyard was running a popular local-area network called Novell, and Stan hoped to install more systems of that kind, now that he was familiar with it.

The technician said he'd check into the matter and call Stan back.

Stan called again an hour later. Another technician answered and told him the company handled a card that allowed IBM-compatibles to run OS/9 and their software. Stan learned that the card contained the necessary Motorola CPU that would simply supplement the 386, making an Intel machine mimic a Motorola.

Stan was reminded of similar attempts to forestall the demise of CP/M, an early operating system for microcomputers. Z80 chips were placed on a card for Intel machines. Z80s and CP/M were dead by the time he finished graduate school. His professors never mentioned OS/9. These auction systems are dinosaurs, he thought.

Barskills wanted ten thousand dollars for OS/9 and its auction software, plus three hundred for each card. Stan said he'd think about it.

He called the company a third time, simply to get the details straight in his mind, and ended up talking with yet another person, a programmer like himself, who told Stan that Barskills was working on a livestock program written in C that would run under UNIX. Stan knew that UNIX was migrating to IBM-compatible micros and might have a future.

"The software won't be released for another year, however," the programmer said, and put Stan on hold.

Then another voice spoke. "Hello, this is Robert Bar, president of Barskills. Just what precisely are we trying to accomplish here?"

"What do you mean?" Stan said.

"You've been picking the brains of my people all afternoon and I want to know why."

"Well, there's a livestock auction in South Dakota that's looking to update its equipment, and I'm trying to locate software that will run on IBM-compatible hardware under Novell." The words came out in a rush, to Stan's dismay. Why can't I hold my own?

"What market are you talking about? Are they currently using my products?"

You mean the duct tape and burned-out bulbs? Stan thought of saying but instead replied, "I don't think I should say."

"Why don't you just tell me the name of the market, and save me the hour it will take to find out for myself."

"No, I don't think I should do that. I have a partner and I don't think he would want me to tell."

"You have a very-small-business mentality," the man said.

"I have a very small business," Stan said.

IN THE KITCHEN, Grace stood at the stove, sautéing mushrooms. Stan, standing behind her, kissed her on the neck. "I read in a magazine the other day that the word 'dam' (D-A-M) in the phrase 'not worth a dam' isn't a curse, but a coin. A coin from the Netherlands. It's like saying, 'Not worth a cent.'"

"Why don't you just say that then?" she said.

"I suppose I *could*, but it wouldn't have that—sting."

"That's what I thought. Well, you won't get away with saying 'dam' for 'damn thing'."

"I won't?"

"Nope. Not around here."

He thought of saying, *You're right, madam*, then did.

After squirming under the force of what she called his earthy upbringing, Grace had come to tolerate, then accept, and finally even engage in conversation at first uncomfortable to her. But she drew the line at cursing.

He kissed her neck once more and rested his chin on her shoulder. Frying mushrooms smell, he thought. In their first year of marriage, she once told him, I got gas today. I'm sorry, he said. No, I mean in the car. Did you roll the windows down? he had asked her. This was a story she had only recently begun to tell others.

"Oh, your weight feels good," she said. "Could you rub my shoulders? My neck must be stiff."

"I *could*."

"Well, *would* you?"

He placed his hands on her shoulders, pressed his thumbs into the muscles, and massaged them.

She sucked in air in a reverse hiss. "The boys just can't do it the way you can. Oh!" She rolled her head from side to side.

"I've also been massaging a problem," he said.

"What would that be?"

"Butech's unfortunate name." Stan called his company *Butech* (with a long U) after the buttes to the south of their house, and in opposition to a futuristic trend in computer store names—*Ultra Tech, Turbo Office Plus III*. There was nothing abstract about a butte, he felt. Wholesale suppliers all over country often mispronounced Butech as Butt-tech, however. Grace was appalled to hear that people had trouble with the name. "I've thought of introducing Butech by referring to butane, but of course butane's a gas. Now I think maybe I should refer to Grassy Butte in the Badlands."

"Grassy butt," she said. He was surprised to hear her say this. "I'm sure that would be a big help."

"Big enough." He grasped her hips and pressed his thumbs into the flesh of her ample and shapely behind.

"I know what you're thinking," she said. "Harder."

He pressed his thumbs into her harder. "White Butte is near the South Dakota border."

"Oh, yes, that feels so good. I must be tense. Now lower."

"And Sentinel Butte, if memory serves, is an erect and watchful guard near Montana."

"*Come, my beloved. With all my heart, I love you,*" Grace sang softly.

Lee entered the room and pinched his nose. "Phew! Mob, what's that smell?"

"I'm frying mushrooms."

"I thought I liked mushrooms," the boy said, still pinching his nose.

"You do. That's why I'm fixing them."

"But I sure don't like the smell of them cooking."

THEY WOKE THE BOYS earlier than usual. It was their monthly trip as a family to Bismarck to visit their grandparents. Stan wanted to check on the network at Lumber Jack, and talk with Jim Fluck, the lumberyard's bookkeeper and network administrator. As they left the house, Vernon said, "I put my magazines in your briefcase, so they wouldn't get dirty. I want to show grandpa and grandma."

"And hope they subscribe," Stan said.

Vernon's magazine, *Why Mom?*, was designed to explain things that kids want to know, as he put it. He would compose, type, and edit the text, print the pages on a computer printer, then fold and staple them as a booklet. He decided to charge subscribers two dollars a year.

Stan dropped himself off at the lumberyard as soon as they got to town. "Pick me up in an hour," he said.

"You think you'll be that long?" Grace asked him. "It's almost time for lunch, and the boys are hungry."

"Why don't you go to the station next door, and get gas in the car," he said. She rolled her eyes as if to ward off being teased, so he replied, "Then we'll go from there."

"Would you show Uncle Jim my magazine?" Vernon asked him. The boys had been to the lumberyard several times and Jim had told them to call him this.

"You'll be back, and you can show him yourself."

"Okay," Vernon said.

To his surprise Stan found a new computer, an Epson 386, acting as the file server, the central computer in a network. The former server, purchased from Mike, sat on Jim's desk, demoted to a workstation. Jim was out on an errand but would be back any minute, the receptionist told him, and invited him to have a chair in Jim's office. Stan sat down, and Jim walked in carrying a plastic bag bulging with boxes of tissues. Jim was on medication of sorts for allergies. "Don't get up," he said. He set the bag on the floor beside his desk.

"I see you have new file server," Stan said.

"We finally junked the Cantronix, thank God," Jim said, removing his jacket. He wiped his eyes with a handkerchief, and exchanged his aviator sunglasses for an ordinary pair. "Actually, it's a workstation now, as you can see. We bought the Epson in town here and haven't had a single server problem since." He wiped his nose and sat behind the desk.

Over the first month of the network's operation, two hard drives in the Cantronix had crashed, interrupting business each time. And in the attempt to replace the drive the second time, a local repairman accidentally cracked the Cantronix motherboard (the main circuit board) which the lumberyard had to replace at its own expense. On top of that, the serviceman charged Lumber Jack fifty-five dollars an hour.

"I warned Jack not to buy a system from Mike," Jim said. Jack was his older brother, the owner of the lumberyard and its namesake. "Sell to Mike, yes. Buy from him? Definitely not. All Jack saw was the huge quantity of lumber Mike was buying for his farm and ranch—railroad ties by the semi-load." Jim's dark eyes dilated wide as the eyes of a storybook animal and watered. He was far-sighted like Stan, his thick glasses magnifying the liquid look.

"So Jack thought it only fair to return the favor, and buy something from Mike."

"I guess. I admit the Cantronix looked good at the time, especially the price, but from the start its connection to Mike bothered me."

After Mike left the computer-chip firm, he bought a microcomputer company with plants in Canada that manufactured IBM-compatible microcomputers. He said he bought it as an investment, then cycled it back out, as he put it.

A Canadian named Jansen bought it. Cantronix, as the company was called, was headquartered in Toronto. Jansen and Mike were good friends, according to Mike, and Jansen offered him wholesale prices. The Canadian rate of exchange on the dollar made the prices attractive.

Stan said, "Mike tells me Cantronix might let us market its hardware in the U.S. under a private label of our own. Mike has a slogan picked out: *Butech. It's a beaut.* I pretend to be amused."

"It's not bad," Jim said.

"Most people have trouble with the name. Even my spelling checker thinks 'Butt' is better than 'Butech'. Once a woman telemarketer mispronounced the name over the phone, then apologized for the mistake, started her spiel for monitor wipes, broke down giggling, hung up, and never called back. Butt wipes, you see. It's not as trouble-free as calling this 'Lumber Jack.'"

"If only it were trouble-free," Jim said, blowing his nose. "Mike lines you up to install the hardware and the network. All right. Then he just presumes I'll install the accounting software. The system starts crashing and where is Mike? In Japan. I just now sent off another Cantronix 286. I've returned computers to them so many times FedEx charges have come to fifteen hundred dollars. And shipments from Toronto are a nightmare. They get hung up in Memphis for days, sometimes a week, for reasons that don't make sense to anybody, including the FedEx people. I've ordered traces on shipments several times."

"So if I get hooked up with Cantronix—"

"Your business could fail," Jim said. "When Mike shows up, I leave."

"What would Jack have done without you?" Stan said, meaning this as a compliment.

Jim had installed the accounting software, despite its unintelligible manuals, with phone calls to the software's maker. His tenacity and uncanny intuitions prompted the company's support team to offer him a job in Salt Lake City. Jim declined. I'm needed here, he had told the hiring executive. He had told Stan, I'm not about to move to Utah and work for Mormons. Jim was a member of the Assemblies of God.

"I don't know what we would have done without your 386," Jim told Stan.

Stan had rented his Zenith to Lumber Jack for a month, at half the price the local stores were charging for such rentals. Stan bought his last year at the college, at a faculty discount of fifty percent. It was the most advanced microcomputer of its kind at the time—an Intel 386, a true 32-bit processor with a 32-bit data bus. It ran at sixteen megahertz, but was faster than a Cantronix 386/20.

"I used to work for Mike." Jim wiped his eyes.

"For Mike? When was that? I thought he was the accountant." Stan said, heaping up questions.

"Several years ago I kept the books for his farm and ranch, and his stores in Mandan. It was misery. Mike wants only executive summaries. He has no sense of the time it takes to do detailed things right. He has a master's degree in accounting, but Candy did the grunt work before he hired me. She took it over again when I left. She does it now. Mike would be lost without her."

"I had no idea," Stan said.

"And that hog farm? What a stench! You can't get the smell out of your clothes." Jim sneezed, as if he'd caught again a whiff of the smell. His nose was chapped and red. He looked better in sunglasses. "Mike had us over a barrel here, until we got the Epson. I'm not blaming you, you understand."

"You've never seemed to."

"I heard from Jack, who heard it from Mike, that you're getting involved with livestock markets."

"I'm handling the hardware and software. Mike's handling the business details. I was hoping that later he'd help with the accounting software."

"Don't count on it."

"I think I need to order three modules—accounts payable, accounts receivable, and a general ledger. The first two make sense to me—the auction pays sellers and receives payment from buyers. I don't know about this ledger. Owen Yuler—he's the owner of the auction—wants a database of buyers and sellers, similar to one he has at home, only more sophisticated. The programs are written in dBASE."

"I've heard of it."

"It's the standard language for PC databases. The modules include the source code—the text of the programs. I'm hoping to customize them for the auction, using a dBASE-compatible language called Coyote."

"And you think Mike will teach them this stuff? He doesn't even use a computer!"

"I've been wondering about that," Stan said. "He asked me once, when Candy was out of the office, where the Enter key was. It's incredible."

"It's not so incredible as you might think, not once you get to know Mike."

Stan heard her voice. The music of it rose briefly in her words to the receptionist, and then she entered Jim's office, herding the boys ahead of her. Stan stood up.

"Hi, Jim," Grace said. "How are you? How's your dad?"

"He's keeping busy," Jim said, getting up from the desk. He went to the door and took Grace's hand, then touched each of the boys. "Sometimes he drops in to see how *we're* doing. Me, I'm fine."

Jim and Grace had known each other long before Stan had known either of them. They went to the same high school in Bismarck, where Jim played the clarinet and sang tenor. He and Grace became reacquainted later, singing together in the Bismarck-Mandan Civic Chorus, after Stan and Grace were married, and Jim's father had built the cupboards in Emma's kitchen.

Jim crouched down and said to the boys, "What are you up to these days?"

"I don't know," Lee said, then his face brightened. "We painted a wagon and the merry-go-round."

Jim glanced at Stan. "An old hay wagon I found," Stan said.

"We painted it light green," Lee said. "It was really fun!"

"Uncle Jim?" Vernon said.

"Hmm?" Jim said, standing again.

"Would you like to subscribe to my magazine? It's two dollars a year. I'm going to publish it every month."

"Sounds interesting. And that's a pretty good price. What's it about?"

"It explains things that kids want to know."

"He calls it *Why Mom?* Actually, it's his second magazine," Grace said. "His first was *Hoo Hoo Owl*—when he was five."

"*Mom*," Vernon complained.

"I'm sorry. I couldn't resist. It was such a cute title. I saved every one."

"The new one has crossword puzzles," Vernon said. "And hidden-word puzzles, and answers to questions kids ask their mothers."

"I'd like to subscribe," Jim said. "When's the first issue coming out?"

"There's one in dad's briefcase," Vernon said. Stan set the briefcase on Jim's desk, opened it, took out the magazines, and handed them to Vernon, who handed one to Jim. "I have some for grandpa and grandma here, too."

Jim took the magazine, leafed through it, then read aloud. "*How is hail formed? Do stripes on zebras match other zebras? What hedge can stop a speeding jeep? Answer: The PT hedge nicknamed 'pain and terror.'* Well." He laid the magazine on his desk, got out his billfold, removed four dollar bills, and handed them to Vernon.

"It costs only two," Vernon said.

"One subscription for me, and one for my dad. He loves this stuff."

"Thank you," Vernon said, handing Jim a second magazine in exchange for the money.

"Thank *you*," Jim said.

"He makes more money than I do," Stan said. "Why is that, Mom?"

"Maybe you'll be a writer or an editor or a publisher when you grow up," Jim said to Vernon.

"I'm going to be a veterinarian," Lee said. "Like grandpa T."

"Can we see the folklift?" Dale asked.

"*May* we," Vernon corrected him. "And it's *fork*lift.," he said, fanning out the bills.

"*May* we," Dale said, swaying on his feet.

"I'm afraid it's not working," Jim said. "Just one of our many problems around here."

Dale's face fell and he sighed.

"But the pop machine's working," Jim said. "You thirsty?"

Dale blinked and couldn't suppress a smile. Happy-and-sad face, Stan thought.

All three boys said they were thirsty. The soda or pop machine at Lumber Jack was something of a curiosity to them. It looked like a normal machine, but its door wasn't locked. You didn't have to put coins in, but merely opened the door. Lumber Jack used it as a cooler.

"Stan, it's lunch time," Grace said. "I don't think they should."

"It's lunch time?" Stan turned to Jim. "Why don't you join us?"

"Aren't we going to grandma's house?" Lee asked.

"They're not expecting us for lunch, are they?" Stan said to Grace.

"No, but—" she answered. She's considering the expense, he thought.

"How about we say lunch is on me," Jim said. "We have to support that beef industry now that your dad is working at auctions, don't we, boys?"

"Dad almost bought a calf," Dale blurted out.

"I didn't know that," Grace said, giving Stan a look Suzanna might give Figaro. He exaggerated a smile in return. "A belated birthday present?" he suggested.

"You weren't supposed to say anything," Vernon said, wagging his index finger at his brother.

"A waggy," Dale said, pursing his lips, shaking his head.

"What's a waggy?" Jim asked.

"You know, when somebody scolds somebody," Grace said. "They stick their finger out and wag their whole arm?" She demonstrated this motion toward Stan.

"Yeah," Jim said.

"Well, a waggy—" Vernon said. "Is when you keep your arm still and just wag your finger. That's what dad calls it."

"And if you just use your little pinkie," Lee said, demonstrating to Jim how to wag that finger. "That's a wiglet."

Jim picked Dale up and settled him on his shoulders. "You're irresistible!" Jim said. He's right, Stan thought, he is. Dale was small and wiry, not an inch of fat on him. It seemed people were always picking Dale up, if he didn't climb up on them first.

"There was this little one-hundred-and-seventy-pound calf at the auction," Stan said. "I got bidding on it, but you will be happy to know"—he said this to Grace—"that it sold for more than I thought we could afford."

"Two hundred dollars," Vernon said.

"Dad told us not to tell Mom," Lee said.

"Okay, okay, that's enough," Stan said, glancing at Grace, who merely shook her head in mock disgust, imperturbable. Why do I always think the worst when she is so imperturbable, Stan thought.

"I'm so-we, Dad," Dale said.

"It's all right," Stan reassured him. "Your mother is smiling inside."

Dale looked at her.

She cocked her head at her youngest son, walked to Jim, lifted Dale down from his shoulders, and ran her hand through Dale's curly hair.

Jim grabbed his coat, a sky-blue jacket with *Jim* embroidered in gold thread over a front pocket, and exchanged his glasses for sunglasses. "I know this place. It has great pizza burgers. Pepperoni, sausage, hamburger. Lots of cheese and tomato sauce and mushrooms. Doesn't that sound good?"

Lee pinched his nose, but all the boys said it did.

Chapter Three: Coding

MONDAY, 8:00 AM Central Time.
"The feds are required by law to provide me with water from May through September," Mike said. He was explaining with irritation his irrigation system, as they drove to Littleton in his "Jimmy." "They have to open Heart Butte Dam on Lake Tschida if I'm not getting enough."
"How do you pump it?" Stan said.
"I don't own the pumps. The feds do. They rent them to me free, but I have to pay the electric bill."
"I suppose the pumps are pretty expensive."
"That's not the point," Mike said, more irritated. "That way they can monitor my usage."
"There are strings attached then."
"You'd better believe it."
"I suppose you had to get some kind of approval."
"Are you kidding? The paperwork's taken two years. Talk to the feds, talk to the state, talk to the county commissioners in two separate counties. It goes on and on—government red tape. They're so slow they creep!"
"That's bureaucracy for you."
"They have their own purposes," Mike said. "Take this highway now. The government didn't build this road so that we, you and I, could drive to Littleton."
"No, I don't suppose they did, but—"
"They built the road for their own purposes. And here we are driving on it."

"I don't know about state highways," Stan said. "But I read somewhere that the Interstate system, the specifications for the concrete—you know, how thick it is—are military specifications. The roads have to hold up under tanks."

"Absolutely. That's what I'm talking about. You don't think semis need concrete that thick."

"I don't know. The Interstate is bad in some places just from ordinary traffic it seems. Maybe they do. It's just something I read."

"While we're on the topic, listen to this," Mike said. "There's this radar-equipped airplane I know about, but it has no radar dish. The whole skin of the plane is the dish, if you see what I mean. They've got six mainframes on board crunching the data. And then there's a fighter jet. The instrumentation is in holograms imbedded right in the windshield."

"Jeez, that's incredible," Stan said.

"How do I know? I'm a military consultant. I get a retainer of ten thousand dollars a month, and two hundred dollars an hour consulting."

"A hundred and twenty thousand dollars a year just in retainer!" Five times what Stan received at the college. Five times what his dad paid himself for working day in, day out, all year long. "You're not pulling my leg, are you?"

"Now listen," Mike said. "I think we need to go over your presentation right now. You've never negotiated business of this magnitude before, have you?"

"No."

"First rule: Don't raise unnecessary fears. People are already afraid of computers."

"You don't think Owen is?" Stan was genuinely surprised.

"I was talking about people in general."

"That's probably true. People in general are afraid of computers," Stan said. "But I think a little fear is good. You have to be prepared for problems. I read an article the other day that said networks for microcomputers are down forty percent of the time. Forty percent! It's not just at Lumber Jack."

"That's another thing," Mike said. "Stick to the project. Don't bring up Lumber Jack. *Concentrate*—you hear what I'm saying? Focus on Littleton." Mike didn't explain why and Stan didn't ask. Reasons for hiding what happened at Lumber Jack weren't hard to find. And hadn't Mike told Jack about Littleton?

"The point of the article was that those statistics don't seem to be halting the rapid spread of networks. I think that's interesting."

"Yeah? And how many people know that statistic?"

"Probably not many."

"Yuler's ripe for a turn-key solution," Mike said. "At twenty, thirty thousand, he'll think he's getting a bargain."

"What do you mean 'turn-key'?"

"We do everything from A to Z, and he pays for all of it."

Mike's customers in California must have been different from mine, Stan thought. His would rather do things themselves than pay him to do them. They changed their own oil, soldered their own plumbing, wired their own houses, dug their own wells. They would ask his advice on what hardware to buy, then order the hardware from catalogs, and install the components themselves. Stan didn't charge anything for his advice.

"I don't know," Stan said.

"Don't know what?"

"If Owen is ripe for a turn-key solution."

"We're going to offer it. Don't try to guess what he might or might not do."

Then Mike described his vision for what he called custom hardware, which meant the scoreboard. "We'll get a fancy display. Not just the kind that shows numbers. The marquee-type, I'm thinking of, with scrolling messages. Cantronix could build it."

"You think so?"

"We could display messages like 'Welcome Seller So-and-So'. Advertise upcoming sales. Advertise for big producers. Let Yuler make a little money. He'd go for it."

Mike probably knew best, Stan thought, but he seemed so condescending. The closer they got to Littleton, the more annoyed Mike seemed to get with his questions and comments.

"YOU THINK twenty megahertz is fast enough?" Owen asked.

Mike and Stan were sitting with Owen at a table in the auction's cafe. In the cafe's kitchen, a woman in a hair net was frying beef on a grill behind an order window. Owen had ordered two hamburgers for himself, and had offered to treat Mike and Stan. Mike declined. Stan went to a cooler and returned with a diet cola.

Grace would look ever so lovely in a hair net, Stan thought.

They were discussing the computer system. Each had a copy of the specifications. Mike sat hunched over in a chair set back from the table, with an elbow on a knee, looking over his copy in a manner that made Stan think he could be titled, Mike, The Thinker.

"Twenty is plenty fast enough," Mike said to Owen.

"You think so?" Owen asked this of Stan.

Thirty-three megahertz machines were starting to appear; Owen must know, Stan thought. He felt uneasy about appearing to second guess Mike, and lack of ease constricted the simple act of agreeing. "Yes," he said, and cleared his throat. "It's fast enough. I installed a similar machine at a lumberyard in Bismarck and speed was no problem." Speed was no problem. True, Stan thought.

"Continue," Mike said.

"I'd like to talk to that lumberyard," Owen said. "Do you mind?"

"Sure. I mean no." Stan glanced at Mike who just stared at the sheet in his hands. "I'll give you their phone number."

"Don't forget now." Stan gave him the number right then and there, and Owen wrote it down.

"The 386 will have two megabytes of RAM (random access memory)," Stan said. "One serial port for telecommunications—"

"Is this 386 an IBM?" Owen asked.

"An IBM-compatible."

"What kind?"

"Cantronix," Stan said.

"Never heard of it."

Mike had said Owen would buy anything, but he seemed cautious, and Stan thought he'd better give Mike a moment to explain the Cantronix and his connection to the company. Owen's hamburgers arrived. He asked the cook for ketchup, and she got a bottle from a nearby table and handed it to Mike, who handed it to Owen.

"The design of the Cantronix 386/20 is state-of-the-art," Mike said. "Just ask the lumberyard."

"Thanks Mike," Owen said. "Go on."

"The 386 will have two megabytes of RAM, one serial port for telecommunications or a serial printer—"

"You haven't decided which?" Owen asked.

"No. There are three other computers in the network, all with serial ports, and there are several possibilities—all good—for spreading the work out."

"Okay, okay, sorry, go on. Mike, would you hand me a napkin?" Mike reached over to a nearby table and handed him several napkins.

"Two parallel printer ports—" Stan said.

"Why two?" Owen said, chewing.

Stan sighed and took a deep breath. "One's built into the motherboard; it's standard equipment. The other port just happens to be on the graphics card for the monitor. Which I hope to get to in a minute. You'll need both ports eventually, I'm sure."

"What about this hard drive?"

"What about it?" Stan asked.

"One hundred megabytes is pretty big, isn't it?"

"It'll do the job. It's ten times bigger than the one you have at home."

Owen bit into his hamburger and waved Stan on.

"There's also a three-and-a-half-inch floppy disk drive—one point four four megabytes."

"The little disk drives. They're great, aren't they?" Owen grinned at Mike with one cheek bulged out like a gopher's.

"Yes, they are. And I've specified a monochrome graphics monitor. I don't think you need color. Not for the file server anyway."

"Why's that?" Owen glanced at Mike as if this were less than he expected.

"This 386 will function as a *dedicated* file server. Once you boot it up, you might as well turn the monitor off. The server will serve the three workstations in the network but it won't be a workstation itself. It's possible to run the server in *non-dedicated* mode, in which case the 386 could act both as a workstation and a file server, but a non-dedicated server would only slow the system down and require more memory."

"Let's see if I've got this straight," Owen said. "There's this 386 and I can't use it."

Mike sighed and rested his forehead on the table.

"You sure you don't want a burger, Mike?"

Mike sat up, calm, and shook his head.

"You'll use the 386, but not as a workstation," Stan said. "It will be a dedicated server. You'll turn the server on and watch for the network to boot up. Then you'll boot up the workstations, and they'll connect to the hard disk on the file server, and the server will—you know—serve them. The worst thing about using a non-dedicated server— and what I hope to avoid—is that if the workstation side of the server were to lock up, or hang, you'd have to reboot the server. And that would bring the whole network down."

"Don't tell me this can happen," Owen said.

"Well it can. I was reading an article the other day—"

"Why don't you go over the workstations," Mike said.

Mike really didn't want him to hear this, did he? "There will be three 286 PCs, each with one megabyte of RAM, one little floppy disk drive, as you say, and a monochrome monitor. There will be a workstation for the block, another for the seller side, and the third for the buyers."

"There are no hard drives in them?" Owen asked.

"No, but there is a modem card—"

"One wide-carriage printer," Owen said, reading from the specifications. "Two narrow-carriage printers, and a cable to the electronic scale—you can skip these. Okay, what's this 'ArcNet' stuff?"

"The network hardware," Mike said.

"I've specified four ArcNet cards, one for each machine," Stan said. "I'll make four separate cables from the hundred and fifty feet of coaxial cable listed on the sheet. The BNC connectors, also listed, attach to each end of a cable, one end of which plugs into a network card, and the other end plugs into an eight-user active hub also listed. The hub is a black box where all the cables meet."

"Let me ask you about the cable to the scale," Owen asked.

"Sure," Stan said. "What?"

"Well, I've talked to this guy and he says that I've got to get a new weight-control box out on the block. Is that true?"

"Yes it is. The control box you have now uses what is called a BCD signal, and you will need a serial signal—RS-232."

"Exactly. That's what he said."

"The cable to the scale will be a serial cable. Now about the scoreboard—"

"No new scoreboard," Owen interrupted. "Nope, not until this thing is up and running. We can do without a scoreboard."

Stan waited for Mike to say something.

"Scratch the scoreboard," Mike said.

"Mike says you're gonna write the software all by yourself," Owen said. "Do you really think you can do that? No insult intended, you understand. It's just that I, well, do you really think you can do it?"

"Yes, I think I can. I'm not planning to write the whole thing myself. Did he tell you that?"

"Yes he did, didn't you, Mike?"

Mike admitted he did. "How long will that take in your expert opinion?" Mike prompted Stan.

"I can get a package that includes the source code. The accounting system is all there—already written, you see?—but the code is modifiable. I'll simply patch whatever new code I'll have to write into the existing code, and the job will be done."

"How long do you think this will take?" Mike repeated.

"I don't know. I can only guess."

"Guess then," Mike said.

"Three months."

Mike turned to Owen. "The contract will include three months for development, starting in October, and three more for installation and testing."

"Okay," Owen said. "That's all I need to know. You're the expert. No, there was something else. Hmm--"

"Once the system is up and running, you'll have access to the data on every weight ticket," Stan said. "Complete buyer and seller histories. Like you were trying to set up at home."

"Oh yeah, now I remember. Some of these have it so that if somebody—the weigher, for instance—runs into trouble, he can just hit a button, and the people like you take over, like, right now. You know what I mean? You're kind of watching the sale from your office, and jump right in when we need you. Is my system gonna have that?"

Stan was encouraged to hear Owen say *my* system. "I've included the modem and the communications software for that very purpose," Stan said. "It'd be like being at your side."

"Oh jeez," Owen said, tapping his watch. "It's getting late. Mike, I gotta talk to you about those hogs. Stan, do you mind?"

Mike produced three thousand finished hogs a year from a herd of three hundred sows. He made a deal with Owen on the spot to deliver finished hogs to the market on Tuesdays, when his truckers could unload several semi loads at a time. The hogs weren't going to be auctioned off. Owen was going to act as a middleman, arranging their sale to a packer in Nebraska. The two of them never returned to Stan's presentation. The sole network from Stan's point of view covered the hair of the cook in the kitchen.

THE NEXT DAY, Mike told Stan he would talk to Owen alone. "Money is my business." Stan agreed it was best.

Mike called the day after and asked Stan to come to the office. He didn't give any details, and Stan didn't ask. Grace wasn't showing, early in her pregnancy, and Stan suggested they all go Bismarck. After dropping them off, Stan drove back to Mandan. The sky was overcast; storm clouds were moving in from the southwest.

Mike met him at an outer door to the office, displaying a toothy grin. "I got him to agree to the hardware and software specifications." Mike held what Stan was sure was a check. "I assured him we'd have the system installed in four months, by the first of the year, followed by three months of testing. Here," Mike said, holding out the check.

Stan took it and followed Mike into his office. Fifteen thousand dollars, made out to Butech. Stan had never received a check for this amount in his life, and should have been amazed, but he didn't know what the money was for, and felt suspicious.

Mike stood at his desk. "I got you four months for development, instead of three. I know exactly how you programmers think." He sat down and eased back into a swivel chair.

# SALE DAY

Stan sank into the chair in front of the desk. "This is wonderful!" he said, wondering what the money meant.

"Absolutely! You just have to know how to stroke the fur in the right direction," Mike said, pretending to stroke a cat on his desk. The old smoothie, Stan thought.

Stan sniffed the check. "Half up front for Littleton, I hope."

"No, half for Littleton and Piper."

"What? Fifteen for both?"

"He wouldn't go higher than fifteen grand for each, and he didn't want any maintenance agreements, but I got him to agree on a payment of a hundred and fifty dollars a month for communications links, once they're in place."

"You call this 'stroking the fur right'? Is this why you wanted to go down alone?" Mike didn't answer. Stan laid the check on the desk, and locked his fingers together as if in prayer. "One hundred and fifty for each market?"

"No, for both."

"That won't even cover the phone bill!" Stan said.

"The phone bills are extra and Yuler will pay them. The communications-link payment is for monitoring the sales."

"That's not even twenty dollars a sale! Some can last up to twelve hours or more."

"You can be working on other things most of the time, I'm sure. Once this takes off, you'll have a dozen markets installed and online. I foresee two thousand a month minimum. Plus new installations and upgrades."

"*Now* you're stroking the cat."

"What do you expect me to do?"

Stan had projected sixty thousand dollars for both Littleton and Piper. With half that up front, he could pay off his debts to credit-card companies, and stay out of debt for the rest of the project. He had allowed more debts to accumulate, rapidly, in expectation of the Littleton money. Now, the way he figured it, he would have three thousand dollars to call his own until the second installment. There were so many upcoming expenses, especially the baby, and he was tempted to say, *This* is the worst goddamn news of the season. He regretted so much saying it to Grace that he managed to restrain himself now.

Stan cupped his hands and breathed on them, as he would in the winter to check on their feeling. "They got forty grand for that dumb system in Montrose. Barskills charges ten just for their obsolete software."

"Listen," Mike said. "Yuler's taking a risk, he's the one funding development. And the software, though it's state-of-the-art, I grant you, is, at this point, just an idea." Stan glanced at the picture of Mike on the desk, bowing to the Orientals. Was he being subservient, or stroking their fur? "I also promised Yuler free upgrades to the software." This came out as if the plastic over the picture had cracked. Stan didn't reply. Finally Mike said, "Do you want to put bread on the table or not?"

Stan stared out the window and noticed a red-and-white pop can toss about in the street. He imagined the can's hollow sound. Mr. Big Westerner, he thought.

"Don't forget," Mike said. "There's another fifteen when we're done."

Little Mr. Yuler was what Mike had called Owen. There was no question this time, though, of who got the better of whom. A blast of wind rattled the windows, and whisked the can out of sight.

"You'd better get crackin'," Mike said.

It was the last week of August and it was starting to rain.

I almost bought a calf from him, Stan thought.

*A PASSAGE from Stan's masters thesis:*
Textbooks on programming recognize six stages of program development
—specifying the nature of a problem
—designing a solution
—coding the design in a programming language
—debugging the code
—testing the program's performance
—documenting in English, or an ordinary language, what the program does.
These stages may seem obviously sequential, but only in retrospect. In reality they interact as aspects of a set of techniques without temporal priority. Perhaps if all the specifications could be described at the outset, and a resulting design entirely encoded, and the code thoroughly debugged before testing, one might reasonably talk of one isolated stage following after another. In actual practice, however, the overall design of an original program emerges only after experimentation with partial code that contains bugs, and debugged modules that aren't tested and have little or no documentation.

"I'M WRITING A PROGRAM for a livestock auction, and I have to read from an electronic scale," Stan said, speaking into the phone.
The floor scale had been his biggest worry. He was trained in software, not hardware. He was a programmer, not a technician. The scale fluctuated, and he figured he'd have to take samplings every so often and then average them. How and how often, he had no idea. Any program he wrote would have to pass certain tests administered by a livestock association before it could be used in a sale, as a spokesman for the association told him. The man said he'd look at Stan's work when it was done.

As it turned out, the program didn't have to take samplings at all. The technician who calibrated Littleton's weight-control box told Stan that the box handled all the samplings itself and returned the final weight on request.

Periodic calibration kept the box itself legal.

"A cable from the scale runs to a weight-control box," Stan said into the phone. "The protocol happens to be BCD."

"Ah, she's old," David said, speaking of inanimate objects, as usual, in feminine terms, which Stan found distasteful. David was trained in electrical engineering like Henry—the hardware side of computer science. He had been a classmate of Stan's, and was now employed by the University, maintaining networks on the campus. He specialized in communications—modems, multiplexers, and communications software. BCD (Binary Coded Decimal) was a set of communication signals, or protocols, that were in David's estimation obsolete.

"Yeah, it's old, like most of their equipment, but I'm planning to install another weight-control box that is RS-232." His instructors preferred this protocol for serial communications. State-of-the-art, as Mike liked to say. "As I understand it, the box retrieves the weight on request." Stan heard clicks of a keyboard over the phone. Was David typing, he wondered.

"So request her, and wait for the weight," David said.

Stan thought of Grace. She would be showing weight soon. David's personal protocols, strange as they were, were tripping weird relays in him. He imagined David twisting the tips of his handlebar mustache, grinning like a Hollywood villain. "Again, as I understand it the box returns a string of characters that represent the weight in two different ways—kilograms and pounds. It returns both at once. I want only the pounds. The string also includes an error code."

"So strip off her pounds and interpret the error code."

"I'm writing the program in Coyote." Stan paused for David's reaction. The clicking continued. "And I have to call the scale program as an external." He paused again to let this sink in.

"Then I'll save the pounds in a file you can open when control returns to Coyote," David said.

"Let me go over this," Stan said. "We're in Coyote. The operator requests the weight; he hits the Enter key. Coyote calls the external program—"

"Call it 'ScaleIn'."

"Coyote calls ScaleIn, which gets the string from the box, strips off the pounds, and saves it in a file."

"If her weight is negative—check for this—there will be a message in an error file indicating her error."

"ScaleIn ends—"

"And control returns to the beast, Coyote," David interrupted. "Your program reopens the file and reads the weight."

"That's it," Stan said.

"Coyote has to call an external?" David asked.

"I'm afraid so."

Coyote's interface with other programs was the crudest sort—an external call. The operating system would shut Stan's program down, then Coyote. Next it would load and run ScaleIn, then shut it down, and reload and run Coyote, which would reload and run Stan's program. Besides being inelegant to an efficient programmer, an external call was time-consuming.

"Pascal okay?" David asked.

"Sure, what else would it be!" Stan replied.

He thought David had a religious commitment to Pascal—not the French mathematician and philosopher, but the programming language designed by Niklaus Wirth. Stan, whose commitments were more in accord with Pascal the man, preferred C. David thought C stood for Crap. In graduate school, true believers in C claimed that Pascal's structure was ass-backwards. David often barked at Pascal's detractors; the department chairman was one.

David was the best programmer in any language anybody in the department had seen. He rarely showed up for class and instead of working for two weeks on programming assignments, as Stan and most students did, he would take off for the Twin Cities and stay most of the week, then return late Friday night and write the assigned program—in C, FORTRAN, FORTH, Assembly, LISP, Pascal, you name it—over Saturday afternoon.

"When do you need it?" David asked.

"By the end of the year. The sooner the better. Do you need more than a day?"

"I am employed, you know."

"You're working on something right now from the sound of it. I can hear typing."

"Ah, she's just a little windowing program for DOS, à la Mac, à la Xerox."

"That doesn't sound like employment. More like fun."

"I'm also installing file servers on the side in my spare time. How's self-employment?" David asked, as if he'd narrowed to the nerve.

"Like unemployment until recently. I'll send you the technical manual for the weight-control box, and the technician's phone number. Anything else?"

"You said livestock. Like in cow?" The university where David worked was nicknamed the Cow College. It was a land-grant university that specialized in agriculture. David and Stan became friends when they were paired up in an assignment to develop a simple input-output program, or I/O processor, which Stan had dubbed the "E-I-E I/O".

"It's low-tech," Stan said. "But it's life."

"Lucky. Sounds great."

Two weeks later Stan received a diskette from David. Stan sent him a hundred-dollar check, but received it back in the mail.

STAN SOMETIMES had to travel out to Mike's farm to talk to him, and a surprising attitude unfolded. Mike had his hired hands watch agricultural videos, and made them take notes. He gave them written exams on what they'd seen, but never let them know how they scored. Stan thought he was expecting a bit much.

One of them, a young man named Skip, told Stan that Mike ran his operation on "schedules." Mike told him, for example, to make hay from alfalfa early in the morning from seven to nine, regardless of the conditions. "Some of those bales come out of the baler smoking!" Skip said. "You point this out to Mike and he'll look at his watch and say, 'Time to do fencing.'"

"Doesn't Mike watch the videos?"

"Well, he must. He gives us all tests."

"Maybe they come with the videos. Maybe Candy makes them up."

"All I know is he doesn't know diddly-squat about farming. Or management."

"What do you mean?"

"Well, we have six young Hutterites working on the farm, trying to escape the strict life in their communities, and they say Mike is worse than anybody they've seen."

"But surely—" Stan began to say.

"When I first interviewed for the job, I told him I'd work for him if I didn't have to abuse my bum leg. I hurt it real bad in a motorcycle accident. It has poor circulation. Anyway, next thing you know, Mike has me putting up rafters for a new hog barn. By mid-morning I can hardly even walk, let alone crawl over rafters."

"I can believe it," Stan said, feeling sympathy down below.

"Then he wonders why the work's goin' so slow," Skip said. "He likes to ride along in the cab when we're combining corn—but that's another story. I've probably said too much already. You can't beat his wages, though, I have to say that for him."

"They're good?"

"Real good," Skip said, revealing a broad grin, lips folding away like the lip of a pail. "Eight bucks a hour, plus housing."

MIKE GAVE STAN a tour of his hog farm—a breeding shed where his boars bred his sows, and a farrowing barn with metal farrowing crates that kept the sows confined while they gave birth to litters. Above each crate infrared warming lights glowed red-brown. Mike reported that his litters amounted to ten on the average. He even had an Intensive Care Unit, where his hired hands administered a regimen of preventative vaccines and medicines to piglets.

He took Stan into a feeder barn where pigs lived on plastic-mesh floors the hired hands could wash down with hoses. The pigs ate ground feed that arrived through plastic PVC pipes in the ceiling. "Ground to within seven microns," Mike admiringly said. One pipe happened to be plugged that day; another had filled a feeding trough to overflowing. There were no hired men in sight, and Mike, irritated, had to hunt down a hired hand and tell him to fix the problems.

Then he showed Stan the finishing barn where he divided his hogs into several groups, depending on their initial weight, and fed them precise quantities of feed so they all finished out at the same weight. "One hundred and fifty pounds on the average. There's no more than a quarter inch of fat on their backs. I raise them lean."

Next was the sow barn. It had a concrete floor with a wide trough down the middle. His hired hands washed the manure on the floor into the trough. At one end of the trough was a huge hollow drum, lying sideways, weighted in such a way that, when it was filled to a certain point with water that sprayed from a nozzle above it, it tumbled on an axle, tipping hundreds of gallons of water into the trough in a rush. The water washed the waste in the trough into a lagoon. A sow was stuck in the trough, on its side for so long it had a sore on its back, rubbed raw in her attempts to get up. The drum tumbled and Stan watched while a deluge struck and swept over her. Mike shrugged.

He raised his hogs in confinement—a "hog factory," he let Stan know. The animals never saw the light of day, never got outdoors until they were loaded on semi-trailers for market. Every barn put out a wicked stench. The air was laden with feed particles, urine vapor, and plain old pig shit. Stan found it hard to breathe after a while, and remembered Jim saying the hog farm stank. Boy, does it ever! he thought. Mike said this was the high-tech way to raise slaughter hogs.

"Here, I bought you more dust masks," Mike told some of hired hands in the feeder-pig barn after the tour. "Take good care of them. They cost twelve dollars apiece."

Later, as Mike and Stan were driving away from the farm, Mike said, "There are only two ways to make money in farming. You run a dairy or you raise hogs. Hogs are more profitable."

"What about cattle? You have five hundred head, don't you?"

"Cattle prices are fantastic right now, but it won't last. Put your money on hogs and dairy cows over the long run."

"Could a person raise hogs like you do but on a smaller scale?" Stan asked, thinking that perhaps he could start raising hogs on his twenty acres.

"No, I've got this down to a science." Mike was suddenly annoyed, as if the problems of the day had caught up to him.

"Sorry I asked."

"You know those dust masks? They only cost two bucks. But if you tell them they cost twelve they'll take care of them."

WITH EVERY TRIP he would take, Stan's pickup, a black 1979 LUV 4x4, lost power. The pickup would slow to twenty miles an hour going uphill. Once when it was parked on a hill, Stan tried to drive forward, but the engine killed before the pickup moved. He got out and found a flat rock the size of his hand wedged in front of a tire. He removed it, appalled that the pickup couldn't overcome such a small obstacle, and tried to climb the incline again—this time in four-wheel drive. The pickup still couldn't do it. He finally backed down the hill to a level stretch of road, took a run, and made it to the top.

"Sounds like the engine is in need of an overhaul," Mike said. On a new desk behind him was a Cantronix 286. Is he going to start using a computer, Stan wondered, equally surprised to hear Mike prescribe an overhaul for the engine. He didn't seem the mechanical type.

"Sounds like it," Stan said.

"I'll tell you what. My mechanic at the ranch can take care of it. A LUV is an Isuzu, you say? I bet I can get parts directly from Japan. The machining—I'd suggest a machine shop in Bismarck." Mike mentioned the name. "Their work's second to none." Mike's mechanic probably informed him of this, Stan thought. The machining Mike referred to was a process of boring out the cylinders of the engine block to receive a new set of pistons.

"What do you think it'll cost?" Stan had already checked at a garage, where a mechanic estimated that the machining alone would run him four hundred dollars. The mechanic quoted Stan fifteen hundred for a complete overhaul, including parts and labor.

"I'll make you deal. You install my tax program on this computer behind me—can you do it this afternoon?—and my mechanic will work on your engine for free. I pay him a salary. You pay for the parts and the machining, and we'll call it square."

"Sounds good to me," Stan said.

Stan installed Mike's tax software, and showed him how to use it, in two hours. Mike had filed for an extension on his income-tax return and the deadline for the return was a week away. For some reason Stan didn't pry into, Candy wasn't available. Mike could type but he was rusty. Stan felt more alien than usual, peering at Mike's finances for the five previous years. The profit-and-loss screen indicated three years of loss, each year in six-digit figures, and two years of profit, each again in the six-digit range. Whether the figures represented Mike's entire enterprise, or just his farm-and-ranch income, Stan wasn't sure. Hog prices and cattle prices were supposed to be good, he thought. Mike was intent on getting the return finished, and said he appreciated Stan's help.

The overhaul to the engine took a month. Parts and machining came to seven hundred dollars—half of what it might have cost elsewhere. Some parts came from Japan. Mike had connections.

"I'll pay you back when the Littleton project is done, okay?" Stan said after the overhaul was completed.

"Don't worry about it," Mike said.

"I don't think the exchange of labor was fair. I mean, I worked for two hours. Your mechanic worked for a month."

"Fair? Sure it's fair. That's the great thing about the free-market system. You and I made an agreement, and we both got what we wanted. This time you just happened to come out on top. A month of work in exchange for two hours. A ratio, let's say, of three hundred to two. It's a classic example." Of the free-market system, Stan thought.

Mike didn't have to work on the engine, of course. His personal time wasn't involved. Stan had saved Mike time, and probably money, by installing the tax software, and coaching him through it. Still, Stan thought, Mike had to pay his mechanic a month's salary for working for me. Mike had to earn that money somehow.

"It's a perfect example," Mike said.

Later that day Candy came into Stan's office for coffee. Mike had offered him an office, a door down from his, possibly to compensate for the way he had given in to Owen. Candy leaned against the doorpost, stirring in the powdered creamer she used, and said, "I hear you came out on top of that deal."

"Did I ever."

"Well, that's the great thing about knowing people who know things. Mike has tons of connections."

"I can believe it," he said, feeling uneasy about her slant. He hadn't intended to take advantage of Mike.

"That's the way Mike likes to work," she said.
"Sometimes he comes out on top."
"Often he does. And that's what makes it so great for people who know him. You're really lucky you do."
"I feel that, yes."
"I mean, look at this office. Mike just gives you the space, lines up the work, keeps your little pickup going. To me, it's little short of amazing!"

*Can't she see I've been working for this?*

If everything went as planned, Mike would make three thousand dollars for less than ten hours work on the Littleton project—a ratio of three hundred to one.

*Not bad, Candy.*

"WE DROVE UP through New Salem for a change of scenery," Grace said, during dinner at her parents' house. "And caught the Interstate there."

"You did?" her mother Emma asked. "What was it like?"

"It was lovely north of our place. Hills, and river valleys, the Heart River, and the curved gravel roads."

"It must be beautiful at this time of the year," Emma said.

"Is there salt on the table?" Henry asked, peering over the glassware and dishes.

"There are two, dear, one on each end," Emma said. "Right in front of your nose."

"Oh." He picked up a combination pepper-and-salt shaker next to his plate.

"Everything is delicious, Mom," Grace said. "I love your cauliflower in cheese sauce. When I make it, it gets runny."

"In New Salem there's the world's largest Holstein cow," Stan said. "A statue, of course, thirty, forty feet high."

"Now boys," Henry said. "How would you ever milk a cow of that size?" Vernon, Lee, and Dale were seated along one side of the table.

"You'd get two fwont-end loadews," Dale said, tapping the tips of his fingers together, demonstrating how to squeeze a cow's tit between them.

"Front-end loaders!" Henry said. "Did you hear that? Ha!" He lifted his napkin from his lap and put it to his mouth. He choked back laughter until he lost his breath, then inhaled and started to cough.

"Henry! My word!" Emma said.

When he calmed down, he wiped his eyes with the napkin. "Imagine, a kid his age knowing about loaders! Where does he get this stuff?"

"We live in the country, Dad," Grace said.

"I've been thinking about getting a loader tractor," Stan said. "And talking it over with the boys."

Henry said, "What else have you rascals been up to?"

"We painted a wagon," Lee said.

"And what would that be for?"

"For hay. If we ever get any animals," the boy answered.

"And a mower and a rake and a tractor and a baler," Stan said, trying to head off talk about animals. Henry had no use for anything that wasn't a machine, a robot, Stan thought. Henry shook his head.

"And we got to go to an auction sale," Lee said.

"Dad almost bought a calf, and told us not to tell mom," Dale said.

"Then Dale forgot, and told Jim," Lee said.

"This little story keeps getting longer and longer," Stan said.

"Jim who?" Henry said.

# SALE DAY

"Jim Fluck," Stan said. "Do you know him? You knew his father. He built your cupboards here."

"I know Jim. He's a fine young man. His father—there is no better finish carpenter in town. I saw their booth at the last Builders' Show—the lumberyard I'm talking about—and from the looks of it, they're doing quite well."

"They're doing very well, and they have most of the bugs worked out of their computer network."

"I'm amazed they'd put up with that for such a long time. Weren't you working them out? How long has it been now? A couple a months?"

"About that," Stan said, wishing Henry would drop this.

"Pass the margarine," Henry said.

Stan, who was seated at the other end of the table, handed a crystal margarine dish to the boy nearest him, and saw it go from one boy to the next to their grandfather. Even the way he spread margarine on bread was careful and deliberate.

"We have an announcement to make," Grace said.

Stan looked up at her. "Grace?" he said. He didn't know if he was ready for this.

"We just got the results back from Vernon's Iowa Basics," Grace continued. "And—guess what?—he received a composite score in the ninety-ninth percentile!"

Stan sighed.

"Why, Vernon, that's wonderful!" Emma said. "Stan?"

"Grace?" Stan said. "Would you pass the ham."

"Sure." She gave him a big grin as she passed him the plate.

"Well I should say!" Henry said. "You keep up the good work, young man."

"Thank you," Vernon said. "I'll try."
"Homeschooling, Dad," Grace said.
"Your kids are smart, is all," Henry said.
"They take after their grandpa," Grace said.
"Me? I've been brain-dead for forty years."
"I knew it," Emma said. "I knew it was something serious. I just couldn't put my finger on it."
"May thinks it's just great the way the boys are learning," Grace said. "She calls them 'my three sons.'"
"May who?" Henry asked.
"Oh, stop it," Emma said. "Stan's mother, for heaven's sake. Your daughter's mother-in-law."
"All right, all right," Henry said, and then added, as if to atone for the lapse, "How are your folks? Have you heard from them lately?"
"Dad's recovering from his stroke pretty well, I guess," Stan said. "He's exercising."
"May says once they retire, they're going to come out to stay for a month at a time," Grace said.
"Well, at least mom said she would," Stan said.
"Why don't you come out, Dad?" Grace asked.
"He doesn't want to ding up his car on the gravel," Emma said.
"Why don't you take mom's car?" Grace said.
"I don't want to ding up her car either. How is the TV working?" Emma shook her head at her husband. "What's wrong now?" Henry asked her.
"We can get only one channel and the reception's pretty bad," Stan said. "But we have a radio with TV bands and we turn that on for the sound."
"The VCR is ready to take," Henry said.
"Oh, goodie!" Lee said.
"Can you rent videos where you live?" Emma asked.

"Oh sure," Grace said. "The hardware store has a good selection, and the grocery store."

"Boys, your grandpa here built the television in the living room from a kit," Stan said.

"You did?" Lee said. "I didn't know they had kits."

"Uh huh," Henry said. "Of course that was years ago."

"I'd like to see one someday," Lee added.

"I made a guitar amplifier from a kit once," Stan said. "When I was in high school."

"I didn't know that," Grace said. "Fifteen years you live with a person—"

"Has it been that long?" Henry asked.

"I soldered everything myself, but broke this one piece. A capacitor, I think it was. It broke right in half. I taped it together but the amplifier didn't work, so I sent the whole thing to the company. Their people looked it over, soldered a few questionable connections, and replaced that part. The amp worked great when I got it back. I couldn't believe it, though—they charged eighty cents for the part, and two hundred dollars for labor!"

"You taped a capacitor together and thought it would work?" Henry said, as if he'd bitten into something bitter.

"I just put things together following the directions. I didn't know much more than that."

"I'll say," Henry said, rubbing his hawklike nose. "Taping a capacitor. My God!"

"I used electrical tape." Stan smiled to indicate his own amusement.

Henry didn't laugh, but shook his head in disgust.

"Stan's gift is more in the area of software—logic," Grace said.

"Well *still*," Henry said.

Stan thought of mentioning Henry's unstructured program, but said instead, "How is Wayne?"

"He's fine," Emma said. "So is the whole family. Patty's cutting back to part-time to be with the children. Martha's in first grade. She's doing very well, and loves to sing."

"The last time Wayne was here, he reprogrammed your Mac. Remember?" Stan said to Henry. "He changed the beep it makes to an elephant's trumpeting call. Do you remember what he said?"

Henry turned the corners of his mouth down and shook his head.

"He said—you must remember—'Macintosh. The serious business machine.'"

"We should be so lucky to have menus drop down from our heads," Henry said. "I would like some more ham." The meat plate passed from Stan to boy to boy to boy to Henry. "Thank you," he said.

"How's the auction project coming along?" Emma said.

"I've spoken to the owner and his bookkeeper, and found out what they want. I've been to Montrose to look at a system there, and called a few companies that specialize in livestock software—"

"And he's signed a contract," Grace said.

"You have?" Emma said. "That's wonderful! I'm so glad for you. Now we have three reasons to celebrate."

"Three?" Henry asked.

"Vernon's score, the contract—" Emma said.

"And our anniversary," Grace said. "It's a lovely dinner, Mom."

"I'm glad you appreciate it," Emma said, glancing at Henry.

"This auction—I suppose it's all IBM," Henry said.

"Uh huh," Stan said. "When I was at the college, somebody did a survey, and found out that engineers and art-production people preferred Apples. Computer-science types and business people preferred IBMs or compatibles. At the auction, there's an interesting serial connection to an electronic scale. It's RS-232."

"You're not going to write the software for *that?*" Henry said.

"No. A friend of mine, an electrical engineer, has already written it."

"I was wondering," Henry said. "I'd like to get a modem, but I can't think of any reason why I need one."

"The Yuler's house—Owen Yuler is the owner of the auction—their house reminds me a lot of yours," Stan said. "Everything's so neat and clean."

"All I have to clean up after is the two of us," Emma said. "And Henry's so tidy, you wonder if he lives here sometimes."

"So what you're saying is that when I'm dead and gone, you won't know the difference."

"I'll know the difference. No more complaints."

"Pass the pickles," Henry said. "I don't complain."

After clearing the table, rinsing the dishes and putting them in the dishwasher, then washing the pots and pans, Emma sliced the dessert—baked Alaska pie. Stan and Grace set the servings around the table.

Stan embraced his wife's waist.

"Happy anniversary," Grace said to him.

"At least I didn't get this date wrong," he told her. "You'll love this dessert," he said to the boys.

"*Come, my beloved. With all my heart,*" Grace sang out.

"Would you hold it down?" Henry said, putting a finger in his ear.

"I think it's wonderful," Emma said. "After three children. To be able to sing like that."

"And three's plenty in this day and age."

"Would you quit harping?" Emma said. "I'm sure they would like to have a girl. Wouldn't you like to have another granddaughter?"

"What I would like is not the point. It's whether they can support a family, on next to nothing, living way out in the country."

"With all the talent in the family, Henry, I'd think you'd like music," Stan said.

"Of course he does," Emma said. "He used to play the piano, and the trombone."

"Let's not go into that. I wasn't any good, and it was a cheap, old, good-for-nothing trombone."

"You're such a perfectionist!" Grace said.

"Unfortunately for us," Emma said. "One winter night, when he was a junior in high school, he was crossing a street from the school to the gymnasium, and he slipped on the ice and fell right on his back!"

"I was carrying that cheap thing. It flew out of my hand, up into the air, and landed on the street with a clang. I lay there, freezing, looking straight at the stars. It broke a weld and dented the slide."

"He never played it again," Emma said.

"Dad had already left us," Henry said. "My mother was all alone with us kids. We couldn't afford to fix it."

"We know the feeling," Grace said.

"That is precisely my point," Henry said, tapping the air.

Stan said, "*The rich get richer, and the poor get—*"

"*Children,*" Henry said. "Ira Gershwin."

He knows a song or two, Stan thought.

"DAD," VERNON SAID, entering the laundry room that doubled as Stan's study.

"Hmm?" Stan said without even looking at his son, all absorbed in his work on the computer.

"How much does a box of diskettes cost?" Vernon said. "The little ones."

"I pay three-fifty for good ones from 3M."

"Hmm," Vernon said, pursing his lips.

"Why?"

"I'd like to buy a box to put my *Why Mom?* files on."

"For backup? That's a good idea."

"No, I'd like to store my files right on the diskette."

"The hard disk's much faster, and it's much easier to use."

"I still want to do it. Then I won't take up your disk space."

Stan turned to him. "That can't be very much, but I appreciate your thoughtfulness."

Vernon reached into his shirt pocket and pulled out neatly folded bills and thumbed through them. "Here's four dollars," he said, holding out the money.

"You don't need a whole box. I'm sure your files will fit on one diskette. At least to start with."

"I'd like to buy a whole box." Vernon held the money out.

"I'll just give them to you. You don't need to pay me."

"I *want* to buy them. I thought you could use the money."

"You're a sweet boy. Come here." Vernon came close, and Stan took his money, then his son's hands, then pulled him into his arms.

"PRAY FOR ME," Grace said. "I have terrible cramps."

She was lying in bed under the covers. Stan had showered, and was dressing in the bedroom at dawn.

"Your period, you think?"

"I believe I'm having a miscarriage."

Stan imagined cramping muscles pushing outward and—the image arrived complete—a little blood clot of a body expelled from between his wife's legs onto a towel in the bathroom. What would they do with it?

A humiliation worse than the pregnancy.

Yet who, besides Grace and he, knew? Who would have to know? Not even the boys knew, or had to know.

He brought her pain reliever and a glass of water and told her to stay in bed and try to sleep. Then he called Mike's office and told Candy he wouldn't be in. He fixed breakfast, then read psalms to the boys. Lee and Dale sat in his lap; Vernon stood at his elbow. Stan turned a page, and read

*You have formed my inward parts;*
*You have covered me in my mother's womb...*
*Your eyes saw my substance, being yet unformed.*
*And in Your book they all were written,*
*The days fashioned for me,*
*When as yet there was none of them.*

He couldn't read on, but sent the boys outdoors, and sat in the chair, meditating if not praying, as his wife had requested. He suffered a sight of that sow stuck in the trough, struggling to get free, rubbing its flesh raw. The water slamming into her full force.

Later that morning, Grace called to him, and when he knelt beside the bed, she said, "My water broke last night. I had this gushing feeling. I think I was about three weeks along."

"I didn't want another child," Stan said. "Now

we're not going to receive one." He knelt and held onto her.

"You don't have to say anything more. I know you were trying."

"Was I? Humiliation—it's a terrible thing to say, even to think. I'm sorry."

"We're being humbled by this."

He lay down beside her, and she rested her head on his chest. He recited the words of the psalm, and saw tears brim up in her eyes and run into her hair. He held her until her tears and trembling stopped and she at last fell asleep. *When as yet there was none of them*, he repeated to himself. *None of them*, he thought. *None.*

## Chapter Four: Debugging

"IT'S HARD TO BELIEVE," Stan said. "Mike wants out of the project!"

"It's not so hard," Jim said. He had come to Stan's office in Mandan, as he'd asked, to talk about a possible partnership.

"According to Mike, the window of opportunity of his involvement has closed. Before he went off to Korea, he suggested you replace him. I need an accountant."

"Is he connected with this in any way?" Jim asked, wiping his eyes with a blue bandanna.

"He wants a finder's fee, ten percent, that's all. The whole project is Butech's. Of course, this office is his."

"If he's involved even one percent, he'll try to run the whole show."

"It's strange to hear you say that. In fact, Mike has never even looked at the software."

"Believe me, that's consistent with his control."

"He wouldn't be a ten-percent owner. The finder's fee is a separate thing anybody might receive. He'd have no more say than Owen Yuler would. He's the owner of the auction."

"I know. He called. I talked with him." Stan glanced at Jim. "Don't worry. We had a good talk."

"As you can see, I've set up Piper's equipment here," Stan said, prompting Jim to look around the room. "And I'm using it to develop the software for Littleton.

Everything's working fine. Okay, I did return a 286 in October. When the FedEx agent in Bismarck saw the Cantronix box, she said, 'Do you know that poor Mr. Fluck? He has returned this kind of equipment many times. He looks so dejected when he comes in.'"

"Poor Mr. Fluck," Jim said.

"And the replacement that Cantronix sent back—it wasn't released from Memphis for five days, just as you said. What I need, now that Mike wants to back out, or has, is somebody to teach them how to run the network and the accounting."

"Where do things stand?"

"I have all the software—DOS, the network, the accounting modules. Since October I've been writing the block program. Cows and bulls are in and out of the block in a minute, and the program's got to respond *that quick*. A friend of mine has written a program for the electronic scale. He makes it look like child's play."

"And your deadline?"

"January 1st. I have one month. After the block program is done, I have to tie its data into the accounting programs, by modifying them but, to tell you the truth, it might be quicker to write the programs from scratch."

"What about your expenses?"

"See, you're the accountant. Well, all the software and hardware is paid for, except the Cantronix equipment. I told Mike I'd pay for it. I insisted he *not* pay for it—you see what I'm saying?—though he's kind of holding Cantronix at bay. I received an invoice from them that charged me full retail prices, if you can believe it, instead of the wholesale price Mike and Jansen agreed on. I showed Mike the invoice, and he said he'd take care of it. I still owe Cantronix six thousand dollars, but they've agreed to wait until I'm paid more."

"Who's agreed?"

"Mike and Jansen."

"They're two of kind, it seems to me," Jim said. "I wonder if their private deals ever get communicated to the business office. What are you living on?"

"Three thousand from the first installment. I'll have three more months of testing in the New Year, but I'll need some of that time just to finish the programming, I'm sure."

"Seven months on three thousand dollar is spreading yourself a little too thin, if you ask me. With a family and all."

"I was sort of counting on problems at Lumber Jack to sustain me. You know, soak you guys further."

Jim grinned for the first time. "How is Grace? I enjoy her bringing the boys by."

"They like your open-door pop machine. Grace is fine. Actually she had a miscarriage in August. It was pretty hard on her. She suffered more from my attitude and me, I'm afraid, than from the money pinch. But, as these things turn out, she's pregnant again. I'm grateful for another chance."

"Another child, you mean," Jim said. Stan felt a gentle correction. "I was going to ask what you'd pay me to hook up with a scoundrel like you, but now I see congratulations are in order." Jim held out a hand and Stan grasped it. "Blessings on all of you. 'Unless the Lord builds the house, they labor in vain who build it.'" He released Stan's hand. "*Household* is what my dad likes to say."

"And you, his son, repeat it."

"How is the homeschooling going?"

"Dale is learning the alphabet. Lee's starting to read. Vernon took the Iowa Basics and had a composite score of ninety-nine."

"My my."

"Vern doesn't just read; he loves to read and, of course, loves to write. They all have Grace's gift for math. And they're learning to work with their hands."

"That's good to hear. Jack and his wife are ready to try."

"Tell them it's the right thing to do. And give them my regards."

"I will."

"Anyway, I'll receive another fifteen thousand when the project is done. Six goes to Cantronix, three to Mike. There'd be six left over. How about four and a half for your part? I'd get the remainder. Fifty-fifty then, you and I, and no further commitment on your part, unless you want there to be."

"I want to be 'involved' with your family, one way or another, but I'll have to think about this."

"Listen, would you just take the modules with you? Install them on your computer, play around with them, get to know them, then when the time comes, you could teach the auction people. Owen seems scatter-brained at times, and hard as nails at others, but Sharon, the bookkeeper—I think you'd like her."

"I'm allergic to livestock," Jim said, rubbing an eye. "Give me the disks."

The door to the office opened, and Candy stuck her head in. "Oh, Stan, you are here. And look what the cat dragged in," she said, opening the door wider.

"Hello, Candy," Jim said. "Long time no see."

"Why is that? Don't you love me anymore?"

Stan wondered what this was supposed to mean, but then Candy put one arm up along the side of the doorway and the other behind her head, bent a leg at the knee, and rested a foot on tiptoe, posing in a manner of a showgirl. "I will have you gentlemen know that, presently, this forty-year-old woman and her lucky forty-five-year-old husband are expecting. Our first. In April. Don't hold your applause. I'm just thrilled."

"Congratulations," Jim said. He went to Candy and gave her a hug, then glanced back at Stan.

"We're both just delighted," Candy said. "But of course Mike's in Korea."

"Then it looks like the grunt work will all fall to you," Stan said, glancing at Jim, who held his arms up as if protesting his innocence and offering a blessing at the same time.

"Why, what a ridiculous thing to say!" Candy said to Stan.

STAN HAD ORDERED computer printers designed to print six lines per vertical inch, and ten characters per inch on the horizontal—the standard design—but the layout of Littleton's preprinted forms, the ones Sharon had given him, didn't fit these dimensions. No matter how he lined them up, columns on the buyer invoice were off a hair; the seller-settlement voucher was off in every direction. He decided that Littleton's forms just wouldn't work. Another expense. The weight ticket had Littleton's name, address, phone number, and Thursday-sale slogan printed across the top, and posed no problem. It was 4" x 6"—plenty of room to print on.

After a day of trial and error, Stan designed new layouts for the invoices and settlements that fit the printer. He ordered three thousand copies of each of these forms, which set him back six hundred dollars.

I've got to go forward, he thought. He would sell the forms to the auction at a ten-percent markup.

# SALE DAY

IN MID-DECEMBER, Stan went through all the boxes of hardware intended for Littleton, and tested each system, monitor, printer, cable, and network card, as he had in October. Installation would begin in January, and he didn't want faulty equipment to embarrass him, or disappoint Owen, or renew the apprehensions of both.

Owen seemed to call every other day to hear how things were going. He would ask questions and then not give Stan time to explain. He had called the lumberyard, as Jim had said, and had learned of their troubles. "Sounds scary," Owen told Stan. "Real scary."

"You have to be prepared," Stan said. "Don't get rid of your weight-ticket printer. You may need it."

"The lumberyard speaks highly of the network, though. And of you, old buddy. Way to go."

Jim had said not to worry, Stan thought.

Stan took a computer out of a box, set it on a desk, plugged it in, and turned it on. The computer emitted a hum. "Not this again."

He turned the computer off, removed the cover, disconnected the power supply from the motherboard, and turned it back on. The fan in the power supply whispered normally. He reconnected the power supply, but the fan didn't move and the humming returned.

He called Cantronix and quit counting the rings when they began rattling like chains.

"Cantronix. This is Martin. Who is this?" Martin was the production foreman for Cantronix, Jansen's right-hand man, the person in the company Stan talked to the most.

"This is Stan, in North Dakota."

"Ah, Stan! How are you?"

"I'm fine." This is true, he thought. The 286 has the problem.

"How's the weather?" Martin asked. "Do you have snow now?"

"Yes, we have snow. How about Toronto?"

"We have a great deal of snow, and very cold temperatures. A good time for a holiday."

"A holiday?"

"You're lucky you caught me. I am on my way to Barbados today. We've given everybody here a three-week vacation."

"You've got to be kidding. Three whole weeks!" The Littleton installation was two weeks away; he'd have to use one of the PCs reserved for Piper at Littleton, if this was the way things were.

"The place is deserted," Martin said.

"I know the feeling." Jim had declined; he was needed at the lumberyard, he said. Mike was in Korea.

"What can I do for you?" Martin finally asked.

"One of the 286s won't power on. It just hums like the one I sent back in October. Do you remember?"

"I remember."

"This one was working in October. Today I take it out and it doesn't. It's just been sitting in a box for two months."

"The power supply maybe."

"No, I don't think so. It seems to work when I unplug the power supply. When I reconnect it, I get nothing except the noise."

"Why don't you send the computer to me?"

"I can't afford the shipping. FedEx charged a hundred and fifty dollars last time. The computer's worth only six." It's not worth a dam, he thought. "Besides, you're all on vacation!"

"We'll be closed until the seventh of January. Have you tried exchanging chips U17 and U18?"

"Are you serious? I'm a software guy!"

"I am going to Barbados today," Martin said. "Nobody will be here for three weeks, and I am saying that if you want to try something, try exchanging the chips. U17 and 18. They're right in the middle of the motherboard. Big chips, labeled U17 and 18. You can't miss them. Do you have a chip puller?"

"Yes, I have a chip puller."

"You say you're a software guy and yet you have a chip puller!"

"For memory chips, for God's sake!"

"The CX-286 is a bad design," Martin said.

Stan said nothing. He was trying to absorb this admission, and imagining an empty Cantronix warehouse, and Martin, the lone middle manager, bundled up against the cold, impatient to get off to Barbados.

"It's a beaut," Stan said.

"What did you say?"

"Have a good time in Barbados."

"And listen, Stan. Don't screw around with U19."

Stan found a chip puller, a simple U-shaped pliers used to pinch and pull chips straight up from their sockets. He located the chips where Martin had indicated, but they were under a metal support that was riveted, not screwed, to the bottom of the computer. There was a two-inch clearance above the chips, and he couldn't get at them with the chip puller without removing the motherboard, and that couldn't be done without removing the cards for the video, memory, and network, the floppy drive, and the power supply—a complete disassembly.

A *very* bad design, he thought.

Who invented terms like *motherboard* anyway, he wondered. Why not mainboard or something impersonal? Video cards were called cards, but they were also called daughter boards. Who in his right mind would dream of circuitry in terms of a mother-daughter relationship? A daughter plugged into her mother's socket. Mom outfitted in DIPS (dual inline packages), so to speak. Chips and dip. Ah, she's a hostess. *Ah, she's old.* Stan remembered David's words and his manner of speaking. David wasn't the only one. The whole industry seemed to be tending in this direction: allusions to family maintaining illusions of family.

"Exchange chips just to turn the damn thing on," he muttered.

Needlenose pliers didn't open wide enough, but with an oversized pair of ordinary pliers he had purchased for extracting staples from fence posts, he managed to get hold of U17 from the side. He felt as if he was clamped unto candy, a sugar lump tacked down to peanut brittle. He had to lift the chip without scratching the package, pop it out without bending its prongs, without breaking them off, God forbid.

He applied pressure and U17 rose and came free. *Your eyes saw my substance, being yet unformed.* The words rose in him. A drop of sweat escaped from his forehead before he could turn his face away, and fell onto the motherboard. He couldn't see where the drop lay in that fragile and miniature world.

"SHE SAYS you're a hot-blooded Icelander," Henry said.
"Well I should say!"

Henry tossed an issue of *TV Guide* on top of the kitchen table, sat down in a chair, picked up the guide, and began to leaf through it as if paper pages offended him.

"That has nothing to do with it," Stan told him. "She was talking about keeping the bed warm at night."

"Yah, keeping it warm."

"Would you let the poor boy alone?" Emma said to her husband.

"He may be poor, but he ain't no boy."

"What a stupid thing to say," Emma told him.

"Stupid? You want stupid? I'll give you stupid. You always defend them."

"You sound like a TV character, Henry," Stan said.

"Is my tape ready to come on?" Emma said. "It's already past seven."

"I program the machines to come on automatically. I'm sure it's taping your— Oh, what does it matter?" He tossed the guide down on the table.

"I don't *always* defend them. I just don't see what can be gained by being...by being..."

"So nasty?" Henry said.

"So unpleasant."

"Ah, unpleasant. Well, let me tell you, it's damned unpleasant growing up poor. It's nasty."

"I wish you wouldn't speak in that manner," Emma told him.

Henry took up the guide again and scrutinized the cover.

"So far nobody has suffered," Stan said. "Not Grace. Not the boys."

"And so, why not just have another child?" Henry said. "Is that it? Is that what you're saying?"

"No, that's not what I'm saying. I'm working. This Littleton project—"

"Puh! Let me know just one thing, if you will."

"Henry?" Emma said in a tone of warning.

Henry glanced at her.

"What?" Stan said.

"Do you know"—Henry began—"where babies come from?"

"Henry!" Emma said, and clenched her teeth.

"Has anyone told you about the birds and the bees?"

I'll never forget this, Stan thought: elegant Emma, my mother-in-law, clenching her teeth.

JANUARY 17th. Stan threaded paper into the computer printer in Littleton's booth, then booted up the block program. "I call it 'Block 1.0,'" he said.

Owen stood beside him, wearing a Thursday-sale cap, looking on as he typed on the keyboard. Exchanging the chips, as Martin suggested, had worked, and Stan put the computer in the booth, where he could keep an eye on it over the three months of testing. He confirmed the program's sale date—01/17/91—and time. He had missed the New Year's deadline, but Owen wasn't entirely ready either. He hadn't gotten an RS-232 weight-control box, so the computer wasn't connected to the scale.

Barskills' printer would still be handling the sale.

"For the first round of tests," he said, "I'll leave your old printer hooked up to the scale and scoreboard as usual, and run the computer in parallel, to see if the system can keep up." This was Mike's idea. But what of it, Stan thought.

"It'd better," Owen said.

"The computer printer will print out simulated weight tickets." He entered data for several trial tickets, his fingers feeling unresponsive as he typed. It was chilly in the booth. The heaters hanging from the ceiling blasted warm air toward the bleachers, but there was a large volume of air to heat. He could see his breath. Owen pointed out his typos, seeming to evaluate his every move.

Stan nudged him aside, checked the printer, and realigned the paper.

The day before, Sharon and another woman, part-time help, had spent the entire afternoon eagerly entering data on eight hundred sellers and fifty buyers—names, addresses, and phone numbers. The office program assigned internal buyer or seller numbers to them. Stan stressed to Sharon what he thought were the defects of the system at Montrose, and how his program was better. He pointed out that the only way into Littleton's booth was from the block or the back yards; there was no discreet route to the office as there had been at Montrose. Sharon appreciated that difference. Gofers are what we've got now, she had said.

Owen's younger brother, Lloyd, was also in the booth, wearing a windbreaker the pale orange of orange sherbet, with Littleton advertising printed across his broad back. He was fiddling with the microphone, which alternated between static and no sound at all. Owen would leave Stan, offer advice to Lloyd, then return and crowd Stan so much he felt his warmth.

"Shit," Lloyd said. "It quit altogether."

Owen stepped away, took the mike from him, and tried it himself. Lloyd located another mike in a box in the back of the booth, and blew dust off it. He plugged this second mike in, but it didn't work either. This equipment, Stan thought. Why doesn't Owen keep the place up better?

"Here, give me that thing," Owen said. Lloyd handed him the second mike, and he blew into it. "Call around," he said to Lloyd. "And see if you can get another one. And take this with you—would ya?—so you know that they match."

Lloyd took the mike from him, jumped out of the booth onto the scale, and left the block's metal pen on a run, bursting the double doors open wide.

"Forget that now," Owen said. "I need a mike." Stan went on typing on the keyboard. "Forget that now, I said." Stan looked at Owen, who had disconnected the other mike from its cable and held out the cable to him. "Here's what I want you to do," Owen said. "Take this cord down to the hardware store. You know where it is, don't you? A block off Main, two blocks south and one west. Take it down there and fix it. The connection's bad, is all."

"Me?" Stan asked. "You want *me* to do it? What about the sale? the test run?"

"Forget that now. You know how to solder, don't you? A computer man like you."

"Yes, but maybe we could tape it together!"

"I don't think so."

"I was just joking."

"Well, take it to the store then, would ya?"

Stan took the cable to the hardware store, and soldered the wires in the microphone adapter at a workbench in the back of the store. Take your time; be as careful as Henry would be, he told himself. What am I doing here? He looked up from the melted metal, and scanned the workshop, taking comfort in its orderly arrangement, yet feeling out of place. What if this thing still doesn't work?

Thirty minutes later, Owen plugged the repaired cable into the mike, and held out his hand. "Computer Man, everybody!" he said in amplified voice.

A few scattered cheers and whistles descended from the front rows of the bleachers from a handful of men. Sales were small in January. Stan was embarrassed. David was a computer man; Martin, a hardware man. Yet if Owen had said, *Let's hear it for Software Guy!* he would have felt even more humiliated. *What a ridiculous thing to say,* Candy had said. She was right, he thought. *Stupid? You want stupid?* Henry had said. *Computer man!* seemed to echo from the big room.

Stan shrugged, then maneuvered past a manual balance scale secured to the floor in the middle of the booth, over old cables taped down, over the new ones hanging at fly-height from the computer and printer, and took up his position in front of the computer, with his back to the block.

Owen started chanting into the microphone. Lloyd served as spotter, and operated the levers controlling the doors. The weigher, a chain-smoker whose nickname was Smoke, ran the weight-ticket printer, prodding cigarette butts in an ashtray.

Owen was selling cows one by one by the hundredweight. Without much enthusiasm, Stan felt.

Smoke tore a sheet from a ticket, folded it in half, and handed it to Stan. Stan typed in 1520 pounds, pressed Enter, then entered 1 head. The screen displayed an average weight of 1520 pounds. He pressed B for Black-white-face, and C for Cow. He entered nothing for Tags or Comments, then entered D-E-W, the first three letters of the seller's last name, DeWald.

The program paused while it looked up the name. He drummed his fingers on the keyboard, thinking, *slow, way too slow.* The program finally displayed a list of DeWalds—last name, first name, city, state, and Zip code, and seller number. He read down the list, then highlighted and selected BOB DEWALD. The list disappeared and the screen displayed the man's name and seller number. Better than Montrose, he thought.

He entered $47.75 for the money, and typed C for Cwt. The program displayed $680.20—the correct total price for the cow. Smoke spoke and held out another ticket. Stan took it and set it aside. He entered 10 for the buyer's pen number, and typed Y-U-L for the buyer's last name. Another delay, then a list of buyer names appeared on the screen, and he chose KENT YULER (a cousin to Owen). The list disappeared, and the screen displayed Kent's name and number in the appropriate fields. The printer printed a weight ticket, and the screen reset itself for the next round.

He folded the first ticket and dropped it down the tube for the yardmen, then picked up the ticket he had set aside earlier. Another of DeWald's black-white-faced cows. The same D-E-W to type as before; the same delay as the program looked up the same names; the same Bob DeWald to select from the list. I shouldn't have to repeat all this, he thought. It's stupid. I'll have to fix that. He entered the pen number, the same as before, and Kent Yuler's name and number appeared on the screen, as if by magic, without the delay of a lookup. The way it should work for the seller, he told himself. Why didn't the seller portion work in this way?

He would fall off the sale's pace every time the seller changed, or the buyer or the buyer's pen number changed. Smoke would tap him on the shoulder and hold out another ticket. Owen yelled, "Crank it up!" a couple of times.

Entries repeated from one ticket to the next were to Stan's advantage, except for the seller. A single buyer would buy all the cows of a seller, one after another, often for the same price. Sometimes bidding would go on longer than usual, and he would catch up. Then he tapped Smoke on the shoulder.

The sale was over in half an hour. Eleven sellers sold twenty-four cows to three buyers, mostly to potbelly Stu.

# SALE DAY

"Remember the next sale is in two weeks." Owen tapped the microphone on the counter, as if rapping a gavel. This drew everybody's attention. "And be sure to pick up your free calendar for '91, if you haven't already." These depicted Herefords grazing against a backdrop of mountains—not a Dakota scene. Their size (3' x 4') was enormous compared to others, and Stan ran into them everywhere—banks, gas stations, grocery stores. Men from all over the region wore Littleton baseball caps. Stan wrote with Thursday-sale pens. Owen didn't seem to scrimp on advertising.

Stan advanced the computer paper, tore it off at a perforation, and gathered the fanfold sheets together. The simulated tickets represented the first real data the system had gathered and stored. Now I can test the office program against the real documents issued today, he thought.

Owen suddenly lifted the sheets from his hand, shook them out, as if he were a herald about to read from a scroll, and examined them as if looking for errors. "My God, if that doesn't look pretty. Come and look at this, Lloyd."

For the first time that day Stan felt relief.

Sharon stuck her head through the double doors and yelled, "How'd it go? I have to get back, but I just had to know."

"It'll never keep up," Smoke yelled back to her, shaking out a match, exhaling a cone of smoke into the air. "Not in a big sale."

"The seller lookup is slow, but I can make it go faster," Stan said.

"Computer Man," Smoke said, exhaling more slowly.

"Computer Man," Lloyd repeated into the mike. He tipped his cap toward him, then swung the mike by the

cord in a circle above his head, as if the mike and its cord were a lasso. Owen was a comedian. Lloyd the clown.
There goes the mike, Stan thought.

AFTER A SELLER would unload his cattle at the market, he would receive a numbered receipt from a yardman. This "check-in ticket" recorded his name, and the number and type of cattle he brought in. Yardmen would keep a copy for their own use, and return a third to the office.
On sale day, the yardmen would herd a seller's cattle onto the block, and hand the yard's copy of the check-in ticket to the auctioneer, who would announce the cattle and name of the seller. Check-in tickets were called "the mail" during a sale. Stan found this amusing.
"Why can't we enter the mail before the sale starts?" he asked Sharon. "Then all we'd have to do at the time of a sale is enter the check-in number. The seller data would pop up automatically. There'd be *no* seller lookup, you see? It would go a lot faster."
She thought about this. "Well, there's the way it's supposed to work, and there's the way it does. Sometimes guys drop off cattle without telling anybody whose they are. Sometimes the yardman doesn't make out a ticket. Sometimes he does, and then loses it. We've sold cattle without knowing for sure who they belong to. More often, the yardman doesn't even bring me my copy, and I have to get the mail from the block after the sale, if I can."
"I see."
"Until there's order around here, I'd forget it."

"SAY IT AGAIN," Stan said. "Car."
"Cow," Dale said.
"Try it again. Carrr," Stan said, emphasizing the R.
"Cowww," Dale said.

# SALE DAY

"Here she comes," Lee said, peering through the car window.

Stan had parked the Ramcharger in the parking lot of a grocery store. Grace had gone alone to buy a few things, and had just come out, heading toward them with a brown paper bag in her arms. The boys were eager for her return. She had said she might buy them a treat.

"Let's try something else. Say 'Thank you for the thing.'"

"Thank you for the thing," the boy said.

"Did you hear that?" Lee said. "He said it!"

Dale repeated the phrase and blinked, as if he couldn't quite believe it himself.

"You'll have to say that for mom," Vernon said.

"Thank you for the thing," Dale said again.

Grace opened the door to the Charger, set the bag on the floor mat, and climbed in. "All right," she said, settling into a front bucket seat. "We can go now. I have no other errands." She reached for a seat belt.

"Mom, listen to Dale," Lee said.

"Shh," Stan said to him. "Let Dale tell her."

"Tell me what?" she said, turning her attentive face toward him.

"Thank you for the thing," Dale said.

Grace looked puzzled and glanced at her husband.

"Say it one more time," he said.

"Thank you for the thing."

Grace's mouth dropped open. "Why! When did you learn to say that?"

"Just now," Stan said. "While we were sitting here waiting for you."

"Now he can say 'thank you'," Lee said.

"It's a breakthrough!" Grace said, addressing her son. "It's wonderful, honey."

"Thank you for the thing," the boy repeated once more.
"What thing, Dale?" Vernon asked and grinned.
"I don't know. Mom, did you buy us a tweet?"

STAN BEGAN by spending two days a week in Littleton, besides sale days, arriving at nine in the morning, and leaving for home at five in the afternoon.

Other days he would drive to the office in Mandan and write or revise programs on the network there, keeping similar hours.

Sometimes he would drop Grace and the boys off at her parents' house first. Grace packed him a lunch every morning, and he enjoyed driving into the sunset at the end of a day. The extra hour he gained crossing to Mountain Time allowed him to get home for supper when they had supper at home.

Sales were held every other Thursday during the winter. There was enough work at the auction to keep employees busy most days, and just enough slackness in that slow season to give them an excuse to chat in the office. *Blah, blah, blah*, to quote Bill Shakespeare.

Yardmen and truckers, and Owen and Lloyd when they were in, would interrupt Stan with questions about the system or programming; or with gossip about local matters he knew nothing about; or with their questions about his opinion on the nationally televised news, which to Stan was gossip of a more extensive and sophisticated kind.

He and the family didn't watch TV, he told Owen. The VCR Henry had given them quit a few minutes into the first videotape they rented—Doctor Dolittle. Stan put the VCR and the TV away in the basement, under a tarp. Out of sight, out of mind, he had told Owen.

I'm impressed, Owen had told him.

Sharon, who was fully working herself, let him be, but he finally decided it was a mistake to try to work at the auction during the day. He began driving to Littleton late in the evening, still twice a week, and would arrive at the auction about midnight. Sharon gave him a key, and he let himself in. He was generally free to concentrate better, but even in the wee hours of the morning there were interruptions.

Truckers drove at night, and wanted to unload as soon as possible when they got in. Littleton's policy was to encourage truckers to call the auction at any hour of the day or night, and usually a yardman would get out of bed, if the hour were late, come to the auction, and help them unload.

Once, at three in the morning, a trucker appeared at the window, and asked, "You work here?" He wore a handlebar mustache, black cowboy hat, and a western-cut jacket. He was far-sighted with magnified eyes like Jim's.

"No," Stan said.

"What you doin' here then? Would ya hand me that phone?"

The trucker called Owen and told him the reason for his running late. He was driving a semi, he said, with a full load of steers from a ranch in Montana. He had tried a shortcut on a gravel road that came to a dead end where he couldn't turn around. The highway patrol finally showed up and, in addition to helping him out of his predicament, fined him for driving the semi on a restricted road. The steers hadn't had anything to eat or drink for twenty-four hours, and looked like hell, he said. Could Owen come down, the trucker asked. He handed the phone back to Stan. "You gonna help me unload?"

"Me? I wouldn't know how."

"What are you? Some kind of technician?"

"A computer consultant. I'm writing a program."
"Damn cushy job."
"Cushy? It's three in the morning."
"You don't have to remind me," the trucker said. "Damn state patrol. Those steers look like hell."

The steers didn't sell at the next sale. Nobody bid on them. The auction bought them, under an assumed name—the name of a real North Dakota farm the auction used that day in its market report. Owen worked out a deal of some sort with Stu after the sale, and Stu took care of it.

It occurred to Owen that Stan could answer the phone in the early morning hours, and forward calls to the yardman on duty, to Lloyd, or to Owen himself if need be; Stan could run the trip software from the office, and tell truckers the best way to come; Stan could offer the truckers coffee when they arrived at the auction, point out the restroom, show them the lounge where they could rest if need be. Stan complied, but it interfered with his concentration and wakefulness.

When he wasn't interrupted, he would become absorbed staring into the monitor—another world, he often felt—and lose track of time. The color of the sky, as seen through the lobby's picture window, would appear to him dark blue, then gray hours later, then light blue. His were digital mornings—now this color, now that—without the normal gradations of dawn. Turning from the screen, he would suffer a dislocation, as if his surroundings were illusions—mere computer graphics. He also began to come down with the chills, always after eating his lunch, it seemed. And he began sleeping, or trying to sleep, in the lobby on the auction's lumpy leather couch under his winter coat beneath the big picture of Owen and Mike, all smiles.

This is taking its toll, he thought.

# SALE DAY

Owen came in once when he was trying to sleep. "Go on down to the house, why don't ya," Owen told him. "I've got an extra bedroom in the basement."

"All I want is a cat nap," Stan said.

One morning at four, he decided to take Owen up on his offer. As he approached the Yuler's front door, motion-sensitive floodlights came on. In the shower of light, he felt greasy faced. The glass storm door opened, but the main door was locked. He wasn't about to ring the doorbell at that hour, and turned away thinking he'd go back to the sale barn and rest on the couch. Or maybe head home.

The overhead garage door was open; Owen's pickup was in the garage. A door in the garage opened into the kitchen, and he let himself in.

In a basement bathroom, he washed his face at the sink and wiped himself dry with a thick and luxuriant towel. In a laundry area next to the bathroom, his eyes fell a pile of white underwear, on the floor in front of a washing machine. A family sleeping upstairs, and he viewing their underwear, he thought.

The bedroom intended for him was off a game room of sorts. Pool table. Dart board. Two glass-enclosed gun cases. An assortment of shotguns and rifles. Stacked boxes of tap-water filters and air ionizers. Stacked boxes of nutrition supplements and vitamins.

Owen's wife's business, he figured.

The phone jangled and jangled again.

Stan didn't think he could take much more. Do thieves ever stop short at the sight of the underwear of their victims, he wondered, or just flee at the sudden sound of a phone?

He heard footsteps on the stairs, and turned to see an arm come through the doorway and turn off the light, leaving him standing in darkness. In the light of the hall, he saw Owen pause with his back to him, then turn so his silhouette filled the doorway. Owen turned the light back on. "Stan! You scared me! I thought it was one of the kids."

"Who left the lights on?"

"Yeah," Owen said with a yawn. "Well, good it was you." He was barefoot, in faded blue jeans and a white undershirt. "Listen, make yourself at home. You found the bedroom, I guess. Take a shower if you want to."

"Thank you."

"I gotta run down to the barn."

Stan took off his boots in the bedroom, turned off the lights, and lay down on the bed in his clothes. The room had no windows. The darkness was tangible. He strained to see through it, but his eyes played tricks with an interior light, as if cathode rays were still ricocheting through his aqueous humor. For a moment he felt he was mere spirit in the black air. His head was aching, his heart was hopping, then he felt his eyeballs, as if drying out from the day's work, suddenly congeal.

THE NEXT MORNING Stan seated himself at the Yuler's dining room table. The clock on the wall read nine. A chandelier above the table cast rainbow-colored patches of light on the tablecloth and carpet. He had showered but was dressed in the clothes he had slept in. One of his neighbors had said that changing a car's oil without changing the filter was like taking a shower, then putting on dirty underwear again. Stan felt this was true. Master Shabby, everybody!

In the kitchen Owen's wife was setting dishes in a cupboard above a counter separating her from him. He had seen her at the auction only once, and all he could now from where he was sitting was a smock from her waist to her neck. She was pregnant.

"Good morning," he said.

"Morning." A voice from behind the cupboard.

"You must be Claire. I'm Stan."

She didn't reply.

"I'd like to thank you for letting me stay the night," he offered.

She bent over an open dishwasher, and removed a handful of silverware. "You have Owen to thank for that," she said, sorting the silverware into a drawer.

"Is he here?"

"No, by now I'm sure he's a hundred miles away." She turned to the dishwasher again and took out several ceramic mugs.

Bottles of vitamins and food supplements cluttered the counter. "My wife is a dealer," he said, and mentioned the brand.

"That also is Owen's affair," she said, setting the mugs in the cupboard. "But I take them."

Owen seemed to be into everything, he thought, like Owen thought Mike was.

An air ionizer whispered on the counter next to a white coffee maker, half full. "Is there somewhere around here where a guy can get a good cup of coffee?" he said.

"Go down to the gas station. Down to the auction." Her voice was weak. Her wrists were thin. Her skin was pale. She was moving in shadows. She came out from behind the counter, and gave him an ambiguous look. "This coffee's cold."

STAN BIT into a blueberry muffin and took a sip from a coffee cup in the gas station's parking lot, replaying his encounter with Claire that led up to the last thing she had said: "Owen invites all kinds of people, but they're his friends, not mine."

He sat alone in his pickup, facing the station's white cinder-block wall, as blank as last night's black bedroom, seventy miles from his gracious wife.

RED HEART-SHAPED BALLOONS floated in mid-air, tied down by thin strings, and bowls of heart-shaped candy sat at both buyer and seller windows. "Happy Valentine's Day," Sharon said.

"Same to you," Stan said. One holiday that doesn't cancel a sale, he thought. He set the last of three boxes on the floor in a corner of her office—one with settlement vouchers, another with invoices, the third with weight tickets, three thousand copies of each. He was in the process of booting the file server, when Smoke leaned in the seller-side window, and crossed his arms over the counter. "What's this, Sharon, grade school?"

"Come on. Cowboys have sweethearts," she said.

"Shit," Smoke said.

"Aren't we surly today. Have a heart." She held out a bowl of candy to him.

"Did you say, 'A hard'?"

"I said, 'A heart'."

"Okay, why don't you give me a piece?" A smile revealed his stained teeth.

She set the bowl down and picked out a heart. "Okay, how about this one. It says, *Be nice.*"

Smoke took a candy from the bowl. "Well I'll be damned," he said, pushing up the front of his cowboy hat. "This one says, *Up yours.*"

Sharon lowered her head and sighed.

Smoke snickered, popped the candy into his mouth, tipped his hat to Stan, grinned, and shrugged his shoulders, as if to say, "What'd I say *now?*" A grade-school gesture if there was one, Stan thought. Then Smoke left.

Sharon sat down at the desk and drummed her fingers.

"What's his problem?" Stan asked.

"He doesn't have a sweetheart," she said, then hid her face in her hands.

"Are you all right?"

She held up a hand to reassure him. "I'm all right."

"Are you sure?"

"Please excuse me." She put a hand to her mouth. She was trembling with laughter. She shook out her hair, wiped her eyes, took a deep breath, then let it out. "Whew! That's better."

Stan glanced at the file server. "It's up," he said.

"Yeah," Sharon said. "But can you keep it up?" She put her hand to her mouth again, blushing, and glanced at him. "Oh please forgive me," she said, then hurried out of the office and hit the door of the restroom coughing. A single shriek of laughter came from the COWGIRLS. The fan in the Cantronix whispered, and Stan looked down to see if his fly was open.

The Valentine's Day sale was small.

The seller portion of the block program didn't require redundant lookups.

The system competed with Smoke.

It stayed up.

## Part Two

A COMPUTER PROGRAM may generate the numbers 1-2-3. What number will it produce next? 4? Let's say it's the number 1, followed by 2 and 3 again. What will the next number be? 1? Maybe, maybe not. The pattern 1-2-3 might be repeated. If the next number is 4, and everything is repeated again, the whole pattern would be 1-2-3, 1-2-3-4, 1-2-3, 1-2-3-4. The next number, however, could be 15, which happens to be the 15th number in the pattern.

But then what will the *next* number be?

If you're not the programmer, Stan thought, you cannot predict it, let alone the pattern to follow. Smaller patterns are drawn up into larger patterns, and you're never in a position to know when a pattern-altering pattern might arrive. Not even a knowledgeable programmer can predict this. The behavior of complex programs, or those written by teams, or modified by many minds over many years, can be baffling.

Stan's program for his master's degree was an editor for indefinitely large text files. It took him two years to write, and by the time he finished, he had performed countless tests, and had become so jittery as a result of failed tests and crashes that he had begun to suffer visions while he was driving, for example, of his pickup engine blowing up without warning. When he was eating, he was afraid the food on the table might explode.

Chapter Five: Testing

## WHAT IS TIME?

Stan's father had once asked him this at a time in Stan's life, his last year in college, when his interests had become so abstract that he was focusing on symbolic logic. He didn't answer. His dad said, Time is when it gets too dark to see, and water you're washing with freezes in a pail.

His dad was trying to be philosophical, he felt, but he thought that by saying *when* in saying *time is when* his dad had presumed time in his definition of it—a naive logical blunder. At that stage, Stan hadn't felt inclined to enter into the homespun ruminations of a vet. His dad's questions about time, the meaning of life, and so on, embarrassed him. This attitude seemed to upset his dad and finally render him silent—a darkening time in their relationship.

Unexpectedly, philosophy of science opened a door and let in light. Philosophy of science was the field of the theory of theories, as he thought of it—how abstract can you get! Yet, as paradoxical as it might seem, his studies in the field offered an outlook he thought he and his dad might both relate to. Stan embraced the view that scientific theories, far from representing *the Truth*, merely modeled the world, as different numerals model a number. Many models were plausible, he thought, several were fruitful.

Theories represent old things in new ways, one philosopher had written. It seemed everybody in academia was bent on multiplying new ways, but Stan began to seek out the old things understood in the old ways—older even than the oldest of theories. Time was originally measured in days and weeks and seasons and years, not factored into picoseconds (trillionths of a second) or light-years. Space was not merely the cosmos, but heaven and earth. Light was not photons, but daylight, moonlight, starlight, and the light from fires and lamps. None of these ancient things in their own terms seemed theoretical.

One day he was surprised to find himself blinking in the light of the setting sun, standing in grass up to his chest, as if he had been placed there a moment before, feeling grass seed pepper his face in the wind. He turned with the wind, and caught a glimpse through the kitchen window of Grace working. In that moment he felt his *overarching perspective* was the expansive blue sky; his *intellectual standpoint* was the dry earth under his feet. This understanding had opened to him, unbidden. He went to the house and told Grace the good news.

He moved his family into the country, fifty miles southwest of Mandan, to a ghost town called Lark, where nobody besides wildlife had lived for ten years. He thought the town was named after the Western Meadowlark, the state bird that sang so sweetly, perched on fence posts, but a man who had grown up in Lark as a boy told him the town was named after an old Scot who once lived in those parts—Mr. Larky. He also told him that soon after the town received its name, a young man said, *I came to Lark to go on a lark, and now that I've come I'm having a lark.*

When Stan and Grace and the boys arrived, there was a white town hall on a crumbling stone foundation, two houses, several outbuildings, including a tipping outhouse, three caved-in basements, open to the wind and rain and their curious boys, and the merry-go-round and water hydrant of the old Lark city park. The place looked more like an abandoned farm than a town. Ten of its twenty acres was pasture. *Time*, as an American novelist had written, *haa had its diminishing effects.* Jeannine DeWald had inherited the town site from her father's estate, and rented a house to Stan and his family for next to nothing, just to keep the place up. The house was in bad shape from years of abandonment. Bat pee from bats in the attic streaked down the chimney and dried there, their brown droppings littering a shelf in a bedroom closet. Sewage backed into the basement when the septic line plugged in the first week. Still, Jeannine's offer was generous and welcome, he thought.

She was a relative of Bob DeWald, and a member of a local Presbyterian church. She invited them to church, and they began attending services and became members.

One day she came by with an old map that named the town's streets and property allotments. A grain elevator had stood on Main Street. Their front door opened onto Dakota. 123 Dakota Avenue became their address.

The UPS man was amused.

"ONCE THE SYSTEM IS UP and running, you need to confirm the sale date and time," Stan told Smoke.

Stan stood at the block's computer and tapped on the monitor's glass, indicating where the date and the time were displayed on the screen. "The screen shows the date and time, but you should check and confirm them. Just press the Enter key if they're right. If they're wrong for some reason, simply correct them. Here, you do this," he said, stepping aside.

Smoke crushed out his cigarette, stood, positioned the stool in front of the computer, and sat down again. He reached over the counter and pulled a pack of cigarettes, with a metal lighter lying on top, next to the keyboard.

"The date is right, so just press Enter," Stan said. "Here." He pointed to the key, and Smoke pressed it.

"Nothing happened," Smoke said.

"Sure it did. You confirmed the sale date, and the cursor jumped down to the time entry. See this little blinking light?"

Smoke squinted at the screen.

"The time is right, too. So press Enter again."

Smoke pressed Enter again, and peered at the screen.

"We're not connected to the scale or the scoreboard yet, so we need to confirm that we're *not*." Stan tapped on the glass again, and read from the display— "*Read from the scale?* N for No. *Write to the scoreboard?* Again, N for No. Just confirm these."

"Press Enter?"

"Yes, twice. Now the next field contains the initials of the weigher," Stan said, pointing to the screen. "Type your initials in, and press Enter."

Smoke looked at the keyboard, then entered H-H with a crooked finger and pressed the Enter key. His name was Howard Howiatow. The screen went blank for a moment, and he glanced at Stan.

"Don't worry," Stan said. A new screen appeared. "Here we are. The weight-ticket screen. Now you can enter the weight and the head count," he said, pointing out the two fields. "Type in three thousands pounds for the weight, and two head. You can use the number pad on the right, or the numerals running across the top of the keyboard. Either is okay."

Smoke typed 3-0-0-0 on the number pad.

"Press Enter," Stan said.

Smoke did, then he pressed 2 for the head, and pressed Enter.

"Now you're getting the hang of it," Stan said. "The system calculates the average weight per head, and displays it on the screen—fifteen hundred pounds. See this?"

"Uh huh," Smoke said.

"Next you identify the animal, or animals. Press R for Red, then B for Bull, for example. All the codes, and what they mean, are listed on the screen. See?" Stan said, tapping the glass. "You'll have them memorized in no time. Go ahead."

Smoke pressed R, then Enter.

"Wait! I said press R then B. Back up, would ya."

"What?"

Stan sighed. "We have to back up. You got the red but not the bull."

"I haven't even done the bull yet."

"I know. But the cursor has jumped ahead to the Tags field already. It skipped the bull."

"Great," Smoke said. "Now what?"

"You can move the cursor back to the Sex field, where you enter the bull, by typing Shift-Tab." *To the sex field. Where you enter the bull. What am I saying?* "Hold down the Shift key, and then just press the Tab key." He showed Smoke where the keys were, and Smoke pressed them and held them both down. The computer started beeping. "Let up," Stan said. "That's enough. Now you're all the way back to the weight!"

Smoke took his hands away. "Jeez."

"Press Enter," Stan said, and Smoke pressed the key. "Now again." Smoke pressed the key once more, and looked over at him. "Don't look at me, look at the screen. Now we're back to the color. Just press R but don't press Enter."

Smoke pressed the key.

"Now notice, after you type these one-letter codes, you don't need to press Enter. You shouldn't. In fact, you mustn't. The one-letter codes jump ahead on their own. After you pressed R for Red, the cursor jumped to the Sex field. Then, when you pressed Enter instead of B for the Bull, the cursor jumped out of the Sex field, without getting the B, and landed in the Tags field."

Smoke lifted up the pack of cigarettes, tapped out a cigarette, and lit it, sullen.

"I know this seems confusing now, but the jumping ahead happens only with the one-letter codes. Maybe I'll change that, require Enter on all of the fields. For now, just press B."

"But not Enter," Smoke said.

"That's right."

Smoke pressed the key, and the amber screen read *Red Bull.*

"Now press Enter to skip over the Tags field."

Smoke did this.

"Now in the Comments field, you can type things like 'Crippled' or whatever."

"Two red and crippled bulls. Puh!" Smoke blew smoke straight at the screen.

"Like us?" Stan asked. Like Smoke, he wondered.

He showed Smoke how to look up the names of the sellers (Bob DeWald was a favorite), enter the money, select the mode of the sale (by the hundredweight or the head), enter the pen numbers, and look up the names of the buyers (he used both Kent and Stu).

Smoke didn't know how to type. He wasn't even familiar with a keyboard. Stan coached him through several trials—Smoke's stained fingers trembling over the keys.

Owen came charging through the double-swing doors, mounted the metal pen surrounding the block, as if climbing a ladder on the run, let loose that piercing whistle of his, and yelled, "Damn it, Smoke. Put that cigarette out. Don't you know you're not supposed to smoke around computers? Stan, didn't you tell him?"

The system might cost him his habit, Stan thought.

Lloyd ran Barskills printer that day. He handed weight tickets to Stan, who gave them to Smoke, who tried to enter the data, but Owen, who was leading the sale, kept egging him on so loud over the loudspeakers everybody could hear. Smoke would lose track of the cursor, and Stan would point it out to him, or reposition it if he skipped a field. Smoke would hunt for each key on the keyboard, then press each one with one finger, but there were few sellers and fewer buyers than sellers. Stan resisted the temptation to butt in when Smoke had to type letters of names, even when Owen told him to.

A couple dozen cows, a few bulls.

After the last bull went out the door, Smoke still had half the tickets to enter.

"You come over and practice, you hear?" Owen told him.

"Who's gonna pay me to drive here and do that?"

"If you want to weigh for me, you come over on your own and get used to this thing."

Smoke picked up his cigarettes and lighter, and left, looking as if he might burn the place down. The system might cost him his job, Stan thought.

"I could put a copy of the block program on a disk for him to use at home," Stan said. "Or wherever."

"Good. You do that," Owen said. "And would you mind typing the rest of these tickets in? Do it—would ya?—and I'll buy a 386, an SX, from you for at home."

He still wants to buy things from me, Stan thought. Owen said nothing to him about the April 1st deadline.

GRACE WAS GAINING weight, wearing her maternity clothes, and showing her bare tummy to the boys. They surrounded their mother resting in a recliner in the living room one sunny afternoon, where months before Stan had read them psalms and Grace had suffered upstairs. Stan was trying to tune his recalcitrant guitar on the couch.

"I love being a mother. I love you, and you, and you," Grace said, giving each boy a kiss. "And you." She blew Stan a kiss.

"And you," Vernon said and poked his mother's belly, indicating the baby.

"And you," Grace repeated, imitating her son.

"Dad," Lee said. "Say that 'stiff standers' thing."

"Why don't you sing it!" Grace said.

Stan glanced aside and set the guitar down. "*What has four stiff standers, four dilly-danders, two lookers, two crookers, and a long wiggle-waggle?*"

"A cow!" Lee said.

"Here's another one. What has two stiff standers, two dilly-danders—"

"Stan!" Grace said, shaking her head.

"Two lookers, no crookers, and no wiggle-waggle, insofar as I know?" The boys looked puzzled and said nothing. "Your mother!" Stan said.

"She's not a cow!" Dale said.

"He didn't say she's a car," Vernon said, wagging his finger, shaking his head at his little brother as his mother had done to Stan.

"I said 'cow'."

"He knows you did, honey," Grace said to him. "Vernon, don't tease him."

Vernon patted Dale's curly hair.

"Your mom's a good milker, though," Stan said.

"Do you speak in the active or passive sense?"

"Both, I'm sure."

"Candy is expecting soon," she said, as if in answer.

"So are Owen and Claire. You're changing the subject."

"No I'm not. Spring is the season for calving."

Lee sat on the couch beside his father, balanced the guitar in his lap, and started to strum it. *"Four stiff standers, four dilly-danders..."*

Their fourth child was due on the 4th of July. Our 4th on the 4th, Stan thought. An easy mnemonic.

THE SECOND SALE in March was a breeze. Lloyd's wife, Debbie, a secretary, operated the computer. She hadn't seen the software before, but she knew cattle and keyboards, names and faces, and didn't depend on weight tickets from Smoke, but entered the data all on her own. Stan was amazed at her skill. Best of all, he thought, Owen didn't intimidate her.

After the sale, Owen told her, "You and your lucky husband deserve a steak dinner. How 'bout it? On me."

It was tempting to join the party but Stan didn't feel he had a right to. His deadline was two weeks away, he hadn't finished the office modules, hadn't even started on some of them, so he stayed behind in the booth when the others left. Owen flung the double doors open. "Next time, Smoke," he said. "You'd better be ready."

APRIL, and the smell of pine sharpened the air. Lloyd was in the booth hammering away when Stan arrived, nailing the last wood trim to a remodeled countertop. Stan swept a hand over the raw plywood, joined well and level. A new blue RS-232 weight-control box perched in a wall bracket beside the old box, which Owen had retained. Wise man, Stan thought.

Lloyd helped Stan move the computer equipment onto the counter, which was wide enough to accommodate all of it. Stan connected a cable, fashioned by David, from the computer's serial port to the weight-control box. Then he mounted a stool and took in the view—the entrance and exit doors, the block, and the bleachers, all clear. "From this perch a guy can see everything. You build this yourself? It's nice."

"Uh huh," Lloyd said. "Thank you."

Stan set the block program to read from the scale. Lloyd stood at his elbow. The weight-ticket screen appeared. "Here goes." Stan tapped the keyboard and waited, staring at the screen until he sensed Lloyd was looking at him and felt he had to return Lloyd's look.

Nothing happened.

"Now what's the matter?" Stan said.

The computer beeped; the weight read zero.

"That thing's not on," Lloyd said.

"What thing?"

"The weight box. It's not even on. Here, let me get it." Lloyd reached behind the box for the switch, and after a pause pressed a button on the front. This is how Smoke must feel sometimes, Stan thought. "Hold on," Lloyd said. "Let me get down on the scale." He jumped from the booth. "Now try it again."

Moments later the weight appeared on the screen. "One sixty seven," Stan said. "Is that about right?" Lloyd was trim and well-built like his carpentry.

"It should be. They calibrated the box when they installed it last night." Lloyd jumped up and down several times. "Try it again."

"I'm going to time this," Stan said, studying his wristwatch. Moments later he said, "One sixty seven again, but it took seven seconds. Barskills' takes two."

"That's pretty slow," Lloyd said. "Let's try it again." They conducted several more trials, and the overall result was the same. Lloyd climbed into the booth, his face indicating a readiness to help all he could. "At one cow a minute, it'll never do," Stan said, shaking his head, glad it was Lloyd he was talking to. "We'll just have to use the old system today."

"I like the new weight tickets," Lloyd said. "Did he have you design them?"

"Owen, you mean? Yes he did."

Owen rolled his eyes when he learned the results of the testing, but he said to go ahead anyway. He insisted that Smoke run the software, but Smoke wouldn't do it. He wasn't ready, he said. Stan started the sale, but Owen changed his mind after selling three cows. It's too slow, he said. He called Smoke from the bleachers where he was sitting with Stu. Stan turned off the computer and pushed it aside, feeling eyes from the bleachers looking down on him. Lloyd set the old printer on the new countertop. Stan connected a cable to the old weight-control box, while Lloyd reconnected it to the printer. If Owen would only listen, we could save ourselves this trouble, Stan thought.

Smoke finished the sale.

"Why's it so slow?" Owen asked him afterwards.

"There's an external call to the scale program—"

"Can you make it go faster?"

"Yes, I know of a way," Stan answered, hesitating to say it would mean rewriting the whole program. "There are a couple of ways."

"Okay, that's all I wanted to know."

He doesn't need to know now, Stan thought.

"There was something else. What was I thinkin'? Oh yeah, the weight tickets, you know."

"Yes," Stan said, expecting to hear a good word like Lloyd's.

"I want smaller ones like we used to use."

"You don't like the ones I already have?"

"Come on into the office, and I'll show ya what I mean. No sense in payin' for all that extra paper."

I've already paid for a wagonload, Stan thought, as he followed Owen and Lloyd into the office.

Owen showed Stan the smaller weight tickets with preprinted areas for the sale data. "Nope," Stan said when he saw them. "I need a ruler." Sharon handed him one. Stan measured the tickets. "They're only one and a quarter inch high."

"What's wrong with that?" Owen asked.

"It won't work in the printer."

"What'd ya mean it won't work?"

"The printer you have can either push or pull the tickets through. Pulling wastes paper, so I put the printer in push mode, which can actually move the paper in both directions."

"I don't follow ya. So just push these little buggers through."

"Haven't you watched the printer work?"

"Well, sure. But just what are you talking about?"

"After the printer prints a ticket, it ejects it up far enough so you can tear it off."

"Right," Lloyd said. "I gotcha that far."

"Now the next ticket, which is blank, is too high," Stan continued. "So the printer reverses direction and pulls the blank ticket back down into position."

"I was wondering why it went in reverse," Lloyd said. "It's the first printer I've ever seen do that."

"Would you let the man finish?" Owen said him.

"But you if pull it down too far, the top of the ticket will get caught on the print head, or on the shield for the ribbon, when it starts to go up. There's no fear of that now, because the tickets are big. But I think the top margin on this would have to be a fourth of an inch, at the least," Stan said, indicating the small ticket. "And that doesn't leave much room for anything else."

"So you're sayin' the weight tickets are too small," Sharon said.

"Well, maybe not," Stan said, changing directions himself like the reversible printer. "I'll just have to play with that size and see. It'd better be blank though. I don't want to have to print within these tight lines."

"I don't care about how blank it is. It's just the size I'm talking about," Owen said flatly. He seems depressed, Stan thought. So he decided to absorb the cost of the first tickets himself.

COYOTE, INC., had issued a new version of its database software, with an improved API (application program interface) which might have increased its overall speed, but it was expensive, and Stan was afraid it might still be too slow.

He finally decided to eliminate Coyote's external call to David's program by eliminating Coyote entirely, at least from the block program. He would write a new block program in Pascal, and incorporate David's code directly into it, making a simple and fast *internal* call to ScaleIn. The new program would get the weight from the weight-control box and immediately move on.

He bought the most recent professional version of Pascal, complete with compiler, assembler, and debugger, and another package of Pascal procedures that mimicked

Coyote commands and manipulated dBASE-compatible files. There was no complete correspondence between the commands of Coyote and these Pascal procedures, unfortunately, and translating the block program from one language to the other made redesigning it necessary.

Stan called the new program *Block 2.0*.

These decisions cost him five hundred dollars. He paid for them, and other expenses, with cash advances on credit cards, and with money earned from odd jobs. Credit-card companies kept offering him cards, basing their offers, he figured, on his credit rating from his years at the college, when he had paid off his debts right away. The odd jobs took time from the project, of course. The advance of the first installment from Owen was gone by now.

The block program wasn't completed by the next sale, and Stan called Littleton Livestock to tell Owen the bad news.

"Littleton Livestock. This is Sharon. How may I help you?"

"Hello, this is Stan."

"Good morning!"

"Good morning," he said, trying to make it sound grim. "Say, would you tell Owen the block program's not ready? I won't be coming down today."

"Don't worry about it. Owen won't be in either. Claire had a baby boy this morning."

Now Rick has a brother, Stan thought. "Give Owen and Claire, and Rick, and their girl—and their baby!—my regards."

"They've named him Michael Owen," Sharon said.

A cigar and a photograph of grinning parents and baby arrived in the mail that very day from Mike. Candy had given birth to their first child, Mike Jr., on April 1st.

"April Fools', little guy," Stan said, handing the photo to Grace. "I'd never name a child after me."

MIKE WAS OFTEN OUT OF TOWN on business for weeks at a time, often out of the country. Candy ran the show, as she put it, when Mike was absent. She managed a large part of their operation even when he was around—or this is what Jim said. She was also busy with Mike Jr., as a new mother. She brought him with her to the office every day. She had a coffee station, as she called it, set up in a small room in the office Stan had, and she continued to make coffee in that room after he settled in. *Help yourself to coffee, Stan. Don't be shy*, she would say. In fact, she sort of forced it on him. *Your cup is empty. Shame on you*, she would say. Or, *I can't drink this all by myself. Help me.* Or, *If you don't help me drink this, it'll just burn.* Maybe the bookkeeper in her couldn't bear to see the coffee go to waste. Yet if the two of them managed to drink all the coffee before the day was out, she made another pot, and started in on him again.

Stan didn't mind. He was uniquely prepared for maternalism of a particular kind in connection with coffee. His dad's mother was a full-blooded Icelander, as his dad's father was, and she had a habit of humiliating even her younger grandchildren if they refused to drink coffee. Stan's little sister once did when his grandma was serving at a wedding reception. *Shame on you*, his grandma said to her, in a tone similar to Candy's. Before Stan was born, before his mother had even dated his father, his then-to-be mother heard a woman on a hospital ward moaning as she came to consciousness after surgery, pleading not for her husband or her children or God but for *Coffee! Coffee!* This woman was Stan's then-to-be grandma.

His grandparents were Lutheran, of course, and grandpa Jonas Thorlofson was reputed to have said, when he was challenged one day: *You're goddamn right I take my religion seriously. Don't you?*

The way they talked had passed from father to son.

Stan thought Candy was attractive when she was pushy, which was most of the time. Mike called her his restless California beauty. She said she couldn't stand the small-town life of Bismarck and Mandan, which seemed to render her more restless than she liked, but more beautiful to Mike. The situation was no-win for her, Stan reasoned.

One day she came to the coffee station carrying Mike Jr., and poured herself a cup. Stan sat at a workstation in the outer room. "The one thing that Mike finds it hard to learn is that he's a father and has a son," she said.

Stan heard her but went on with his work. He had come across a report on a cupboard door at the auction that indicated Littleton Livestock had sold 45,000 head of cattle between October and December the year before. He was trying to determine whether or not the hundred-megabyte drive in the server was big enough to handle the data for that many.

"Stan!" she said, calling from the other room. "Do you mind if I ask you a question?"

He wasn't sure. She might needle him about the pickup, the office, the Littleton project. He glanced at the picture Grace had framed for his office—he in the work belt, the boys in their aprons, in front of the painted wagon. "Sure!" he yelled back. "I mean no. Go ahead." He pushed his chair away from the workstation, and leaned back.

Candy got into a chair close to him, sat down, and leaned forward, holding the baby. "Mike wanted Mike—

this Mike," she said, glancing at the baby. "He wanted him baptized, and I'm not sure it was right."

"Mike wanted him baptized? I didn't think he even went to church." Mike had told Stan in one of their meetings that alcoholism was the most serious problem in rural communities, especially among young people. Mike thought the churches were way out of touch with what concerned people most.

"He doesn't. And I was raised a Baptist."

"I see what you're saying." Baptists didn't believe in baptizing infants; they baptized adults.

"Now the minister in Bismarck, the Presbyterian one, our friend, George—oh, of course, you already know him—he said it was okay. He baptized him right in the house!"

"In somebody's house, that's okay," Stan said. "You remember the Philippian jailer? St. Paul baptized him and his whole household late at night, in their house. That isn't a problem."

"Oh, I'm sure it's okay."

Stan wasn't sure what she meant. "Did George tell you that baptism can make matters worse for a child if he doesn't 'own up' to his baptism, so to speak, later in life?"

"Why no, he didn't. *That* can't be true. Mike was baptized when he was baby—his mother's a Catholic. Most people are baptized as babies, aren't they? Isn't that true?" Without waiting for an answer, Candy stood up from her chair, and adjusted her hold on the baby. "I'm sure it'll all work out just fine." She walked out of the room, closing the door to the office with a careful click of the latch.

Candy was Baptist. The Flucks were Assemblies of God. Stan was Presbyterian; so was their mutual friend, George. The Yulers were Baptist—a recent development in Owen's life, Stan had heard. From gossip about it, Owen had been a big drinker, but had quit, and now put Bibles in Littleton's lobbies and lounges. Stan hadn't seen any.

Mike surrounds himself with all these professing Christians—what does that mean, Stan wondered. Why have his son baptized? Belief, superstition, custom; to pacify his mother, to agitate his wife; regard for his mother, due regard for his minister friend; all the above. Lots of models, he thought. Who knows what the truth is?

That was Pilate's response.

GRACE TOLD PEOPLE she was expecting a firecracker: *Our 4th on the 4th*. On Thursday, April 25th, she went into labor ten weeks early. She had been crouching on the kitchen floor, wiping out a lazy Susan, working at midnight, when her water broke. They had hoped to have the baby at home.

She phoned a rural hospital twenty-five miles away and made arrangements, her plump image reflected in a window as if superimposed on the darkness outside. Stan helped her pack a suitcase. They went to the Ramcharger, where she spread a bath towel on the driver's seat, climbed in, and settled herself behind the steering wheel. She insisted on driving herself; he would stay with the children. Feeble light from the house fell over her features. Stan closed her in. "'Beloved, don't delay,'" he said.

"God be with you," she said, and drove off. The car's lights disappeared behind trees near the highway. Then the phone rang. Oh no, the nurse said; she should go directly to Bismarck. Sixty miles in the opposite direction, Stan thought. Driving in her condition—all for nothing.

He called Evelyn Ream, a friend from church who lived half a mile away, and within ten minutes she arrived to stay with the boys. Grace arrived home an hour later.

Stan took over the driving, and listened to his wife talk about a sharp curve that she had slowed down to sixty to make, and of a deer that had reached the other side of the highway just as she passed it. The dashboard's pale light illuminated her face.

Soon the deputy sheriff stopped them, as Stan was speeding down the dark, empty highway through Flasher. Stan explained their predicament, and the officer instructed him to turn on his flashers, then let them go.

*Turn on my flashers in Flasher.* Coincidences of this sort annoyed him, but once he and his wife were on their way again, he welcomed the steady blinking of the indicator lights in the dark capsule of the car. The only vehicles they passed were amber-lighted semis, and trucks, hauling what things who knows where at that hour of the morning.

They reached the hospital in fifty minutes. Grace was confined to a bed in an attempt to retain as much amniotic fluid as possible.

"I was expecting a firecracker," Grace told the doctor examining her. "But nothing like this."

"Acting a little bit too independent, I think," the doctor replied. "The child is in the best place for now."

The hospital room was high-tech and expensive, but Stan found it hard to admit it might be a luxury. His child's life was at stake. "I'm glad we kept our insurance paid up," he said.

Over the weeks in the hospital, Grace read books, listened to cassette tapes of music and sermons, received visitors (her mother came almost every day), talked with the nurses, and rested and waited. Stan found himself repeating under his breath—*You have formed my inward parts. Cover me in my mother's womb.*

THEY HAD WANTED to put in a garden. Mr. Miller, a retired man from town, used a roto-tiller to till up gardens, but he wouldn't break sod. Mr. Day, a retired farmer and their nearest neighbor, was sorry he couldn't help them out; he hadn't owned that kind of equipment for twenty years. Chuck Ream, their next-to-nearest neighbor and Evelyn's husband, said he would be right over.

  He arrived, slim, tan, and wrinkled, in a beat-up straw cowboy hat, on a weathered orange tractor, an Allis Chalmers D17. He looked over the spot where Stan planned to put in the garden. "In this wide open area between the two rows of trees," Stan told him. Without a word, Chuck drove away, disappearing behind a grove nearby; the tractor slowed, then idled. Several minutes passed and he reappeared, pulling a rusty two-bottom plow that squeaked on its metal wheels. The curved moldboards of a plow of this type cut and turned the sod. "It's from the forties," Chuck said. He finished plowing and drove away.

  Stan stared at the uneven overturned earth—grassy clods, row upon row, sixty square feet, wondering, What do I do now? Sixty feet square, he corrected himself, pounding on a clod with a shovel, shaking dirt loose from the sod. Sweat pooled on the lenses of his glasses, which kept slipping from his face. Bending was painful. He heard a tinkling sound growing louder and, looking up, saw through the trees Chuck returning with something behind the tractor, rows of concave steel discs that pinged on the gravel and rocks of their road. The discs broke up the clods, smoothed the dirt, and leveled the garden off.

  "What do you want for your trouble?" Stan asked.

  "Nothin'. Welcome to the neighborhood."

STAN AND HIS SONS visited Grace twice a week, and she eagerly followed their stories. Vernon would explain how he and the others helped in the garden. Lee would tell how they fixed meals and ate them without her.

Dale wouldn't spontaneously speak or even go to his mother.

"And how is the block program coming along?" she asked.

"It's almost done," Stan said. "I wish I could determine the speed without going to Littleton. It should be a lot faster without that stupid external call."

"I'm sure it will be. I'm praying for you."

"And Owen. He wants that small weight ticket. Which may be a problem, but we'll see."

STAN SET UP OFFICE in the basement of their house in Lark in order to be near the boys and keep up the garden. The basement was unheated and he put in a small wood-burning stove. An image of a fully clothed man playing a lute behind a woman reclining naked was cast into both sides. Stan had no time for guitars; his wife was in a hospital bed. The pastoral life isn't a lark, he thought. He burned rotted boards he had stripped from the hay wagon, and imagined the naked woman welcomed the warmth, as he did.

The foundation of the house had a pyramid of concrete, four feet high, along the south wall to keep the house from sliding downhill, and the corners of the north wall had one-inch cracks near the floor. Stan heard water from melting snow pour into the basement through the cracks late one night, and had to scramble to get cables and box after box of their stuff and Littleton's up off the floor.

Water would also rush down makeshift pipes to the septic tank outdoors when the boys drained the sink in the kitchen after washing the dishes, or flushed the toilet, or washed the clothes. The well's jet pump would kick in when they turned on the water, to water the garden or get a drink or make coffee for Stan. When they thumped down the stairs from the second story like a herd of elephants, or got into arguments, he would tramp upstairs and straighten things out, then return to the crypt, as he came to regard it. Sunlight entering through oversized windows accentuated the cobwebs overhead but the spring light cheered him.

The block program retrieved the weight in a blink, to everybody's surprise.

"HOW LONG do you think this will take?" Stan asked.

"It all depends," Chuck said. He slowly got down on his knees, sat back on his heels, and removed the cover from a box that held a metal clipper wrapped in stained paper. The box cover read

*Sunbeam Corporation*
*formerly*
*Chicago Flexible Shaft Company*

Stan waited for him to say more, but he didn't. "Depends on what?" Stan said.

"On how it goes," Chuck said, unwrapping the clipper and examining it.

"Yes, I suppose how long it takes will depend on how it goes. How does it usually go? How long does it usually take? You must have some kind of idea."

"Oh I don't know. Two or three weeks maybe."

Chuck rotated a metal pin on an end of the clipper, and the blade on the other end wobbled back and forth.

"Okay, that gives me some idea. More likely two weeks?"

"More likely three."

*Why didn't he just say that to begin with?*

They were in one of the rooms in Chuck's sheep barn, and two sheets of plywood lay on the floor. A half-horse electric motor was bolted to a shelf high on one wall. Attached to it were a pair of chrome shafts forming an arm and forearm, with gears at the elbow. The free end of the second shaft, the forearm as Stan thought of it, touched down on the plywood, and from its hollow end oil oozed.

Chuck reached for what looked like a metal three-pointed star—a screwdriver with tips of different sizes—and loosened a screw on the clipper.

"All right," Stan said. The Littleton project might be slipping away, but he felt he was getting somewhere with Chuck.

"How many sheep do you have?" he asked.

"One hundred and forty, not counting the bucks, which are five." Chuck removed from the clipper what appeared to be a comb and laid it down on his pant leg. The comb, bright chrome and four inches wide, had eight teeth, crusted with something like wax. He gave a twist to a knob on the top of the clipper, removed a blade with several triangular teeth, and set that down beside the comb.

Stan crouched beside him and picked up both parts. "What are these called?"

"The one with the sharp teeth's the cutter, and the other's the comb. I have to replace them." Chuck selected a new comb and began to fasten it on.

Stan set the cutter and comb down on Chuck's denim pant leg, and stood up. "You think this'll take more than two weeks?"

"When I was young, I could shear a sheep in five minutes. Now it's fifteen. And when I have to catch them first, and put the wool in the bag myself, and clean up for the next one, maybe I get two done an hour."

"Well, if I catch them, and put the wool the bag, and clean up, how many do you think you can do? An hour, I mean."

"Four if we're lucky. But I don't believe in no luck." Chuck placed a new cutter in the clipper, centered it, and tightened the knob.

"Can't you hire somebody?" Stan said.

"At twenty-five cents a pound? Shearers charge a buck-fifty a head. Not when wool prices are down." Chuck squirted oil onto the clipper from a long-spouted oil can, set the can down, rotated the end pin, examined the way the blade moved, and adjusted the knob.

"And it has to be done, doesn't it? The days are growing warmer, and so are the sheep!" Stan could make two hundred dollars on a good day, but he was volunteering his time to Chuck, partly to help him out, but also for the experience. Grace wanted to raise sheep. While she lay in bed, Evelyn helped take care of the boys, and often invited them over. The boys were in the house helping her prepare lunch. "If we can do thirty a day, shouldn't we be done in five days?"

"That all depends," Chuck said, and said nothing more.

"On what?" Stan said, realizing he had raised his voice.

"You can't be here every day," Chuck said, in the same flat tone as before. "You'd better see to your wife."

I'm exasperated with him, Stan thought, and he's thinking of my needs. "True," he admitted. "We visit her two days a week."

"And we can't shear wet sheep."

Stan thought this through, and said as if to himself, "So it might rain, and they'll get wet, and then we can't shear them. They'll have to dry off, and the whole business might take... Well, who knows?"

"It all depends on what the weather might do."

"Are the sheep in the barn?" Stan said.

"I drove them in last night. This old barn—it leaks. But it didn't rain, thank the Lord."

"What can I do?"

"There are wooden gates and some steel posts in the other room, where the sheep are."

"Should I make a corral of some sort?"

"Yeah, we need to go do that," Chuck said, rising up off his heels.

"I can do it myself, if you have something else to do. Just tell me how."

Chuck settled back on his heels and sighed. He's not used to giving directions, Stan thought. To people at least. Or giving these kinds of directions to people. "Okay then," Chuck said, shutting his eyes tight, baring his teeth, placing a wrinkled hand on his hat, thinking hard. "Set three of those gates in a line by the door. This hinged door right here, not the sliding one on the east. Make a sort of a chute to it—this door, I mean. Put posts in the ground to hold them up. Wire the gates together. There's wire on the gates. Then make a kind of half circle with the rest of gates, and hook them to the chute. I use that half circle to catch them in." He took his hand from his hat and opened his eyes. "Did you get all that?"

Stan opened the door between the two rooms. Some of the sheep were lying down with their feet under them; others were standing. The ewes had produced about two hundred lambs that spring, and the lambs were mixed among them. He entered the room, and the sheep lying down got up on their feet; they all bunched up against the far walls, most sheep facing away from him. The steel posts and wooden gates, panels measuring three feet by four feet, were leaning against the wall near the sliding door. Stan set up the panels that would guide the sheep to the smaller room where Chuck was preparing to shear them.

"SUNBEAM used to be the Chicago Flexible Shaft Company?" Stan asked him. "When was that?"

"The young shearers have flexible shafts. Mine're stiff, like my back." Chuck bent over and picked up the hollow end of the shaft, then pulled on a string weighted with round metal washers. The motor started; the gears began to clatter. He stood and, inserting the metal pin on the end of the clipper into the hollow end of the shaft, shoved the shaft and the clipper together in one quick motion. The cutter burred back and forth in a blur.

A dangerous tool, Stan thought.

Chuck bent over again and pulled on the string. The motor slowed and then stopped. With a gentle twist of the wrist, Chuck disconnected the clipper, and let the driveshaft swing down to the floor. "Bring 'em on in. I'm finally ready."

The last time Stan had handled sheep was in high school when he had showed a black-faced, or Suffolk, ewe at the county fair. He had received a blue ribbon for the ewe, and a red ribbon for showmanship, but no spectators in Chuck's barn looked on as the sheep approached the chute warily, then bolted away when Stan tried to crowd them in further. He finally got ten sheep corralled in the chute area, and wired the half circle shut. He waded, as if through snow up to his thighs, to the front of the sheep, and wrestled a ewe to the door of the shearing room. He was breathing hard. The air in the barn was humid from the warmth of the sheep but it was nothing like the air in Mike's hog barns. Sweat dripped from his face onto the wool on the sheep's back, his forearms glistening under flecks of manure. His T-shirt was soaking wet. The feel of live wool in his hands, and its smell, reminded him of the feel and smell of wool scarves over his face in past winters.

This is hard work, he thought. Writing programs, for all its demands, was a sedentary job. Then again, sitting for hours was hard on the crotch.

Chuck plumped the ewe down on her rump, resting her back against his legs, pulled on leather gloves, and leaned over her. He pulled the weighted string that started the motor, and snapped the clipper into the drive shaft. Here we go, Stan thought. The sheep must have had a similar thought. She emptied out onto the plywood a bunch of round turds, then peed.

Chuck ran the clipper down along the right side of the sheep's belly. The wool exposed to the weather was white gray, but the wool revealed by the clipper was cream yellow. Chuck swept his hand across the sheep's belly in horizontal strokes, the tool clacking louder when he'd push through clumps of wool matted with dirt. He grabbed this wool and tossed it aside. He clipped the wool off the back legs and hind parts, and with care avoided nicking the ewe's udder, or bag. He clipped around the stub of her tail. The room was filled with machine noise, but the sheep before its shearer was silent. Chuck straightened up slowly. Shearing would seem hard on the back, Stan thought. Chuck grabbed a foreleg, clipped it, then the other. He clipped the wool off the ewe's shoulders and chest.

Chuck adjusted his stance and, with his free hand, grabbed the ewe's snout. The ewe, with what looked to Stan like strain in her eyes, struggled while Chuck held the clipper away from her. Then, forcing her to straighten her neck, he ran the tool up from her chest to her throat. The clipper disappeared in the luxuriant growth, then reappeared at her jaw. Chuck got down on a knee and, with the clipper still burring, parted the wool with both hands. The wool was about three inches thick, Stan thought; and the parting reminded him of the Red Sea as

Hollywood had parted it. Chuck had not only nicked her neck; there was a slit in the skin near her throat, a narrow red oval about three inches long.

    Chuck shook his head, and let go of her snout. She brought her head forward and blinked, licking her chops. Chuck clipped the wool from between her eyes, from her cheeks, from around her ears, and from the remainder of her head and neck. Holding her by the neck, he stepped around in front of her and, in long horizontal strokes clipped the wool from her sides and back. From one side of her body to the other, he ran the clipper across her backbone, near to the skin, and on the backswing folded the wool over. Her skin was loose and pink. The skin was also baggy near her rump and Chuck pulled it taut. The last strokes of the clipper hit into the plywood. Sixty years old and he can still touch his toes, Stan thought.

    Chuck reached out and pulled on the string. The trilling noise of the gears and the clipper seemed to die away in receding rings of sound, then there was silence, except for a breeze coming in through the top half of a divided door and a bleat of a sheep. The ewe lay surrounded by her own wool as if she lay on a big pillow, a yoke on an egg. Chuck removed the clipper from the drive shaft and set it aside. "Hand me that spray can," he said, pointing toward the wall by the half door.

    Stan got the can and gave it to Chuck, who sprayed dark blue aerosol on several nicks and on the cut near the ewe's throat.

    "It's an antiseptic and an insect repellent," Chuck said. He let go of the sheep and nudged her with his foot. She got up on her feet—without her wool looking more like a goat. Stan opened the half door and stepped out of the way. The ewe didn't move. Chuck gave her a pat on the rump and she hopped over her wool and, with clattering, slipping hooves on the plywood, ran and then jumped through the door just as Lee stuck his head in. He disappeared for a moment, then he and his brothers stepped into the room. "Whew," he said wide-eyed. "That was close."

Vernon looked out through the door. "Without her wool on, that big udder makes her look like goat."

"Great minds think alike," Stan told him.

The ewe stood near the barn, looking around, and let out a bleat, then another. "She's looking for her lambs," Chuck said. She bleated again. "And they're in the barn."

"That sounds more like a 'maa' than a 'baa'," Vernon said, imitating the typical child's storybook sound.

"Maa," Lee said, mimicking the ewe. "Maa."

"She's nursing twins," Chuck said.

"She looks funny," Dale said. "And those blue spots look funny."

"I hate when I cut them. Their lanolin is a God-given healer, but I gotta keep the flies off until the cuts close up."

Chuck directed the boys to pick up the belly wool and other small pieces, and put them in a small burlap bag in the corner of the room. The fleece on the floor Chuck gathered together and tied with brown paper string. He tied a loop in the string and placed the loop over a hook of a hanging scale depending from a hook in the ceiling. "Twelve pounds," he said.

"Is that good?" Lee asked.

"It's pretty good. It's usually ten."

Outdoors, beside Chuck's old Ford pickup, stood a metal stand, seven feet high, with a round base and top, that held open the mouth of a large burlap bag. Stan carried the fleece out to the stand, held it above his head as far as his arms could reach—raw wool covered his face—

and dropped it into the bag. Stan entered the barn just as Vernon finished sweeping. To Stan, the room smelled of sweat, body odor, oil, turds, pee, wool, and raw lanolin. He felt a smattering of grease on his face.

By the end of the morning, the boys were taking turns jumping inside the big bag. They would crawl over on top of the stand from the top of Chuck's pickup, drop down into the bag, and disappear from sight.

"Pack 'em down good," Chuck told them. The bag bulged and swung from their jumping. "Especially around the outside."

When the clipper got too hot to handle, Chuck replaced its cutter, and when its comb got gummed up with lanolin, he scraped the comb clean. Sweat beaded his face and spotted the back of his shirt. He drank ice water from a plastic thermos, and offered Stan and the boys some.

At lunchtime, they drank ice water from pint jars. Evelyn served a cold macaroni salad with small cubes of Cheddar cheese, bologna, sweet pickles, and peas, all mixed up in salad dressing. "This salad is second to none," Stan told her. "Could I get the recipe?"

"Your boys already have it," she said. "Thank you. It's also Chuck's favorite."

Toward mid-afternoon, Stan was packing the wool down in the big bag. The boys were too lightweight. At the end of the day, Stan and the boys were tired and dirty and happy. As they drove out of Chuck's yard, Chuck yelled to him, "And check them for ticks!"

"How did it go?" Grace asked when he called her.

"We sheared twenty-four sheep," Stan said.

"I HEAR MUSIC," Lee said.

Mozart's *Requiem* was playing when they arrived at the door to her hospital room: *Kyrie, eleison.* Lord, have *mercy.* The door was open wide. The curtains were open to the south, letting in sunlight, and the floor reflected the light. Vernon, Lee, Dale, and Stan moved through the doorway. The linoleum tile squeaked, clean underfoot. The cardboard guitar case Stan carried bumped into the boy. Grace was sitting up in bed. Emma was seated in a far corner.

"Hi, Grandma," Vernon said, and Emma smiled at him.

"Well, hi!" Grace said. "How are my boys? Come give me a kiss." She turned off the music.

Vernon went to the bed and kissed her on the cheek. Lee circled to the other side, climbed up beside her, and gave her a kiss. Vernon helped lift Dale into his mother's arms, and Dale snuggled in next to her. Vernon picked up get-well cards in her lap and looked through them.

"We got to see Chuck shear his sheep," Lee said.

"You did?" Emma said. "That must have been interesting."

"It was."

"Maybe someday we'll have sheep," Grace said.

"And we got to jump on the wool in a great big bag," Lee said.

"But I got a tick in my hair," Dale said.

"But dad got it out," Lee said.

"Yah," Dale answered, pronouncing it like a German, as his grandfather would.

"Oh how I miss you when you're not here!" Grace said, kissing Lee, then pressing her lips into her youngest son's curls. "And you brought the guitar!"

"I bought some new strings for this old beater," Stan said, taking the guitar from the case. "And I brought you a song. I didn't know Emma would be here."

"Oh, don't mind me," Emma said, and seemed to take inward humor from the remark.

"How nice!" Grace said—in a manner that had prompted the nurses to tell Stan of her good spirits.

"Psalm 133," he said, putting the guitar's strap over his shoulder. "Is a song of ascents."

"Dad's gonna sing it," Lee said.

"Well, I'm going to try," he said. "Here's hoping you rise." He cleared his throat and sang to Grace.

> *Oh, how good and sweet it is*
> *When brothers dwell in unity*
> *Like the precious anointing oil*
> *On the beard of Aaron.*
> *Like the dew of Hermon*
> *Like the dew of Zion*
> *For the Lord commanded there*
> *Blessings—life forever.*

"It's lovely," Grace said when he finished.

"It certainly is," Emma said.

"The melody's lovely," Grace said. "I can't wait to sing it."

"It's not as lively as Mozart's song for the dead," Stan said, trying to modulate the effect of their praise.

"Mom and I were the ones listening," Grace said, admonishing him.

"Dad made you a tape," Vernon said.

"Of him singing?" Grace said. "Wonders never cease!"

"Yeah," Vernon answered. "And we put our funny commercials on it for you."

"There's one about the oil on the *bread* of Aaron," Stand said.

"Oh you silly boys. It's always something or other," Emma said.

"They're really funny," Lee said, shaking his head as if he still couldn't believe how much fun they had had making the tape.

Brothers in unity, Stan thought.

"Dale, what do you think of the tape?" Grace asked the boy, squeezing him tight.

"Funny," he said, dead serious.

"Listen to this card," Vernon announced. "It says on the outside, *Get well.* On the inside, it says, *Or else!* And there's a guy with a club." Vernon and Lee laughed. Vernon showed the card to Dale, who took it and merely shrugged. Lee asked for the card, and Dale handed it over.

"Sounds like your father," Emma said. "Get well or else!"

"Has he been here to see you?" Stan asked.

"No," Grace said. "But I understand. He doesn't like hospitals, sick people, all that."

"He should come all the same," Emma insisted. "You're his daughter."

"Those beautiful yellow roses, there beside the window, are from him," Grace said, and looked ready to cry saying it.

"They were his idea," Emma said.

"Look at the window," Grace said to Dale, pointing toward it.

"Yah," he said.

"Do you see those precious hand prints on the glass?" she said to him again.

"Yah."

"I asked the cleaning lady not to wipe them off," she said, putting her lips to his head. "They're yours."

## Chapter Six: Documentation

A SELLER'S SETTLEMENT VOUCHER was a check, minus the auction's commissions and various fees. These were no simple matters to calculate, Stan saw. A notice posted on the auction's bulletin board in the lobby listed the commissions and fees, but the thermal copy was faint and some of the figures were crossed out or changed with a pen. Sharon stood beside him, deciphering the notice.

"Our commission on most of the cattle is one-and-a-half percent of the first four thousand dollars of gross sales, and one percent after that." She read this from the notice.

Stan realized he hadn't been taking into account the lower one-percent rate, and had been overestimating the auction's commission on bigger sales, such as Mike's. "But there's a three-dollar minimum?" he asked.

"That's what it says. There's also a two-percent commission on breeding stock sold by the head, and a three-percent charge on bulls or registered stock sold by the head." Registered cattle were purebreds or full bloods with papers certifying their breeding. "The hog and sheep rates are crossed out, I guess because last year we didn't sell any horses or sheep, and only five hogs."

"But what if you do? The software has to be ready, just in case."

"I guess you'd better include them then," she said, and rattled off the values of the crossed-out rates.

"This yardage charge is for penning the animals until they're sold, right?"

"Uh huh. Seventy cents per day per head for cattle and horses. For hogs and sheep it's less, but you can't see it. There's also a charge for feed, which used to be fifty-five cents a day per head for cattle, but now it's sixty. But still twenty-five cents for hogs."

"You made a buck twenty-five on feed from those five hogs last year," Stan teased.

"We also charge insurance on livestock—ten cents per hundred dollars of gross sales. Then there's the check-off, but we just collect that." These mandatory assessments, or check-offs, were levied for the promotion of the beef and pork industries. The sales ring charged the sellers and sent the money to the appropriate association. "The beef check-off is a dollar a head," she added.

A no-sale fee of five dollars was also charged to a seller who decided, after all was said and done, not to sell.

"It's possible for a seller to end up owing *you* money?" Stan asked.

"Not likely."

Stan clutched his skull. "Instead of a settlement, I'd have to issue a seller an invoice!"

There were fees for veterinary services, the rates of which were posted separately from the market's, and for brand inspection—an attempt to reduce the sale of stolen cattle. The market itself issued checks to truckers hired by sellers, but the money came out of the seller's settlement.

And settlements were often "split" between two (or more) sellers—landlord and renter, parents and children, brother and brother—which meant multiple checks. Fifty-fifty was the most common split, she said. Owen wanted a statement attached to each check. The statement would itemize an individual sale, and report gross sales, fees, and net sales. Settlements presently were calculated on adding machines, and checks and statements were written out in longhand.

Sharon's signature, looping and bold, would still be necessary on computer-generated checks, Stan realized.

"How do you keep this all straight?" he asked.

Sharon could work out a settlement on a calculator, and probably do simple ones in her head, but she hesitated to confirm the algebraic formulas Stan devised. She could compute a settlement; that was it. "I leave the mathematics to you," she said.

"I want to start using check-in tickets," Stan said. "Things will go much faster."

She closed her eyes, grimacing as if he had named the impossible.

"Can't we just try it?" he asked.

"If that's what it takes to get the ball rolling, I'll just kick ass around here if those yardmen give me any lip." She sneered, up to the challenge, and snapped her gum, *pop.*

"What is it that Owen says about you?"

"I'm one in a million!" She put a hand on Stan's shoulder. "Don't tell him I said that!"

BY THE TWENTY-EIGHTH DAY of separation from Grace, the seedlings of green and wax beans had started to leaf in the garden, along with a vined weed locally called Creeping Jenny. On the same day, the placenta began to detach from Grace's uterine wall, threatening to suffocate their child. Stan raced into Bismarck, and Grace gave birth by Cesarean on May 23rd—a sale day at Littleton.

The baby, a girl, weighed four pounds. She lay in a bassinet in the Neonatal Intensive Care Unit. She lay on her chest, asleep in an isolet, as they called it, a casket of clear plastic. Her lungs weren't fully developed and her eyes had been damaged by administrations of oxygen. She wore chest patches wired to a monitor that recorded her breathing and heartbeat. She would have to wear these for six months more, Stan and Grace learned. She was otherwise healthy.

They named her Rose.

Grace arrived home three days later, bereft without her daughter, too sore from the surgery to walk up the stairs to their bedroom. The boys made her a bed on the couch in the living room. They prepared meals for her with Stan's help, but it was too painful for her to sit at the table, so they all ate in the living room. Stan played the guitar but Grace couldn't breathe well enough to sing—again, the pain.

She expressed milk from herself over the day with a clear-plastic hand pump and froze it in freezer bags.

"How is my little guy nursing?" Stan asked of the hand pump.

"You, you're just terrible," she said. She pulled out on the pump and a stream of white fluid shot into the cylinder.

"I know the number-one cure for mastitis," Stan said.

"What's that?"

"Careful massage several times a day. The oftener the better. Let me know when you need it."

"I don't have mastitis."

"No, you're a *good* milker."

"Lank you," she said.

THEY TRAVELED to Bismarck twice a week, bringing the milk she had frozen. They held and fed and prayed for their daughter, who was still in the Intensive Care Unit and would remain there until she had enough strength to nurse on her own.

In the ICU, Stan cradled his daughter's head in his palm. The rest of her body lay over the length of his forearm. Both he and Grace were dressed in light-blue hospital gowns and Stan's hands smelled of the antiseptic soap he had to wash with.

"She's so small," he said, feeling a precarious fear over the miniature balanced body.

"She's darling," Grace said. She sat in a wood rocking chair beside her daughter's isolet.

Stan looked up and saw her parents walk past a visitor window toward the room, wearing blue gowns, and felt his throat seize.

"She's growing," Grace said. "I can tell."

"Your parents are here!"

"Where?"

"They just walked past the window. They must be right outside the door. They're dressed to come in."

The door opened and Emma, then Henry, entered in their blue gowns. Henry was wearing a gold-banded tan hat with his.

"Dad!" Grace said, and stood.

Henry waved a bony hand.

Emma glanced at her husband. "Why Henry, you still have your hat on!"

Henry raised a hand and felt for his hat, then looked down at the incongruous gown, and shrugged at the mismatch. "I guess that's the best place for now."

"I'm so glad you've come," Grace said, and went to her father and kissed him on the cheek. "And Mom, thank you." She went to her mother and kissed her on the cheek.

"He comes with me every day," Emma said, turning to her husband.

"I didn't know that," Grace said. "You're going to make me cry."

Emma embraced her daughter and gently stroked her hair.

"I can't to bear to think of this little girl lying here all by herself," Henry said. "Surrounded by all this equipment." He stroked her hair with one finger.

"She's not alone, dear," Emma said.

"Without family then." Henry kissed the fingertips of his hand, placed them on his granddaughter's head, then brought his hand back to his nose and sniffed his fingers. "That's quite a smell."

"What a head of hair, huh?" Stan said, holding Rose up to the light of the setting sun. "And the color—it's silver."

"It's ash blond," Grace said.

"I think it's more platinum," Emma said.

"One of the nurses says it's blue-blond," Stan said.

"It's strange, is all I can say," Henry said.

The infant's hair, iridescent in the sunlight, glowed with a million brilliant filaments, blood-filled prisms in the sun. Rose squirmed and squinted in the light. She opened a sleepy tiny eye, and Stan said, "Peek-a-boo, I see you."

"I-C-U, Mom," Grace said with a wave, indicating their surroundings.

"Oh, Stan," Emma said. "How can you think things like that?"

"What are you saying?" Henry asked, stroking his granddaughter's hair.

"Where have you been?" Emma said.

"Mom," Grace said. "He's here."

"I'VE WRITTEN the new block program in a language called Pascal," Stan said. "It's much faster. The office program is still in Coyote, however, so there are drawbacks in the form of new features."

He was speaking with Sharon in Littleton's office. He felt he could talk to her without the usual distractions. He was seated at the seller-side workstation; she was beside him with a notebook in her lap. Except for the auction dog curled up in the sunlight across the threshold of the auction's front door, they were alone. He couldn't tell if she got his joke. She was in earnest to learn.

"Both programs use what we call indexes. Here, let me show you." He picked up a pen, and she gave him her notebook. "Suppose the weight tickets are stored on the hard disk in a random order." He drew five boxes labeled *4, 2, 1, 3, 5.* "Not in numerical order. You see what I mean?"

"Gotcha," she said.

"The weigher, however, views the weight tickets in numerical order, from one to five. The first ticket the weigher sees is the third ticket stored on the disk."

She snapped her gum to show agreement.

"An index file tells the program which ticket to present next. The index for these tickets would be 3, 2, 4, 1, 5." He drew another set of boxes. "The first ticket the third one in the file. The second just happens to be second in the file."

"And the third is the fourth, the fourth is the first," Sharon said in a singsong sort of way. "Gotcha."

"The block program and the office program share the same file of weight tickets, but each program uses its own index. Pascal has its, and Coyote has its. I wish it were Pascal for both but, anyway, every time the block program produces a new ticket, it updates its own index file, but not the index used by the office. The ticket is out there, but Coyote's index doesn't know it exists."

"So what does that mean?"

"Well, let me show you a new feature. I call it a monitor. You'll be able to monitor the weight tickets from inside the office." He typed on the keyboard, and the screen displayed a window of weight tickets.

Sharon studied the screen, dumbfounded, and said, "Where did these come from?"

"I entered them this morning. Notice at the top of the window a command I call 'Refresh'. It's paired with F5. If you press F5, you will get a fresh view of the tickets—an up-to-the-moment display. Watch." He pressed the key, and the window displayed the same tickets as before.

"Nothing changed," she said.

"That's right. No ticket has been added since I made these this morning. Now, I'm going to go add one or two more." He got up from his chair.

"Out on the block," she said. "You'll be a few minutes."

"No, I can run the block program right here—on the buyer-side workstation."

"You can run the block program from here?" She seemed genuinely perplexed.

"Sure, any workstation on the network can run the block program, as long as you don't try to use the scale." He added two weight tickets and returned to his seat. "Okay, now go ahead and press F5."

The new weight tickets appeared in the monitor window. "I see," she mused. "I can monitor the whole sale right from this chair. I'll be able to tell when a seller is done. Maybe make out his settlement before he gets in here."

"And notice F2," Stan said. "F2 is Edit. You can edit the tickets from this monitor window. You know, if Smoke should happen to make a mistake."

"What do you mean 'if'?"

"The only way the office program can keep up with new tickets is to recreate its own index in its entirety from scratch. Coyote has a command for re-indexing the file, and it's called upon every time you refresh the window. This solves the problem of indexes, but this solution is not without problems of its own." Stan paused for a response.

Sharon stared back at him.

"While you're refreshing the monitor, the system software locks the block program out of the weight-ticket file temporarily."

"So?" she said.

"So, the more tickets there are, the longer it takes to make a new index, the longer refreshing the monitor takes, the longer the block program gets locked out of the file."

"Could that slow the sale down?"

This was the one thing that Owen would not abide, Stan knew. "The odds are small that you would refresh the monitor at the precise moment Smoke is storing a new ticket," he said. "It may happen, of course, and only for a few seconds, but it won't happen often."

There was another drawback, but he didn't try to explain it to her, because it wasn't something she needed to know. (But did she need to know what I just finished telling her, Stan wondered.) Sale after sale, he thought, the file of weight tickets would grow, and the larger it grew, the longer the block program could get locked out.

Stan felt forced by this prospect to create an individual file for each separate sale, in order to maintain files of manageable size. There might be forty different files over a year's time, complicating the generation of year-end reports, and buyer and seller histories—what Owen seemed most interested in.

Right then Owen came bustling through the lobby door with Lloyd right behind him. "This time, I told her, it's gonna be different. I'm gonna be there on his first birthday. I'm gonna be there for his basketball games. I don't always have to be gallivanting around the damn country, looking at cattle, now do I? I don't." He was speaking loud enough for anybody to hear. "Oh, Stan!" he exclaimed. "Now what the hell is wrong?"

WHEN ROSE WAS ONE month old, Stan brought her and her monitor home. It was June 20th—another sale day in Littleton. These coincidences, Stan thought—grateful to have what he felt was an authentic excuse not to be at the auction.

Dale was no longer the youngest in the family, and was pleased to give up his crib for the baby, the new life in Lark, whom Dale called Wose.

Two weeks later the family presented her at the front of the country church north of Carson, after a sermon explaining the promises and threats associated with baptism. Stan held her, while Chuck, an elder in the church, assisted the minister, holding a cut-glass bowl of water in both hands, with a towel draped over one arm. Without his cowboy hat, Chuck's tan stopped at his eyebrows; his forehead looked as bright as baby skin.

Well not *that* light, Stan corrected himself, studying the face of Rose asleep in his arms.

The minister read a vow, and Grace and Stan promised to train their daughter in the nurture and admonition of the Lord. The congregation took a vow of a similar kind. The minister received Rose into his cradling arms. She let out a wail at the touch of the water, and several in the congregation laughed. Chuck and the minister shook hands with Stan, Grace, and each of the boys. The minister leaned over Rose and twiddled at her tiny hand with his forefinger.

There was a fellowship dinner in the church basement after the service—hamburger hot dishes, chicken, and ham; sweet breads, buns, and sourdough rolls; vegetable casseroles, raw vegetables, salads; apple juice, grape juice, tea, and hot chocolate; apple pies, chocolate cake with white frosting, chocolate cake with chocolate frosting, and cookies. Coffee strummed away in two large percolators. Stan savored Evelyn's salad.

After the dinner, Grace and the boys sang Psalm 133 while dessert was being served. Stan accompanied them, looking out over the tanned farmers, their wives and their children, at Chuck (holding Rose) and Evelyn Ream, the minister and his wife, and others. Faces reflecting many moments of mercy, Stan thought. When they had finished singing, he said, "The psalm expresses what we feel about you. Maybe someday we can sing it together."

Dale came up to Stan while the dishes were being dried and put away in cupboards and the tables wiped off. "Dad, was I baptized?"

"Of course you were, dear. You weren't baptized here but, sure, you were baptized." Dale stared up at him as if caught in an entanglement of fear. "Anything wrong?"

"No," Dale answered, then twisted his fingers together, bit his lip, and looked away.

Chuck came over to Stan and said, "I understand from your boys that that psalm contains a recipe for oil on *bread*. Ain't that right, Dale?" The boy nodded, rubbed his nose, then nipped on a fingernail.

"On the bread of Aaron," Stan said.

"Dripping down on the hem of his garment," Chuck said. "That's baptism—a clean christening into the Lord Jesus Christ."

Dale looked deep in thought, drawn into himself, and then he smiled at Chuck and ran off.

"I'M AT A STANDSTILL here," Stan said, and shoved again at the door to the grain-elevator office in Lark. The wood door was weathered, and two of its three panes of glass needed glazing again. The third opening was covered with a warped board. The bottom of the door scraped over the floor as he finally pushed it in, gouging arcs in the floor's soft wood. Fir, he thought.

He entered the room, expecting his dad to follow. Sig stood out in the grass looking up at the building, himself looking like somebody else. He had recovered from a stroke and, with exercise and a change in diet, had lost thirty pounds.

"It's in good shape," Sig said. "The steel siding looks good."

"One panel was loose on the roof, but I nailed it back down."

Sig placed a hand on the doorframe and stepped into the doorway, outlined against the brilliant day. Seeing his dad's careful manner, Stan realized there was a step up. "The floor looks good too," Sig said.

"These fir floors—here and in the house—they need new varnish or a floor covering of some kind. The boys are always getting slivers."

"It looks solid, though. I don't see much damage in here. A little in the ceiling."

"Come on in, why don't you? It's perfectly safe." Sig was wearing his usual wool shirt and work pants but also white tennis shoes. When did he start wearing those, Stan wondered. "The building is sixteen by thirty. I'm hoping to make this big room into a computer lab. The small room's my office."

"There's plenty of light."

"There are three windows, these big ones here, on the west, and the door," Stan said, then was embarrassed at stating the obvious. "There's another door on the north, and a little east window inside my office."

"It's very good lighting."

"The walls, as you can see, are in fair shape. I plan to paint over the faded blue with almond, repaint the ceiling white, and sand and varnish the floor. Here are bookshelves built in, and there are more shelves in the office and in the house. It's the first time I've had all my books out of boxes since I don't know when."

"I didn't know you had so many books. There must be a couple thousand. Have you read them all?"

"Not all. Parts of most of them, though. I've read maybe half."

"Good for you," his dad said.

"It's an old grain-elevator office."

"I saw the sign above the door outside."

"There was a fire here once that burned down the main house and a corner of this building. I replaced ten feet of charred studs. There are still blackened boards in the attic, but they're structurally sound. Come on and I'll show you my office." Stan led him across the larger room, past the bookshelves, to a door. "This is an exterior storm door," Stan said, placing a hand on the latch. "It also catches on the floor. Watch out for the extension cord." They entered the room, a small one partitioned off in the corner of the building. His dad stepped carefully over the extension cord on the floor, more cautious since the stroke, Stan noticed.

In the office was Stan's computer, a lamp on the same table, a chair, a filing cabinet, a loveseat, a space heater, and a set of shelves fashioned from concrete blocks and wooden boards. "I tried to keep it simple. It's twelve by twelve—three sheets of sheetrock each way."

"You did this yourself?"

"I got most of the studs from an old shed I torn down. The walls are insulated, but they need paint. This was the burned-out wall," Stan said, pointing to traces of soot.

"It all looks very well done. How did you get the walls so straight by yourself?"

"I used a plumb line and a level. The boys were a big help."

"The right tools for the job."

"The work belt you sent, I want to thank you for that."

"You're welcome."

Stan turned away, uneasy. "I went over all the wiring. The outlets are new and so are the switches. And I replaced any wire that was burned or melted away. A lot of wire in the attic was ruined by the fire."

"That's something I never did understand," Sig said. "Electrical wiring."

"I can't say I understand it, especially two- and three-pole switches. I just follow the diagrams; it all seems to work."

"What's the point of the extension cord?"

"That's the weird part of it all. The rural electrical co-op won't hook up the service until a state electrician approves the building, and the state electrician won't approve it until the co-op hooks up the service. They both think I should run a line from the house. Meanwhile, this extension cord. Actually, three hooked together run from the house."

"I think you should do that."

"What?"

"Run a line from the house. It'd be underground?"

"I was told it would have to be."

"So you don't really know if the wiring works."

"I do. I tested it. I put a plug on the end of a short piece of wire, and wired that into the service panel, then plugged the other end into the extension cord. All the lights work, all the outlets, all the switches—everything. With the extension cord, unfortunately, I can run only the computer or the space heater, but not both. In the winter, I mean. The screen gets all snowy when I try to run both. Not enough juice, I guess."

"You've done a lot of work. I'm amazed there wasn't more damage. It must have been some fire."

"Was it ever a mess in here! There were these old receipts all over the floor, and envelopes. And the boys found—oh, I don't know—maybe a hundred purple four-cent Lincoln-head stamps. There were cat turds hard as marbles, and bird nests of mud, and flyspecks everywhere on the windows. We swept up dirt and dust and turds and broken glass."

"It's too bad you don't have a line from the house yet."

"Oh, and I have flood lights outside above the door we came in, and a weather-proof exterior outlet."

"Yes, I saw that as I came in." All he said sounded so measured, so cautious.

"I'm hoping to make a computer lab. I have my 386, a Korean-made XT-compatible with a 20-meg hard disk, a fifty-dollar IBM XT with two floppy drives, and what's called an IBM PS/1 with a small floppy drive."

"It's all Greek to me."

"I'm just saying I have the makings of a computer lab, if it doesn't get obsolete before I can use it. I have to try to do something in addition to the livestock auction."

"How is that coming?"

"Maybe by August it'll be done. How's the sales ring at home?"

"That's been closed for years. Didn't you know? Every now and then somebody tries to revive it, but local farmers— They want some place close to buy from, but when it comes time to sell, they run to Grand Forks. It's quite frustrating."

"Littleton sold 45,000 head in three months at the end of last year."

"The herd size is much bigger out here on this range land."

"Some guys around here do their own pregnancy tests and even C sections," Stan said. "Do you think you could teach me to do that? The local vet left a year ago, and nobody's replaced him."

"No, I don't think so. If it comes to that, if you need pregnancy tests, I'll just come out and do them for you myself. How much land do you have?"

"Twenty acres. We're renting, you know."

"You can't do much on twenty acres. Do you know the county averages for grain?"

"No."

"I think it's a half to a third of what we get at home. Where are you going to get land? You can't buy it, I don't suppose. Is there any crop land to rent?"

"Not that I know of. Maybe there is."

"Your mother's quite concerned about you," his dad said, and suddenly the caution was gone and his voice had changed. "About Grace and the boys, and now Rose. A young family living way out in the country. And the medical expenses."

"We have insurance, left over from when I was teaching. Grace and I feel that, whatever comes, we have to dig in our heels, settle, and stay put. We can't keep moving around."

"Maybe you could get a place near Bismarck or Mandan. And get a good job working with computers. You're trained for that."

"I've tried. When we first settled here, I tried that. I interviewed for half a dozen computer jobs in Bismarck. With the state—Central Personnel, the Attorney General's office, the Highway Department, the Water Department. They required a two-year degree. I interviewed with a coal company and two electrical companies. They required a two-year degree. I finally interviewed with one of the hospitals for a position as a network coordinator—what I've been doing for over a year. They required a four-year degree. Every place I tried said I was over-qualified."

"I don't understand this 'over-qualified' business."

"I don't, either. It's like they want to pay a certain level of salary for a two-year degree, and they don't want a person with an advanced degree. I said I'd take whatever they'd offer, but no—"

"It doesn't make sense to me."

"Besides, I figure I would need a salary of twenty-four thousand a year to make it worthwhile. I'd have to buy a better pickup. Then there'd be the gas. And the time on the road. I'd be away eleven hours a day. That's not what I want for the children. We're homeschooling."

"Why not go back to teaching? There are colleges in Bismarck. Your mother thinks that's your gift. And I'm inclined to agree."

"I *am* teaching. You're teaching. How many times I've heard you say that! Mom's teaching. The difference is you're teaching in the real world—where I want to be."

A gust of wind rattled the east window of the room, and cottonwood branches bumped on the roof overhead.

"Time out," Sig said. Which meant time for his nap, Stan thought. "Your mother took Grace and the children to town," Sig added.

As they were leaving the building, Stan pointed out the new glass in the west windows, and a new lock on the door.

"These old signs on the side of the building—" his dad said. "Don't let your mother see them. *Drink Pepsi in bottles, Drink Coca Cola, Buy Rhinoflex Tires.* They're probably worth something. Antiques, you know. I think antiques are just old things nobody wanted."

"When are you going to get a computer system for the vet clinic?" Stan asked.

"Six megacycles, three tricycles, and a bicycle. It's all Greek to me," Sig said. "I'm an antique. Let the young docs do that."

"YOUR DAD MIGHT have been a university professor," his mother said.

At the kitchen counter, Stan plugged in an electric kettle to boil water for coffee. He used a spoon to measure coffee grounds into two cups. Then he sat down at the kitchen table across from her, just the two of them.

"He was quite gifted in anatomy," she said. "He was being groomed for a position in the University by the head of Anatomy."

"*Groomed* by the *head* of anatomy?" Stan said.

"He used to kick himself for becoming a practicing vet. 'I'm always practicing,' he'd say, then he'd ask, 'When do I get to start the real thing?' Your dad!"

"He's been doing the real thing for thirty years."

"I know it, but if the truth be told it was the will of your Grandpa Jonas that absolutely ruled your dad. Your father had this extraordinary gift. His memory of physical details was phenomenal. I worked as a secretary for the University, and I know. His professors would tell me what a find he was. And you know his rapport with people. But no, Grandpa Jonas wanted his son to be a veterinarian, and by golly that's exactly what he became! Mostly to please his father."

"Grace's dad, Henry, was trained as an electrical engineer, and yet somehow, I don't know the whole story, he ended up managing a dairy farm and a processing plant. It's brought him and Emma no end of grief, though she seems able to bear it better than most."

"No father should have that kind of control over the gifts God gives to a son. Your dad was such a happy young man when I met him, a lot like you. He was so excited by this recognition of gifts he didn't even realize he had. And then to have to endure all those late nights at the clinic and out on the road! But endure he did, and made a life out of his disappointments for the sake of us all." His mother spoke with no emotion Stan could see, as if she had distilled her thoughts over the years to an essence of calm.

"I didn't know," Stan said. "Or maybe I did. He could get so angry at times. I can still hear him."

"You won't hear that anymore. He's a changed man since the stroke. It was like a slap in the face, or on the behind. He has been chastened, humbled in a way I recognize more than he does."

"He seems awfully cautious," Stan said. "In the way he talks, even in the way he walks."

"He's awestricken, is what it is. He walks as if he's walking every moment of his life on water. It takes faith in the Lord, and I see it growing in him." Then she added, "He was so sorry he couldn't be here for Rose's baptism." She drew in a breath at this, as if her emotions had at last been touched, and Vernon walked into the kitchen with his work apron on, carrying a copy of his magazine.

"What do you have there, honey?" May asked, transferring her attention from her son and husband to her grandson between words.

"I want to thank you for the work apron," Vernon said. "I like to wear it sometimes when I'm working on my magazine."

"It is work, isn't it?" she asked.

"This is next month's issue." Vernon handed the magazine to her. "I thought if I gave it to you now, I would save on postage."

"A little businessman here," she said, opening the booklet. "*Why do balls bounce? Answer: A ball has air in it. When you throw it at the floor, the floor tries to push out the air, but the air is locked in the ball. This pushes the ball up.* Well, now I know. Let me see how your apron fits." She put her hands on Vernon's hips and turned him slowly around. "You boys are so slim. I thought it might be too big on you. But I see that you've grown."

"It's big on Dale," Vernon said.

She got up and went to the counter. The kettle was steaming. "Should I just pour the water into these cups?"

"If you don't mind grounds in your coffee," Stan said. "They'll sink in a bit."

She poured the water into the cups and brought them to the table, and Stan took one and blew across the grounds floating on top, then took a sip. Cowboy coffee. "Dad sure looks in good shape. When did he start wearing tennis shoes?"

"When he started to exercise." Stan watched her warm her hands on her cup. "Of course, he doesn't wear them to work. He exercises a lot. He has a rowing machine and a treadmill, and he lifts weights."

Stan heard footsteps descending the stairs, then laughter, his dad's voice.

Sig entered the kitchen with his arms curled in front of him like a weightlifter. Dale hung upside-down from one arm, Lee from the other. Both were wearing their aprons and grinning wide. "I'd give my right arm to be ambidextrous," Sig said, glancing at Stan as though to check his memory on this old joke.

Before his stroke he'd been thought of as a joker, a clown, a sought-after party guest, Stan recalled. "You know, people," his dad would say. "It's not good to tell ethnic jokes anymore, on the blacks or the Jews or the Indians—or even the Norwegians and Swedes—unless the ethnic group is long gone, like the Hittites. So there were these two stupid Hittites, Ole and Lena—"

"Grandpa's sure strong for an old guy," Lee said.

"For an old guy!" Sig said. "Look at this monkey!" He meant of course Dale.

"Thank you for the thing," Dale said.

"Mom, did you hear that?" Sig asked his wife.

"What, honey?" May asked.

"Thank you for the thing," Dale said. "For the wouk apwon."

"Thank you," Lee said, letting go his grandpa's arm.

"Dale can pronounce his T-Hs!" Sig said, curling Dale up in his arms; he clenched his teeth, and started to tickle him.

"Stop!" Dale said, biting his lips to suppress the laughter.

"What's the matter with you? Aren't you ticklish, Dale *Th*orlofson?"

"Did you get a good enough nap?" May asked her husband.

"I got a good one," Sig said, setting Dale down. "And I'm rarin' to go. Where is the gracious one?"

"She's up with the baby, taking a nap," May said.

"Would you like some coffee, Dad?" Stan asked.

"Would I like some coffee? Would I like some coffee?" He kept raising his voice, as if playing a part in an opera. He dropped it to a whisper. "Yes, please." Stan got a cup from the cupboard. Sig said to May, "It's quite an impressive building he's got down there. Lots of books. You should go see it."

"I know he has lots of books. Where have you been?"

"If she goes down there, she'll see those old signs," Stan said, shaking coffee grounds into the cup.

"Oops," Sig said, and put his hand over his mouth, pretending he'd said something he shouldn't have.

"Old signs?" she said.

"Old metal advertisements," Stan said.

"Pepsi and Coke signs," Lee said.

"Antiques," Sig said. "You know, old stuff."

"I'm not interested in any old stuff," May told him. "I mean, besides you. Not signs anyway."

"Here's your coffee," Stan said.

"Thank you, velly much. Once upon a time, there were six antique dealers who got stranded on a desert island. And they all made a good living for two years."

"Selling to one another!" Stan said.

May groaned. "I bet I've heard that one a hundred times over! Your father, I should perhaps let you know, is something of an antique collector himself. You should see his new collection of steam engines."

"I have lots of little gadgets and toys to hook up to them, too," Sig said, without a pang of conscience. "It's quite a collection. I'll show you the next time you visit."

"I want to visit the clinic again the next time we come," Lee said.

"Sure," Sig said, resting his free arm on Lee's shoulder. "We have cages for all kinds of monkeys."

"I wish was a veterinarian," Stan said. "Then I'd take over for you."

"That would be nice," his dad said, with a sudden softening in his voice. "I should have been a professor."

"You can still teach your grandsons," May said.

"Listen to this, Mom," Stan said. "Lee, what do you want to be when you grow up?"

"A veterinarian!"

May put her hand to her mouth. "Just like Stan used to say when he was your age." That took her by surprise, Stan thought.

Sig put his cup down, and Lee stepped onto the insteps of his shoes. Grandpa and grandson held onto each other, as they walked around the kitchen table.

"It almost moves me to tears," May said, blinking.

"If I wait for you to join me, I'll be an antique for sure," Sig said to Lee, setting him down. "Well then, the first thing you need to learn, if you're going to be a good veterinarian, is anatomy. So listen now. *What has four stiff standers—*"

"A cow!" Lee said.

"You already know that one."

"Dad taught us," Lee said.

Grace appeared at the door, sleepy-eyed, her hair mussed and twisting in whorls of radiance the sun lit. "What's all the racket in here?"

"Ah, I'm sorry," May said. "Did we wake you? Sig is being silly."

"No, you didn't wake me. I had a good nap. I must have been tired."

"I'm sure you were," May said.

"Okay," Sig said, turning to the boys. "Do you know the dairyman's handshake?"

"No," Lee said, shaking his head.

"I had forgotten this one," Grace said.

"First, you lock your fingers together like you're going to pray," Sig said. "I know you boys pray." All the boys did this. "Now turn your palms out, away from you, and hold your thumbs down," he said, demonstrating with his hands. "Now, I just pretend I'm milking your thumbs. Ch, ch. Ch, ch."

"Like mom," Dale said.

"Dale!" Grace said, putting a hand to her mouth.

"What do you mean?" Sig said.

"She has two dilly-dandews," Dale said.

Sig clapped his hands together and lifted his chin. "Ha!"

"Shh, Dale!" Grace said, then sighed.

"Oh, these farm boys!" May said. "Come here, you with the popcorn hair." Dale went to her and crawled into her lap. "Thank you for the thing," she whispered in his ear, wrinkling her nose, and poked him in the ribs.

"And you'll need to know the vet's handshake. Have you shown them that one?" Sig asked Stan.

"I hope not," May said, glancing up.

"Is it bad?" Grace asked. "I don't know how much more of this I can take."

"No, I haven't," Stan said. "Shall we demonstrate?" He stood in front of his dad.

"One veterinarian makes an O with his arm, like a monkey scratching his ribs," Sig said. Stan made the shape with his arm. "And the other vet puts his arm through the O and reaches way in." His dad put his arm through the opening up to his shoulder.

"Oh dear," Grace said.
"What are you doing?" Lee asked.
"It's a pregnancy-test handshake," Stan said.
"Not to be confused with a rectal exam," Sig said, removing his arm.
Right, Stan thought. "Nice to meet up with you, Doctor," Stan said to his dad. "Glad you made it back." Then he grinned at Grace, who was trying to tidy her hair.
"Good to see you, Dr. Proctophilus," Sig said. To the boys he explained, "That means 'rectum lover.'"
"*Thereby hangs a tale*," Stan said, glancing at his mother.
"These men," May said to her. "Honestly!"
"We're not real doctors, as you know," Sig said, shrugging his shoulders. "We're just practicing."

ON VALENTINE'S DAY, six buyers bought cattle from twenty-five sellers. Stu made purchases for three different outfits—a feedlot and two meatpacking plants. The market sold 313 head that day: 3 yearling heifers, 125 steer calves, 125 heifer calves, 11 bulls, 16 cows, 9 steers, 13 heifers, and 11 Holstein milk cows. The calf-and-steer report was as follows:

| Head | Weight | High/cwt. | Low/cwt. | Average/cwt. |
|---|---|---|---|---|
| 12 | 600-650 | $93.50 | $63.00 | $86.12 |
| 85 | 651-700 | $90.25 | $85.00 | $88.10 |
| 30 | 701-750 | $87.25 | $86.00 | $86.30 |
| 38 | 751-800 | $89.25 | $83.50 | $88.42 |
| 94 | 225-599 | $118.00 | $59.00 | $104.36 |

Valentine's Day grossed over $180,000—a small fraction of the annual gross sale of sixteen million. The office program generated this information as part of a market synopsis, to Owen's delight. "Now we're cookin'," he said.

"GRACE, it's beeping again."

She was warm in the bed beside him, sound asleep on her back, (dead to the world, as she'd say), snoring. Stan was a light sleeper. The alarm on his daughter's monitor sounded whenever her heartbeat dipped below forty beats a minute. He would wake first and then wake Grace. The LED clock on a nightstand beside the bed read 3:30 AM, the second time that night Rose's alarm had gone off.

"Grace," he repeated louder. "Her beeper again."

"Okay, I'm up," she said, bounding up from the bed in the darkness. She had flung off the sheet. He pulled it back over himself, feeling uncovered and chilled.

"Do you want me to turn on the light?" He spoke out into the darkness, not knowing for sure where she was.

"Please, don't." She was near the door to their bedroom, her footsteps and the diminished sound of her voice from the hallway: "I'll find my way."

The monitor also signaled any irregularities in Rose's breathing. Grace would go to her and rub her head and her feet, all she could do, until her breathing or her heartbeat returned to normal, as they always did.

He had looked into buying a monitor instead of paying the two hundred dollars a month to rent one, but the cost was ten thousand dollars. More than all the hardware for Littleton and Piper combined.

"WATCH, EVERYBODY," Lee said.

Stan sprang off a diving board and performed a jackknife. Underwater he heard an explosion that released the splash and when he surfaced, he heard clapping. Lee was clapping. The boy held his hands above his head, standing in water up to his neck, and pounded his hands together. Attention I don't deserve, Stan thought, feeling a warm sensation ooze from his groin, as if he were relieving himself in the cool water. He swam toward his son, who dropped out of sight underwater. Henry and Emma had pool in their back yard.

Vernon bumped into his father, wearing black goggles, swimming with his face down across Stan's path. He raised his goggled face, apologized, and swam on.

Dale lay along an edge of the pool with a hand in the water, blue goggles pushed up on the top of his head. Dry curls stuck out from under the strap in the back. He raised a hand, and fired an orange squirt gun at Lee, who had surfaced. Stan reached Lee, raised him from the water, and tossed him into the air, seeing Lee pinch his nose before he went under.

"I'm squooting you," Dale said. Stan felt a tiny stream on his back. Lee rose from the water, waded toward his father, and said, "That was fun. Will you do it again?" Stan swung around and reached for Dale, but his son backed away, grazing Dale's puffy trunks. "I just missed you, Mr. Little Bloomers," he said. Dale aimed, and Stan got it right in the eye.

"Not in the face," Grace said.

"So-we," Dale said.

"I'm all right," Stan said, rubbing the irritation away. "I forgive you." He turned to Lee and tossed him in the air.

"Honey," Grace called. "I have something to tell you." She was sitting down in a lawn chair, settling Rose in her lap. Rose's lap and legs were wound with a blanket tapering to a soft point. She looks like a genie, Stan thought. He waded to the side of the pool and, squinting against late afternoon sunlight, said, "You're pregnant again."

"No, silly. Not while I'm nursing. Would you come here and sit down?" He raised himself up out of the pool, took a towel from a pile of towels on a table, and sat in a lawn chair beside her. "Dad said when he was young he had his heart set on electronics," she began. "But one thing led to another and he ended up taking over the dairy plant and farm, when he could've been designing computers."

"I've gathered that much," Stan said.

"Mom!" Lee called. "Watch how long I can stay underwater."

"Okay, honey, I'm watching."

Lee took a deep breath, pinched his nose, and went under. A moment later he stood up, swept his hair back with both hands, then wiped his face. He cupped his hands around his eyes and squinted against the sunlight, smiling.

"Very good. You'll have good breath support." She turned to Stan. "He told me he admires what you're doing, doing what you feel called to do."

"He told *you* that, or told Emma?"

"He told me. Mom thinks his visits to the hospital were a breakthrough. He would hold Rose in the rocking chair and joke with the nurses—you know how he is. The next minute, he'd rock and he'd weep, in a private sort of way, but mom knew, she said. She told me she couldn't remember a time when he's acted that way. He also told me he's realized, after all these long years, that he's had everything backwards—electronics first, people last of all."

Dale crouched at the edge of the pool, pushing a blue paddleboard along the water's edge, making a motor sound with his lips. Vernon glided to one side of the pool, then kicked off toward the other, doing a sidestroke. Gifted, Stan thought. God-given talent. Gold sunlight annealed the pool's blue fluid surface. Water anointed with light. A communion of oil and water, when the oil is light.

"Hi, Mom," Grace called out. Emma, wearing sunglasses, shut a screen door behind her. She stopped to check her geraniums in a planter on wheels, then considered a small plot of petunias at her feet. "Your flowers are lovely!" Grace called. She kissed Rose's hair softly. "So are you, sweetie."

"Grandma, watch," Lee said. "I can hold my breath underwater."

"Go ahead. I'm watching." Emma walked toward the table and lawn chairs, keeping her eyes on Lee as he pinched his nose and went under again. When he came up, Emma said, "Very good. I'm so glad you're enjoying the pool."

"Dale, can I borrow the goggles?" Lee called.

"Show," Dale said. He ran around the edge of the pool, and handed the goggles to his brother.

"Don't run, honey," Grace said. "The concrete is wet. I don't want you to fall in."

"Here, take my chair," Stan said, standing when his mother-in-law drew near. She thanked him and sat down. Stan sat in the grass.

"Your father likes to see the water get churned up like this," Emma said. "Then the dust and the seeds don't settle quite as much."

"The pool looks clean to me," Stan said. "Near perfect."

"The boys just love it," Grace said. "Maybe next summer Dale will be tall enough to stand on the bottom."

"Maybe the year after next," Stan said.

"Henry was petite like Dale as boy," Emma told them. "But when he went into the Navy, right after high school, he just shot up."

"Henry's taller than I am," Stan said.
"But he's shrinking," Emma said. "We both are."
"Hello, down there." Henry stood on a deck a story above them, with his hands on a wrought-iron railing. "How are the swimmers?" He was again wearing his hat.
"Grandpa, watch." Lee said. He went underwater, he came up, and Henry said, "You'll be swimming in no time."

Henry started down a metal spiral staircase, and each step he took gave off a soft resounding sound as if from a gong. He stepped into the grass, repositioned a sprinkler, then walked up behind his wife and put his hands on her shoulders.

"Did you just get home from somewhere?" Emma said, craning her head around to speak to him.

"No, I went to the grocery, but that was hours ago."

"And you've been wearing your hat all this time?"

"I'm wearing my hat?" Henry asked, first glancing, then reaching a hand to it.

"Oh Henry, it's been there the whole time!"

"I'd forget my head if it wasn't screwed on."

"At least you'd know where your hat would be." At the apparent image of this, Emma had to laugh.

"On my head."

Dale came up and asked somebody to tie the string on his swimming suit tighter. Henry's fingers trembled at the effort, but he tied a tight bow, then poked Dale in the belly. Vernon demonstrated to everybody how he could swim in one breath from one side of the pool to the other.

"She's starting to fuss," Grace said, speaking of Rose. Grace removed the blanket wrapping her daughter and set it in her lap, unbuttoned her blouse, and undid the clasp on her nursing bra. The baby waggled her head against her mother's blouse and started to mouth it. "She's rooting," Grace said, throwing a corner of the blanket over her shoulder, covering Rose and herself, and settled back in her chair.

"Have you seen Grace's magic trick?" Stan asked.

"Magic trick?" Henry said. "No."

"It's not magic," Grace said.

"A fussy baby goes under the blanket," Stan said. "And, voilà, a quiet baby comes out."

"It's not magic," Emma said, uttering a soft cluck. "It's love." Mother hen, Stan thought.

"Do you swim very often any more, Dad?" Grace asked.

"Oh, sure. Every day if the weather's nice."

"Do you dive?" Stan asked.

"Oh no, not anymore."

"He swims laps," Emma said. "I like to rest in the floating chair and watch him."

"She's very good at it," Henry said.

"MERGES ARE EASY," Stan told him.

"Whatever you say, computer man," Smoke said.

"Suppose you want to merge two groups of steers into one. You go into 'merge' mode."

"Merge mode? How d'you do that?"

"Notice these various F-keys across the top of the keyboard," Stan said, pointing them out.

"F-keys? Like F-words?"

"The F stands for Function. F5 is for Merge." Stan pointed to the screen where the key was explained.

"Sounds like an F-word to me. Maybe this baby will come to me!"

"Just press the key, would you?" Stan was feeling that here was the main obstacle: *That I, one Smoke by name, present a wall.*

Smoke pressed the F-key. "Next time let's enter some heifers."

"The word MERGED appears on the top of the screen," Stan said, ignoring Smoke's comment. "Do you see where it is?"

Smoke said he did.

"At this point, we are ready to count the first group of steers and weigh them," Stan said. "We're not reading from the scale at the moment so, please, just make up some numbers."

Smoke entered a weight and a head count.

Stan continued: "While the steers are being driven out, and the second group is being driven in, you'll have time to enter the check-in ticket number, or look up the seller, and enter the type of steers they are. Just make something up."

Smoke entered the make-believe data.

"Now you're done with that ticket," Stan said. "Press the PageDown key."

"The steers haven't been sold," Smoke said.

"Right, but they've been counted and weighed, so now press the PageDown key. Right here," Stan said, pointing the key out to Smoke, annoyed.

"I know where it is," Smoke said, and pressed the key.

"The second and third tickets are even easier to fill out," Stan said. "Just enter their weights and their head counts. The seller data from the first ticket will be plugged into the final one automatically."

Smoke filled out two tickets as Stan directed.

"After you're done with the third ticket, press the F5 key for Leave Merge. Now the key means *leave* merge mode. F5 is a toggle." Stan pressed the key himself. "A fourth and new ticket appears, do you see? All the steers put together. A merged head-count and weight—that they are steers, that the seller is this guy, all of it's here."

"And the rest is the same?" Smoke said.

"The rest is the same."

"Hey, this is easy."

"Why don't you practice. I'll give you a hand."

"You know, that disk Owen gave me from you?" Smoke said.

"What about it?"

"I ain't got no computer, man."

Wouldn't you know it, Stan thought.

**INVOICES AND RECAPS** documented the buyer side. Often a buyer would buy several lots for himself, and direct them all to a single pen. Buyers such as Stu would buy for several companies, and instruct the yardmen to put his purchases in different pens.

An invoice described the worth and contents of a pen, Stan thought. An invoice might contain several lines, representing the separate lots of cattle in a pen, each line including a description of the seller (name, seller number, type of cattle), along with a head count, total weight of the lot, the money, and the lot's total price.

An invoice would also include the average weight of the animals in the pen, their average cost, the grand total of cattle in the pen, the grand total weight, and the grand (or gross) total cost of all the *lots* in that pen.

There were various charges added to this gross total purchase. The result was the net total purchase. At the bottom of an invoice appeared the net average cost of a single animal in a buyer's particular pen.

A buyer's commission was one of the charges it was possible to add to an invoice. Feedlots and meatpacking plants paid buyers commissions for buying for them, a nominal percentage of the gross total purchase. The first time Stu received a computer-generated invoice he studied it hard, and then said, "What's this?"

"What?" Stan asked.

"This goddamn commission," Stu said, flinging the invoice in through the window.

"The commission?" Stan asked, picking the paper off the floor, grateful there was nobody else in the office or lobby.

"It's ten times too damn high!"

"Wouldn't you like to make a commission like that?" Stan said, in a light-hearted way.

"Shit" was all Stu said to him. He hadn't been shortchanged, but Stan guessed Stu thought his boss would think he was trying to pull something over on him.

"Here, let me correct it and give you a new one," Stan said. He corrected the calculation of the commission in a line of the program and reprinted the invoice.

"You really know how to piss a guy off," Stu said when Stan came back to the window. Stu grabbed the invoice right out of Stan's hand and walked off, muttering. "Royally," he said, then slammed the door to the lobby.

You're full of it, Stan thought, then realized he had two more of Stu's invoices and his recap to give Stu. Would he be back, Stan wondered.

Is this the sort of thing Henry meant by a rough crowd?

AUGUST, and Stan felt the pace picking up at Littleton. On sale days, the place was hopping with ranchers and truckers, buyers and yardmen, young men and maidens, old men and children. The smaller weight tickets Stan ordered had arrived, and he was back to working days in Littleton.

Owen and Lloyd were in and out of the offices, and on the phone, more often, too much on the move to interrupt him.

Area auctioneers stopped by to chat. One from Carson approached Stan and suggested he write a program on laptops for use at farm auctions.

The brand inspector would lean in at a window, and tease him about his last name ("You're one of those frozen Norwegians."), and pester him about his unfinished program.

In August Marlene appeared wearing a candy-apple-red dress, cut to a height that had gone out of fashion—a miniskirt—and in addition wore high heels, and ungainly, dangling earrings of bright red. She was the "buyer-side gal," as Owen dubbed her. Her nylons, tinted pale red, sheathed long firm legs. She spoke through her nose, in the manner of Edie Adams in a cigar commercial. *Why don't you pick one up and smoke it sometime?* Something about Marlene jogged this memory. Stan felt his throat constrict when she was near, though it might have been her perfume. Her fragrance filled the office and seemed to lure to her window cattlemen with no real business there, as a heifer in season might lure bulls to a fence line. She treated them with cozy familiarity, but they didn't tease her, seeming to treat her as if she were holy.

The office was a sanctuary of sorts, and Stan felt that some men who came to the window, a chink in the wall, wished to trade places with him. They were on the outside looking in; he got to train her.

In slower seasons Sharon had handled both seller and buyer sides by herself, in blouse and blue jeans. Now she started wearing a dress and nylons, à la Marlene, who had caused all manner of things to pick up once she appeared at Littleton Livestock.

The Indian women rested in the booth when large lots of calves came onto the block. "I'm Marjorie—call me Marge—this is Tina," the older one said, introducing them both. They wore blue jeans and jackets. Marge was short, a frizzy brunette, a chain-smoker like Smoke. Once Marge told Stan, "I'd learn to type if I could get an inside job." She called him Sweetheart, Honey, Doll. She said she was rooting for him. Tina, the younger and taller of the two, was taller than Stan, with a thick black braid down her back. She said nothing, except in whispers to Marge, and smiled faintly at her companion's remarks.

When he wasn't on the run, Stan sat on a stool in a corner of the booth, by the back door. Opposite him, an electric wall clock had stopped at 3:30. Its hollow plastic face, smudged and dusty, was illuminated from within, advertising the pep you get from colas in bottles. It was an antique. Stan sipped from an aluminum can.

STAN MET DR. KELLY, a veterinarian from Mandan, called "Doc" at the auction. The vet spent most of his time in the yards, of course, but sometimes came into the booth. "I know your father," he told Stan the first time they met, while the sale was in full swing. They both had to speak up, listening with an ear cocked to each other.

"How's that?" Stan said.

"He was on the examining board at the time I was licensed. We've talked at conventions."

"I've been to some."

"So you're into computers. So is my son. He's at UND, majoring in philosophy, and English. He likes to write poetry."

"I was in philosophy, too, with a Greek language minor."

"A what?"

"Greek. A Greek language minor."

Doc shook his head, but didn't say anything more. Perhaps he just didn't hear, Stan thought. "You don't look old enough to have a college-age son," Stan said.

"Now you're here," Doc said—as if not hearing—and lifted a hand, indicating the sales ring.

"I think it's sort of a circle. Philosophy these days is all language and logic. From logic to programming—it's not a big jump."

"I think that University is liberal."

Stan followed Doc's lead. "I went there, too. One teacher—his lectures were always political, no matter where he started. He would start with Plato, and end up in Grand Forks, or start with Wittgenstein, and end up talking about the airbase outside Grand Forks. Was the community phone book militaristic? It might have had a picture of a B-52 on the cover."

"I went to SU," Doc said.

"So did my dad. It's where I went for computers."

"I just put in a computer," Doc said. "It's working out great."

"My dad doesn't want one. He wants to retire."

"I don't blame him. Your dad's been around a long time."

Doc Kelly stepped forward and talked briefly to Owen, then came back, waved goodbye to Stan, and left by the door beside the stool where Stan sat.

THE BOOTH WAS GETTING CRAMPED. Owen, Lloyd, Smoke at the computer, and two or more spotters crowded the front counter. Barskills' weight-ticket printer sat under black plastic at the back of the booth beside an amplifier, mikes, and dusty boxes. The floor was strewn with cables, some taped down, others loose as snakes.

There was also the ancient manual balance scale, five feet long, four feet high, a foot wide, with a floating metal beam. The scale was solidly set into floor right in the booth's center. Stan supposed they kept it for a backup. Perhaps law required it, he thought. If the power were to go out during a sale, nothing electronic would serve, and they would have to revert to the manual scale.

Owen once told him, "We used to just wait for the power to come back on again." In the history of Littleton Livestock, the power was out for over an hour only once. "We have a backup generator now. Can you believe it? Those old timers! The time it took to sell an old cow!"

The scale was no obstacle to those in the front, or to those who came in the back door, but it was to Stan. Owen would ask him to run an errand; the Indian women, looking for tickets that Smoke hadn't removed from the printer, would call Stan to the back door; Smoke would call him forward past the immovable scale; and Owen would summon him to ask how Smoke was doing.

SOMETIMES A BUYER would like the looks of all the calves in a lot, except one—a cripple, for instance. Then the yardmen would drive the other calves out, and the weigher would weigh just that one. After that, the block software would produce two tickets—one with the weight of the single calf, and another with the weight of the rest. The creation of two lots, and two tickets, from one lot was called a split—not to be confused with a settlement split in which two or more *checks* were issued to *sellers*.

Complications set in when a buyer called for splits while the weigher was *merging* two or more lots. A buyer would want to merge several lots into one, but perhaps split off from each lot peculiar calves to be merged into a lot of their own.

*Block 2.0* could merge splits as well as split merges. Smoke was familiar with the block program's routine by now, but he had little experience with merges and splits in real time. He would start a split, then get confused. Stan would coach him through it. If Owen insisted, Stan would take over for Smoke and finish the transaction.

Settlements were issued, invoices, recaps. Marlene caught on quickly; she liked computers. The market report was ready minutes after a sale. Owen was happy. Sharon phoned the report in to the newspaper. Why not fax it, Stan thought. Why not fax check-in tickets into the office from the unloading chute? Or use walkie-talkies, or an intercom of some kind? Settlements for truckers and Doc Kelly were still calculated and written by hand.

One afternoon Mike even called the market and congratulated Stan, the giant businessman beaming down at one little guy.

THE FIRST CRASH of the system came in August, but not during a sale. Stan was entering fictitious weight tickets in an attempt to methodically test the office program's handling of settlements and invoices. One moment he was entering tickets, the next thing he knew the DOS prompt appeared. The block program simply quit, the computer froze, and he couldn't soft-boot. He had to turn off the computer and turn it back on.

He suspected the Cantronix XT workstation, and replaced it with another originally destined for Piper. He thought the computer was the most likely culprit, but he couldn't rule out the file server, the network hardware or software, the operating system, Coyote, or his programs— any of these might be to blame. Re-indexing or locking the weight-ticket file might have caused the system to crash. A spike or a drop in electricity might have done it. It might have been a fluke. He couldn't rule anything out, and decided not to tell Owen.

"WOULD YOU GO?" Grace said from her side of the bed. "It's the fifth time tonight."

It was Rose's monitor sounding again. Stan reached for his glasses, set them in place, and saw that the clock read 2:20 AM. Five times already, he thought. He rose from the bed into a warm summer room.

"Just rub her head or her feet," Grace said.

He turned on a light in the hall and it cast a panel of light on the floor through the doorway to his daughter's room.

He had gone to bed early that evening, right after supper, finding it suddenly difficult to lift his arms, to keep his eyes open, as exhausted as if somebody had pulled a plug and drained his energy to zero. Yet disturbances from Grace's restless night had disturbed his sleep, also.

Rose lay squirming. She lifted her head with her eyes closed, turned a grimacing face toward him, and put her head back down. She's in pain, he thought. He put his hand on her head and rubbed her soft hair, then pressed a button on the monitor in the crib at her feet. The button was supposed to reset and silence the alarm, but the alarm didn't stop.

"Now what?" He pressed the button again, but the alarm kept sounding. "God, not this," he whispered. "Not now."

Rose lifted her head and set it down, facing away from him. He folded the edge of the blanket away from her feet and massaged them. He pressed the reset button a third time—still nothing happened. "Goddamn thing," he said under his breath. "Grace! Come here!" He uncovered his daughter and laid the blanket aside, took her warm little body up from the crib, along with the wires running in under her clothes, and turned the monitor off.

Grace arrived at his side. "It wouldn't go off," Stan said. "I hope she's all right."

"Here," Grace said. "Lay her back down."

Stan laid his daughter down on her back in the crib. Grace hiked Rose's T-shirt up under her neck, undid a cloth belt that bound her small chest, repositioned two plastic patches that four wires were plugged into, and refastened the belt. She tugged the T-shirt in place and, turning Rose over, lay her facedown in the crib. "Would you turn it back on now?"

Stan pressed the monitor's red power switch. Red digital numerals blinked, then came on again. The monitor was silent. Rose raised her head and laid it back down.

"Sometimes it's not Rose," Grace said. "Sometimes it's just the connections."

"She squirmed out from under the patches?"

"She's really restless tonight, but if she's squirming around it means her heart is all right. I can always tell that."

THE FIRST BIG SALE of the year was announced on the radio, as Stan heard in his pickup on the drive to Littleton that morning. The auction was going to begin at noon, August 29th, and was expected to last past midnight. There would be more than the usual number of livestock, and Owen's expectation of spring calves was materializing; when Stan arrived in Littleton at ten, semi-loads of these were being moved into the yards.

To the north of the building, truckers idled their semis, and ranchers in pickups pulling gooseneck trailers waited in turn to unload. More semis were parked for buyers to the south. The lot in front was filled to capacity with the trailers and pickups and cars of area ranchers.

# SALE DAY

Stan parked his pickup on the west edge of the lot, where gravel gave way to grass.

The three-foot letters of *Littleton Livestock* didn't seem so imposing displayed over the tops of trailers and pickups, and the sounds of unloading—the shouts and whistles, the bellowing cattle, the clanging of metal—and of trailers pulling away from the unloading chute empty.

Owen's pickup, bright red and clean, was parked at the auction's front door. Sharon's familiar voice sounded over the PA as Stan entered, paging him. The hallway was lined with men, some standing, others leaning against the walls, some on benches. Many glanced at his briefcase. A traveling salesman? Stan felt they were judging him.

He went to grab a quick cup of coffee in the cafe, which was busy, smelling of coffee and food frying. Cooks in hairnets, sounds of silverware and plates, men talking at tables. As he waited at the cash register, Stan recalled Owen's eating a hamburger; Mike's head down on the table; the day it all started.

"OH THANK GOD, YOU'RE HERE," Sharon said, looking distraught, as Stan walked into the office.

"Something wrong?" he said.

"You bet there is. Marlene, well, sweet Marlene decided to go on vacation this week. She does this every year, always at the same damn time. I forgot all about it until she didn't show up. I called your house right away but you'd already left. Boy, am I sorry."

"What can I do? Can you run both sides yourself?"

"For a while, I suppose. But later, uh uh, no way on earth could I do it." She shook her head to emphasize this.

"I'll handle the buyer side then, whenever you say so," he said. "But I'll need lots of help." She was called away to a window, and Stan set his cup on the table. The hub, the server, the workstations, the printers were already on. "Is Smoke here?"

"He's supposed to be out there practicing," she said over her shoulder.

Stan went out of the office and paused in the lobby. Sharon was registering buyers, handing out numbers written with a bold black marking pen. Kids were drinking pop. A line had already formed outside the men's restroom. A few buyers who were registered, such as Stu, were slouching on couches in the buyer's little lounge after light lunches. Some were using the phones. No Bibles in sight, Stan noticed.

A TIME OF HARVEST had arrived—not of barley or wheat or sunflowers or corn, but of calves. The bleachers were filled from the first row to the last. The crowd must look like a ripe field to Owen, Stan thought, as he looked out over the front of the booth. Faces in the crowd seemed to close in on him. Most looked eager, a few weary, as if the sale of their cattle—the culmination of the year's work—was one more chore to be endured.

Smoke labored through the sale of many cows and bulls.

"Yardmen!" Sharon's voice called out over the loudspeakers. "Bring in your check-in tickets. Check-in tickets, as soon as possible, keep bringing them on in."

THE YARDMEN DROVE STEERS onto the block. The back door to the booth opened and Doc Kelly stepped in. Stan greeted him, moved over to let him through, and noticed Doc was breathing hard. "How's it going?" he asked Stan.

"So far so good."

After catching his breath, Doc said, "These are my steers."

"So I gathered."

The veterinarian stepped up to Owen and peered over the counter. He gestured to the cattle, and Owen said something to him that Stan didn't hear. Doc set his hands on his hips, and glanced at Stan in what looked like disgust. Smoke announced that there were sixty-nine head. He had merged several groups of steers into one.

"Sixty-nine?" Doc said, looking at Smoke. "There ought to be seventy."

Smoke checked the numbers again. "Doc, what we've got is sixty-nine head." Stan looked over Smoke's shoulder; from the ticket numbers, he had to agree.

Doc's Hereford steers, weighing in at an average of nine hundred pounds, were sold and driven from the block. Doc stepped back from the counter, glancing at Stan with a harried look, and moved to the back of the booth. Just as he opened the door to leave, Owen called. "Doc, like I told you, the steers are too big. If they were lighter, like I said, you'd make out much better. Think about it. It stands to reason."

Stan followed the Doc out the door and down wooden steps, the first time he had gone into the barn. Doc stopped short at the foot of the steps, and Stan had to put a hand on his shoulder to keep from losing his balance. The doctor let go a string of curses, stepping from under Stan's hand, and Stan lost his balance. He stumbled off the step and fell on his knees to the ground. He winced at the pain in his jeans.

"Are you all right?" Doc asked, placing a hand on his shoulder.

"Yeah, I'm all right." He got back on his feet and dusted his jeans off. "How about you?"

"I'm okay. Pardon my French."

"Sure. My dad raised steers one year when I a boy. He felt once was enough."

"It's just that I'm missing a steer and what does he do? He tells me—right in front of everybody—they're too big. Well, maybe they are."

"I don't think anybody heard what he said, except the people in the booth."

"Maybe not. But I'm sure I brought seventy."

Away from the glare and the heat and the noise, Stan realized he had been nervous and warm. He felt a chill in the small of his back in the cool of the barn. It was good to get away from Owen and Smoke and the whole damn business of buying and selling. Not everything is a commodity, he thought. "I'd like to help you," Stan said. "But I think I should get into the office."

"You've done quite enough." The doctor patted Stan on the back, turned, and strode away into the dark interior of the barn.

Stan never knew whether Dr. Kelly returned to his work, or went to recount his sold steers. He never saw him again at the auction. I didn't do anything, Stan thought to himself. Besides stumble and fall.

TO GET TO THE OFFICE from the booth, Stan knew he would have to squeeze past Owen, jump onto the floor scale, try to slip through the block's gate, where cattle often stood in the way, and walk in front of the bleachers toward the double doors. In front of the eyes of all those people, he thought. What he decided to do instead, since he was already in the barn, was follow the buyer-side alley to the outdoors.

Outside, he realized he'd have to climb over the sides of a pen to get to the office. It wasn't until he started climbing up that he noticed a Holstein in a far corner, a black and white milk cow holding her head to ground. She was wary. He jumped into the pen. The cow flinched, and held her head to ground.

"Whoa girl," Stan said, in a tone he hadn't heard himself use in years. The cow seemed bewildered. "Whoa boss." Auctions may change over the years, Stan thought; they may get computers, but the scared cows and frustrated veterinarians, and the way you can quiet them down—those things don't change.

"Stan Thorlofson, come to the office." Sharon's voice split the warm air. "Stan Thorlofson, please."

As Stan and the cow moved to opposite corners, one of his boots stuck in the manure of the pen, and he pulled his foot right out of the boot. Balancing on one leg, he hiked up his baggy sock, reinserted the foot into the boot, and extracted the boot in pain with a sucking sound. Don't forget the manure, Stan thought. Manure and old wounds don't change. The cow held her head to the ground, as if even that truth were not to be trusted.

In the office, Sharon called him over to the seller-side workstation. "Look at these numbers. What is Smoke doing?"

He looked at the screen, and saw what she meant—enormous head counts, average weights ridiculously small, zeroed out check-in numbers. "I had no idea. He seemed to be doing okay."

"He's out of control," Sharon said.

"I told him before the sale not to worry. That you would correct any mistakes he might make."

"So now he's just making things up!"

Stan retraced his path back through the pen with the Holstein, and entered the barn. The Indian women came up to him before Stan reached the back of the booth, and Marge, the older one, said, "We need them weight tickets. We can hear where to put the stock, but we ain't got no tickets."

"I don't know," he said. "Let me find out."

He entered the booth with the women behind him. Owen was chanting; buyers were bidding. The weight tickets were bunching up behind the printer. Stan moved past the scale in the floor, then disentangled and folded the tickets neatly, and was about to rip them apart and give them to Marge, when Smoke looked over his shoulder. "Don't!" he said. "They're all messed up!"

"You're telling me. What are you doing?"

"Take a look!" Smoke said, indicating the tickets with a lift of his chin.

Stan looked at the tickets. The buyer data from one sale was printed on a ticket with the seller data from the next Each ticket contained half the data from two different sales! That's why Smoke hadn't torn them apart. The little weight tickets had become misaligned in the printer.

Stan was realigning the paper when Owen said, "Sold. Move 'em on out." The pneumatic doors on the buyer side opened and, while the calves were being driven out, Owen glared at Stan. "What *is* the problem?" With one hand he muffled the mike.

"The weight tickets," Stan said. "They're out of alignment; they're too small. I thought this might happen." Before he could explain further, Smoke said, "What's this?" and raised his hands from the keyboard as if a bandit held a gun on him. Stan looked over Smoke's shoulder and saw the DOS prompt. "Oh great," he said. "The system's crashed. You're out of the program."

"What?" Owen asked, craning to hear.

What can I say, Stan wondered. The tickets were crap. The system had crashed. The data was—*smoked*.

Owen handed the mike to Lloyd, came over to Smoke, and looked at the screen. "Oh my God. The thing has gone down!"

"I'll have to reboot," Stan said.

"People," Owen said. "It's time we put an end to this craziness. Smoke, Lloyd, hook up the other one. This has just gotta stop."

Stan watched Smoke push the equipment aside then restore the Barskills printer to a place on the counter as Lloyd reconnected the scale's cable to the old weight-control box. Stan saw whispering among the close faces of the crowd and heard scattered laughter from the bleachers. He turned off the computer and the printer and tore off a length of the misaligned weight tickets, turned to the back of the booth where the women were standing, and rammed his groin into the metal scale set in the floor. It didn't give, not a bit. He tried to peel the white layer of tickets away from the three parts beneath, blinking back tears, then gave up, and handed the tangle to Marge, who gave him a knowing look.

"Don't tear them apart," he said. "The tickets. I think you'll see why."

He eased himself onto the stool, and Marge and Tina studied the tickets.

"I wish I worked in the back right now," he told them.

"Cheer up, honey," Marge said, holding up the ribbon of tickets. "It's not the end of the world. We can use scissors." Pain cut through his abdomen. His work on the project was over, he thought, and this arrived with a sense of relief. The block caught his eye—a thick blanket of new wood shavings on the scale floor, the smell rising from pine, the naked warmth of the shavings' color under the spotlights—and the faces in the audience were radiant, flesh and blood flushed in reflection. It wasn't so bad, he thought.

The sale had come to a stop. Owen, looking pale, thumped the mike in his palm as if it were a club. He glanced at Stan once, waiting for his help to get things ready. "Buyers! Sellers!" Owen suddenly said, turning his back to Stan. "If you're interested in computers, this is the moment you've been waiting for. A complete hardware and software package. State-of-the-art, I mean top-of-the-line equipment. And guaranteed for the life of the party! Who'll give me a dollar?"

It's not worth a dam, Stan thought. The whole business. The whole damn thing. Grace was right. It wasn't worth a cent.

"Two bits," a man shouted, and Stan recognized the person as Stu.

Without hesitation Owen cried, "Sold!"

THE SKY WAS BLUE tinged with gold that afternoon in August in southwest North Dakota. Alone in Lark, Stan sat down, bareheaded and barefoot, on the doorsteps of his hillside house, and watched cars and trucks move east and west along the highway against a background of buttes to the south rising to gold blue. He opened a volume of Shakespeare's plays he had folded shut on a pair of pliers and, taking up the tool, removed from the ball of his right foot a fir sliver the size of a stick pin, then set the pliers aside, and located the lines in *The Third Part of Henry the Sixth*, where Henry's queen tells him to hold close his lips, and Lord Clifford tells him to be still. Shut up and die, in other words. The weakling king abruptly disappears from the scene (a field of battle in Act II) and reappears several scenes later, alone, with time for contemplation, and says

> *Here upon this molehill will I sit me down.*
> *To whom God will, be the victory.*
> *For Margaret my queen, and Clifford, too,*
> *Have chid me from the battle, swearing both*
> *They prosper best of all when I am thence.*

"Prosper best of all when I am thence," Stan repeated, baring his teeth in a stab of pain. Where Mike and Owen and everyone wants me, he thought, making a mountain, he realized, of the man-on-the-molehill's self-pity. Henry continued

> *Would I were dead, if God's good will were so—*
> *For what is in this world but grief and woe?*
> *O God! Methinks it were a happy life*
> *To be no better than a homely swain.*
> *To sit upon a hill, as I do now,*

"As I do now," Stan said, and looked off toward the highway. A truck, as if the size of a toy, glided east until it disappeared from sight, and from that point of departure Stan traced, or retraced, the rising contour of the land to the top of a butte where its tip touched gold blue. He read

> *To carve out dials quaintly, point by point,*
> *Thereby to see the minutes how they run:*
> *How many makes the hour full complete,*
> *How many hours brings about the day,*
> *How many days will finish up the year,*
> *How many years a mortal man may live.*

Mortal Mike, the corn counter, the thinker, Stan thought. So many plants to a row, so many rows to an acre, so many acres, or so few. A twenty-acre townsite was nothing, he felt. Lark was nothing any more, no bigger than the toy-sized cars and trucks that drove past on the highway under the lift of that sky. An accountant? To give an account before the years give out. Begin before the end, or it will be too late.

*When this is known, then to divide the times:*
*So many hours must I tend my flock,*
*So many hours must I take my rest,*
*So many hours must I contemplate,*
*So many hours must I sport myself,*
*So many days my ewes have been with young,*
*So many weeks ere the poor fools will ean*
*Ean, yean,* to bring forth young. "The young—poor fools," Stan said. "We're all like sheep"
*So many years ere I shall shear the fleece.*
*So minutes, hours, days, weeks, months, and years,*
*Passed over to the end they were created,*
*Would bring white hairs unto a quiet grave.*
Time was not created for this, Stan thought. Man's chief end is to glorify God and to enjoy Him forever, the Presbyterian catechism stated. *Henry!* Emma clenching her teeth. *You really know how to piss a guy off royally!* Stu. *You're goddamn right I take my religion seriously!* Grandpa Jonas's declamation.
*Ah, what a life were this! How sweet! How lovely!*
*Gives not the hawthorn bush a sweeter shade*
*To shepherds looking on the seely sheep*
*Than doth a rich embroidered canopy*
*To kings that fear their subjects treachery?*
That depends, Stan thought. "That depends," he repeated out loud, shaking his head, dismayed at this weakness of absorbing the voices of others. What voice was his own, he wondered. The king insisted however:
*O yes, it doth—a thousandfold it doth.*
*And to conclude, the shepherd's homely curds,*
*His cold thin drink out of his leather bottle,*
*His wonted sleep under a fresh tree's shade,*
*All which secure and sweetly he enjoys,*
*Is far beyond a prince's delicates,*

*His viands sparkling in a golden cup,*
*His body couchèd in a curious bed,*
*When care, mistrust, and treason waits on him.*
"And dust," Stan said. "Dust waits on him." Him? There it was, his voice, disparaging and self-loathing. There it was, dust in the air, he saw, a field of minuscule gold spangles. The cut grass had gone from green to gray brown, and big round bales dotted the plains like buffalo grazing. A golden cup? He was no more a computer man than this Henry was an heir to Henry the 5th.

That depends, Stan thought. "On what? Goddamn it!" he cried, an arm outstretched, as if to nail the curse to a wall. "Leave me alone," he whispered. Meaning whom? Did Chuck's mannerisms bother him that much? Grace? My love? And then, as if his dad had grabbed him by the arms and begun to shake some sense into him, had taken him aside to give him the licking he deserved—no, he heard his grandpa's voice in confession of sin to *his* son, to Sig: Honor your father and mother, that your days may be long upon the land the LORD gives you. Grandpa Jonas's individual accent set Stan's hair on end: Honor your *föður* and *móður.*

I've failed to honor them, he began. The vanity, the dirt, I have cast on your name. Please let me tell them, let them live long upon the land, North Dakota.

The Ramcharger suddenly appeared at the turn off the highway, then dust rose behind it as it gained speed. Grace and the children were returning from town, coming home. A living voice abided, Stan realized, and had been passed down from father to son. *I depend like a fleece from a scale, I hang upon your every word.* More dust rose, as if incense were rising from a golden bowl.

Stan rose, came down off the steps, and collapsed, his right ankle turned under. I see the heavens, he thought as he fell. The ground was sacred, he felt, even where his hands touched down. A vast sparkling ocean, still and serene, rested overhead, he knew, as he knew in his legs a wavering in a beam of earth founded on water. A groaning from his groin, as if from a wagon under strain, rose from beneath a load of voices he felt he carried. Then he was down on his belly, licking dirt from his lips, cast down at the bruised feet of heaven finally touching the earth, setting it apart, raising dust, all of it holy, all over the land.

Chapter Seven: Rest

THE PHONE RANG and Stan picked it up.
"Hello, this is Owen Yuler calling."
"Yes?"
"How are you?"
"I'm okay. Owen? Are you there?" There was no answer, and Stan wondered if the line had gone dead.
"Listen," Owen said. "I'm pretty disappointed with the way the sale went. What?"
"I was, too," Stan said, thinking somebody must be bugging him.
"It just can't do the job, can it?"
"The software, you mean."
"I mean the software, of course."
"Smoke can't even type!"
"Yeah, but—"
"Marlene goes on vacation!"
"I know, I know, listen, would ya?"
"And those damn little tickets!" Stan felt shame over his face, as if a searchlight had passed over him. An inner accusation followed—*to revert to this in a matter of hours!* "I'm sorry, Owen. Could we get the people together and practice? What did you say?"
"I said I don't think so. How much longer can this go on? It's almost September."
"I don't know how much longer. I really don't."
"*That's* my problem."

"It's mine too, Owen. I—"

"I'll tell you what. There's a system I'm looking at that's really simple. Stan, you should see it. Even my boy could run it. I've got the guy here, he's installed twenty systems in four states already, and he's ready to start as soon as I give him the go-ahead."

"He's in Littleton! Right now?"

"Right here in the office and, Stan, we're working on a deal. He's looked at your software and, I'll tell you what, he's impressed. He likes a lot of your features, and I'd hate to lose them, too. His system though, it's so easy you wouldn't believe it. He wants to incorporate some of your ideas, hire you, and even buy your software. Stan, are you there?"

"He wants to buy my program and hire me?"

"Sounds pretty good, doesn't it?" Owen said, jumping on Stan's tone.

DON LAWSON, who was from Colorado, had installed systems in twenty auctions over a seven-year period, with few complaints from his customers, he let Stan know. He had heard about Owen's troubles, was in the area, and decided to drop in. So here he was and Stan had driven to Littleton to meet him.

"Simplicity is the key," Don said. "The operator can run the software if he can use a calculator."

"Can Smoke use a calculator?" Stan asked Owen.

"All he'd need to know is the number pad," Owen said.

"That's right," Don said. "And a dozen numeric codes."

"You think Smoke can learn the codes?" Stan added, addressing Owen.

"Sure he could."

"They're not hard, and there are only six fields to fill in—not a dozen—and that saves time," Don said. "Do you know C, buckaroo?"

"Yes," Stan said, as if to squelch Don's manner.

"My program's in C, and runs under Concurrent."

"Ever heard of it?" Owen asked Stan.

"No." But with a name like that, Stan reasoned, it must be able to serve as a network.

"I like Don's software, but I want your hardware. It's already paid for." Owen glanced at Don.

"I usually supply the hardware," Don said. "But I'm curious to see how my program will run under DOS and—what do you have here?—Novell?"

"Right. A local-area network."

"Would you be interested in programming for me? Maybe incorporate some of your ideas into my program?"

"Possibly. Owen said you might buy my software."

"Owen's looking out for you, my friend. He's a real wheeler-dealer."

Stan released Owen from the contract then and there, without consulting Mike, and helped Don install his software.

Rumors of Littleton's troubles had reached even Colorado, and relief arrived for Stan in an outpouring the moment he walked out the market's door.

"YOU SOLD HIM OUR HARDWARE?" Mike flopped back in his chair, his mouth open. He blinked and let his arms hang at his sides, as if paralyzed.

What an act, Stan thought.

Candy sat on a couch in Mike's office, with Mike Jr., on his back beside her. "You're really wet, aren't you, sweetie?" she said, lifting him by his heels, which tucked his chin to his chest, and removed a disposable diaper.

"All the hardware and software for fifteen thousand dollars. What he invested in the project. It was only fair."

"He was under contract to us!"

"I know, but it's almost September and he wanted out."

"So this other guy's software," Mike said, pausing as if to get this all straight, "is running on our hardware. Incredible!"

"It's really incredible, Stan," Candy said. "We paid for that hardware." Mike Jr. kicked his pudgy naked legs and whimpered.

"I know and I asked you not to," Stan pointed out.

"I've just lost ten thousand dollars," Mike said, and his look seemed to say it was the greatest loss he had ever suffered.

"Ten? I thought it was six."

"It was ten, let me assure you."

"Yeah? Well, what about me?"

"What *about* you?" Candy asked, fanning the baby with a new diaper. Suddenly Mike Jr. started to cry.

"I've lost a whole year's worth of work."

Mike said nothing.

Candy taped the diaper on the baby and snapped the snaps on the legs of his outfit.

"I'll try to pay you back," Stan said.

"With what?" Mike said.

"We paid ten thousand for that hardware," Candy said. "Or was it twenty? I think it was twenty."

"Who am I talking to?" Stan asked Mike. "You or her?"

"You are talking to me," Mike said, tapping a finger to his chest.

Candy raised the baby, now quieting down, to her shoulder, crouched and snatched up the folded wet diaper, and walked out of the office. "I'm sure it was twenty. Not to mention that pickup."

"The good news is that the guy wants to buy my software and hire me as a programmer."

Mike sat up and drew a pen from his pocket, tapped it on the desk, then clenched it between his teeth, and said in the manner of a mobster, "Go on."

"He wants to incorporate some features of my program into his. He said maybe he could market my software to smaller auctions and sell his to larger ones. He's also running an obsolete operating system, and I think he wants to upgrade everything."

"How much is he willing to pay?"

"For the software? I don't know. I'm thinking of asking sixty thousand. Then I'd offer to buy back Owen's hardware, and reimburse him for the time and the trouble, reimburse you—"

"He won't pay that kind of money," Mike asserted, sure of himself.

"Maybe not. But we shouldn't try to guess what he might do. He's also offered to hire me at thirty dollars an hour, and said he'd guarantee a minimum of twenty hours a week. I could pay you back, and pay for the pickup."

"What have you done for him?"

"I installed his software on the network, switched a couple of modem cards around, and reconfigured the communications software. I also gave him the parameters for the electronic scale. He's working on that right now."

"And he's paying you?"

"He agreed to pay me thirty dollars an hour."

"Will you let me handle this?" Mike said.

"Handle what?"

"His offer to buy the whole system. I hear this stuff all the time—promises, promises. But when you ask for specifics—an offer in black and white—they back off. Do you have the guy's number?"

"Not with me. You can call Littleton."

"I'm not going to play games with this guy. We make our offer. He makes a single counter offer. No negotiations. We take it or leave it. I'll give him until five o'clock next Friday to fax me the offer. One week."

"All right," Stan said, and thought, suddenly Mike is my partner again. Oh boy.

As he sat watching, Mike called Littleton. Don had left. Mike got his number from Sharon and called Don at his office but Don wasn't in. He was still on the road somewhere between South Dakota and Montana at the time, Mike relayed to Stan, and couldn't be reached.

Don had a partner, it turned out, who wasn't as interested in Stan's software as Don was. They learned that much. The partner agreed to make an offer, if an offer was to be made, in the manner Mike demanded.

NEXT FRIDAY at five no fax had arrived.

"You were right," Stan said.

"This happens all the time," Mike asserted again.

"Now that you've got the knife in, I suppose you'd like to thrust it up."

"No I would not," Mike said calmly.

A WEEK LATER, after an hour's negotiation in Littleton between Stan and Don and Owen, Owen offered to lend Stan fifteen thousand dollars at no interest, so Stan could buy back his system and use it to upgrade Don's software.

As an incentive for the loan, Owen was to receive Don's system—new hardware and all—at a discount of ten thousand dollars and get free upgrades as Stan developed them. Don said he would hire Stan for at least twenty hours a week, at ten dollars an hour, so Stan could pay back the loan. The advantage to Don was one more system installed in South Dakota.

"This is getting too weird," Stan said, and Don and Owen, by saying nothing, seemed to agree.

THE BLOCK PROGRAM had created files of weight tickets spanning January to August. Data from the last sale was corrupt and incomplete, but Sharon's diligent editing, and her entering the missing tickets by hand, brought the files up to date.

There were enough tickets saved over the months to justify converting them from their dBASE format to a generic form that Owen could manipulate on his computer at home. Stan wrote a conversion program at Owen's request. In went Coyote's data; out came the output, which became input to First Works.

Stan designed a First-Works database similar to the one he'd designed for the auction. He also created report files that extracted information from this database in a dozen of ways. He copied the database and report files onto a disk and mailed them off. Owen finally has a buyer-seller database, he thought.

Owen called and said he was pleased to get it. That was the last time they spoke with each other, and Stan imagined Owen managing connections between buyers and sellers, guiding truckers to Littleton Livestock, talking on the phone through a mouthful of beef, or chips. Half a year's weight tickets, Stan thought, a humble conclusion to what might have been.

Stan sent Don a bill for one hundred and ninety dollars. Ninety bucks for installing his software, sixty for reconfiguring the modems and communications software, and forty more for a round-trip to Littleton.

He waited a month for payment, then called Don.

"I'll tell you what," Don said. "I'll pay you for the installation and mileage. That's the best I can do. How 'bout it, pardner?"

"Why not the communications work?"

"I haven't used it. I haven't transferred a single file, not a golblame thing."

"Why not?"

"They're not using the software."

"They're not? What are they using?"

"Their old system. I'll tell you one thing: that Owen scares me."

"What do you mean?" Don's news had set Stan's thought about Owen back to square one. *Damn!*

"He doesn't know what he wants. Listen, about the invoice. Knock off sixty dollars and I'll pay it. What do you say, buckaroo?"

Stan reduced the bill as Don requested but never received a cent in payment from him.

One day, sorting through his mail, Stan opened a diskette mailer from Martin, and pulled out a diskette labeled *Scandisk*. A note on the disk read

*Stan*

*Suspecting a virus*

*At C:\>, type scandisk*

*Martin*

He also opened a bill for ten thousand dollars from a collection agency in Canada. He showed the notice to Mike.

"Cantronix has gone bankrupt," Mike said. "I already paid this."

"Are you helping them through bankruptcy?" Stan asked, smiling as pleasantly as he could. Mike frowned.

# SALE DAY

OVER THE DAYS Stan prepared to fence the creek pasture, his three sons were excited. On the day he was ready to begin, they wanted to come along and help and, in the shed across from their house, Stan handed them tools. They hurried to put them in the back of the pickup and returned for more, rebounding from collisions with one another in good humor. Besides several spades, a tape measure, hand saws, gas and oil cans, levels, hammers, screwdrivers, pliers, and a fence stretcher, they managed to carry a post-hole digger, a fence-post driver, steel bars for tamping dirt, and a chain saw. Then they helped him load a neighbor's gas-powered auger, which was connected to an engine on wheels, some fifty-pound spools of barbed wire, and a five-gallon bucket of water for moistening the soil. These were Stan's tools of intention to teach his sons about the world.

In the pickup Dale was squashed against Stan's side and, as they drove from the yard, Dale cried, "I want to be by the window on the way back!"

Stan already had in place in the pasture two-by-fours, steel posts, and railroad ties. He had bought twenty-four ties from Mike, who had gotten them from Lumber Jack, and for ten dollars apiece Mike delivered them to the pasture and unloaded them himself the night before. Mike said, Two hundred and forty dollars is two hundred and forty dollars. Every little bit helps, he added.

"The ties are eight feet long and eight inches thick," Stan said. "Some weigh two hundred pounds."

"I want to see them," Lee said, and craned his head to look out over the dashboard.

Vernon struggled with something in a pocket of his jeans, then freed a piece of black plastic—a toy building block. The boys passed the block back and forth, studying it as if conspiring over what they would build next.

"How are we going to lift the railroad ties?" Vernon asked.

"By hand," Stan said, pleased his son had said *we*.

To put up a stable barbed-wire fence Stan had to construct braces to bear the pressure of the wires once they were stretched taut. The braces had to stand secure, and not give way, under hundreds of pounds of tension, so he decided to set two railroad ties deep in the ground as posts, then span the distance between them at chest height with another tie, forming a girderlike H. He believed this would bear a fence.

After installing a second brace some distance away, he tightened a wire from one brace to the other, drawing it in a straight line between them. Then, alongside the wire, he pounded steel posts into the ground, one every seven steps. He attached two more wires, tightened all three, and clipped them in place to the posts.

"That's done," Stan said. "What do you think?"

"It's great," Lee said.

"The rest of the fence line will take some time," Stan said. "The creek meanders back and forth. We have to cross it three times! And every time, we have to make two braces, one above each bank. That's six braces, right there, plus an end brace where we start, and a corner brace on the other side of the pasture."

"What's a co-new bwace?" Dale asked, and Stan explained.

"It looks like, if you do that, you're gonna fence in the merry-go-round," Vernon said.

"We are. We're going to make the park part of the pasture. That water hydrant—I want to get it running. Then we can water the sheep when the creek freezes over."

"We can still go on the merry-go-round, can't we?" Lee asked.

"Sure. The fence is to keep the sheep in, not to keep you out." He smiled down at his sons.

STAN LET VERNON DIG through the sod with a spade, then placed the tip of the borrowed gas-powered auger in the depression. He started the engine, positioned the handlebars near chest-height so the auger was upright, and squeezed the throttle. The auger ground down into the soil, which was dry, spinning dirt into a growing pile at the hole's edge. When the handlebars finally pressed into the sort dirt, he pulled the auger out, shut off the engine, and widened the hole with the spade.

"Why are you doing that?" Lee asked.

"Because it's too narrow for a tie."

Stan poured water into the hole, to moisten its bottom, and the boys took turns using the manual post-hole digger and drew up mud. When they were finished, he dragged a tie over and lifted one end, feeling as if his jeans might pop, or the internal mesh below give way.

The tie's tarry weight slid through his gloves and thumped to a stop. "Hand me the level," he said. When the tie was in place, they pushed the dry dirt back in and tamped it down with a steel bar. Once the hole was full, they stomped on the dirt with their feet.

Stan stood back and eyed the post, then he passed around a thermos of lemonade prepared by Grace. The work, warmth of the sun, and the breeze over the open pasture made them thirsty. It had taken a good hour to put in the post, and it was time to talk. "Dale," Stan said. "Are you a member of the church?"

"Yes," Dale answered. Chuck had visited the day before, and had asked the children whether they were members of the church or not. Dale had said no.

"When did you become a member?"

"When I was baptized," Dale said. His blond curls wobbled with the wind.

"That's right. But is baptism all you need?"

"No," Vernon said. "You need to trust Jesus."

"If you need trust to Jesus to be members of His church, why did your mother and I have you baptized when you were babies? Do babies have faith?"

"Of course not," Lee said.

"We were baptized because Christ's church always has children in it," Vernon said.

Chuck had grasped Dale's slender shoulder and said, Remember this boys: the Apostle Peter said that the promise is to you—here he was speaking to the grownups—*and to your children*, as many as the Lord your God shall call. Son, you *are* a member of the church!

"May we go over to the creek?" Vernon asked.

"Yeah," Lee said. "We want to see it."

"I guess so," Stan said. "Be careful. The banks are steep. And keep an eye on Dale."

By the time he pressed the auger into the earth, the boys had reached the creek and were throwing stones—or so it looked from where he stood. He called to them and they waved back.

He got the auger stuck in the ground, and managed to free it, noting as he worked that the boys were in sight. But when he reached for the spade, he saw they were gone.

He ran toward where he had seen them, calling their names, and they rose into view from a bank of the creek as if rising up through the pasture itself, and waved again. He stopped and raised a hand.

They'll be okay, he thought, and turned back.

The second tie lodged itself into the hole at the wrong angle then, over the top of it, Stan saw Lee coming toward him in a run. Stan ran to meet him.

"Dale fell into the creek!" Lee yelled, and when Stan got close to Lee, he saw he was crying. He urged him to follow and when he got to the bank, Vernon was holding Dale's arm, helping him climb up the dusty side of it. Dale's clothes were soaked. He was standing barefoot with his shoes and balled-up socks in his hands, shivering.

"What happened?" Stan asked.

"We were bending over to look at a minnow trap in the water," Vernon said.

"I fell in headfust," Dale added, his lips quivering.

"Weren't you scared?" Lee asked him.

"No, I wemebewed to twust."

Stan lifted him up, smelling marsh water in his hair, and carried him across the pasture. Stan removed his wet clothes and wrapped him up in a jacket, his hair already drying in ringlets, and let him sit on his lap in the pickup on the drive home.

THAT NIGHT, when the boys were asleep, Stan went into their room. On the floor, in the middle of a flat plastic green platform, all on its own, was a miniature merry-go-round. Several platforms lay on the floor, and on these were constructed fence braces of plastic blocks, and corner braces, and tiny posts strung with strands of string.

Stan picked up a diminutive auger connected to a motor on wheels, then a red fence stretcher—too large for the scale of the fence but no bigger than his hand.

There was a plastic figurine beside a pile of black blocks like railroad ties and, on an adjoining platform, three figures planted firmly beside a trail of blue blocks that zigzagged across a miniature pasture.

Dale lay asleep.

Three years old, and he falls headfirst from the sky into an "unfathomed creek," Stan said under his breath.

That moment when you go under, upside down, your hearing upset, vision out of control, and stop breathing (for how long?) or start to choke, helpless as a sinking stone, hope thrashing in your heart, and gulp a mouthful of air and marsh water, yet remember to trust.

*I wemembewed to twust,* this tenderest son had said.

He lay his hand on his son's perfectly shaped skull and blessed him, feeling the boy's warmth and fine hair rise and curl around his fingers.

"HAVE YOU SEEN THIS?" Jim asked, as Stan walked into his office.

Jim handed him a newspaper, and on the front page of *The Mandan News* Stan saw a photo of Littleton Livestock. A poor shot but unmistakable—the large letters on the side of the building, the wide parking lot, a pickup parked near the front door. The caption read: *Littleton Livestock Auction Under New Management.* The date on the paper was Wednesday, November 13, 1991.

"It says here he sold the business and moved to Colorado," Stan said, trying to take in the whole paragraph in one gulp.

"Where he's bought another," Jim said.

"His brother Lloyd is the new owner," Stan added, as he read on.

"Who would have guessed?"

"Don Lawson told me Owen didn't know what he wanted but, you know, I think he did—a system up and running before selling out."

"Stan, whoa now. Isn't that pure speculation?"

"It could have been for his wife's sake, I realize. I wonder if the auction in Colorado has computers. I bet it does. I—"

Jim's phone rang and Stan paused. Jim pressed a button, lifted the phone, and covered the receiver. From the next room, the receptionist called, "Jim? It's Mike Becker on the line. Should I tell him you're here?"

"Put him on hold. Or better yet, tell him I'll call back later. I'm busy with Stan." Jim set the receiver down, and Stan heard the receptionist give Mike the message.

"What does he want?" Stan asked.

"He says he needs an accountant familiar with the ranch and the farm—with the whole operation, I guess."

"Are you going to help him?"

"This one last time. Yes, I will."

"LITTLETON LIVESTOCK. This is Sharon. How may I help you?"

"This is Stan Thorlofson."

"Why, Stan, what can I do for you?"

"I was just calling to see if you were still there. Still working for Littleton Livestock."

"Are you kidding? They couldn't keep this place up without me!"

"I'm sorry I couldn't get things working. Of all the people I imagine I've affected, I think most about you."

"Oh, don't! Now that Lloyd owns the market, his wife Debbie quit her job and works here. She's running the computer on the block. We're having a great time!"

"What computer?"

"Yours. We still have your whole system, and Don Lawson's software. Lloyd bought the whole package from Owen, and it's working just fine. Both here and in Piper. I love it! So don't worry about me."

"I'm going to send you a disk," Stan said. "It's called Scandisk. I'll put in a note on how to use it. If you have any trouble, give me a call."

"I'll keep an eye out for it."
"One more question. What about Smoke?"
"That fellow," she said and cleared her throat. "He is no longer employed here."

MIKE ACCEPTED TEMPORARY appointment to the department of Economic Development and Finance in a neighboring state. He became the department's director, in fact. The state's governor fired the previous director, and selected Mike to fill out the term.

Once in office, Mike invited Stan to interview for the position of a computer-network administrator. He told Stan to come up and see him in his office on the second floor of the ED&F building.

STAN SPOKE with a receptionist on the ground floor when he arrived. She called up to Mike and then asked Stan to have a seat in the lobby. Her red-orange hair and rhinestone-studded horn-rim glasses matched her painted fingernails, which she positioned with care in contact with the phone and her keyboard.

Indian, or Native American, watercolors decorated the lobby walls. One was a portrait of a beautiful woman in braids, wrapped in buffalo hide, superimposed on a larger portrait of a buffalo's head. Another pictured the ghostly soul of a dead man ascending in the smoke from a teepee.

From a low table in front of him, Stan picked up a report describing the number of business owners in the state who were women, or minorities, or both—depicting the distribution of ownership, or lack of it, in pie charts and bar graphs.

From what the reports and the art in the lobby suggested, a Native American woman had a good chance, if not the brute power, of getting a bigger piece of the pie.

Men, even Indian, it seemed to Stan, were going up in smoke.

He wondered, waiting there, how the mixture of state money, sleek techno-furniture, and erotic animism saturated the mind of the woman at the reception desk protecting her nails.

Mike's agency was clearly positioning itself (as Mike undoubtedly saw it) to gather the disadvantaged into its arms. But the receptionist and Marge and Tina seemed worlds apart: nail polish against cow shit. There was no place in the scenario for Grace, who had aspirations, which she considered worthy, of being a wife and a mother.

What am I doing here, Stan wondered.

He took an elevator to the second floor and its doors opened on Mike. After bowing to shake hands with Stan, Mike guided him through a labyrinth of partitions that formed miniature "workspaces," the tails of his gray three-piece suit flapping over his tail from his tall frame as he walked. They walked into a huge room where Mike flopped into a chair behind a desk, as if he were still in blue jeans and a flannel shirt.

"So how's our finest network administrator?"

"I don't know how you can keep on like this," Stan said.

"You have to 'go with the flow'," Mike said with upraised hands, indicating his surroundings.

Stan had meant his flattery.

On the wall behind his desk was a photo of Mike shaking hands with the out-of-state governor. How he flatters himself, Stan thought. "It's strange to see you in this setting," Stan said. "A free-market capitalist, a Republican entrepreneur like you, accepting a Democrat appointment. To this department of all places! Don't you find business awfully slow?"

"And you, willing to interview for a position in it! Cut the ideological crap."

Indeed, I shouldn't be here, Stan had to admit.

"Every state is divided into two groups," Mike said. "The haves and the have-nots. We need to insure that as we enter the twenty-first century, and the technological future, that this great state of ours is not left diddling away in the dirt. I'm assembling the experts here to show how to do it."

"Sounds pretty paternalistic," Stan said, imagining again the young Hutterites who worked on Mike's farm.

"You're damn right it's paternalistic! The farmers in this state—they don't know what the hell they're doing!"

"And you do."

"Marketing. I'm talking about marketing!"

At least he isn't talking about farming.

"Let me explain the department here. I have two deputy directors. A statistical expert with a Ph.D. from Stanford, and a financial whiz with a Ph.D. from the U. of M. They're both top-flight in their fields. You'll fit right in. I know how you academics think."

Stan was surprised to hear Mike considered him an academic. But how does he think academics think?

IN AN INTERVIEW with the statistical expert, the expert asked Stan, "Are you familiar with—what is it now? Base something. God, what is it?"

"10 Base T?"

"Yeah, that's it. Are you familiar with that?"

"I've heard of it, read about it in magazines, but I have no firsthand experience."

"Me either," the man said.

The financial whiz told Stan, "I don't quite agree that we need a network administrator, or even a network."

She couched this in a whisper after Mike and the statistical expert left Stan in the room with her.

Stan waited two weeks, then called Mike's office to ask about the position. Mike wasn't in, but his secretary took Stan's name, and said Mike would get back to him.

Two weeks later, he called again. Mike was in a meeting, his secretary said, but she'd give him his message and Mike would call back as soon as the meeting was over.

Stan called another week later, and the secretary told him that Mike had told her to tell him that they had decided not to put a network in after all.

AT THE TURN OF THE YEAR, Rose had outgrown the abnormalities of her lungs and eyes. Her monitor didn't sound in the night, and she slept quietly.

"LET'S GET HER UP ON THE TABLE, then I'll prep her," the young woman said.

Stan helped her lift the sheep onto a stainless-steel table, where it lay flat on its side with its head and neck stretched out. It was a ewe, in premature labor, suffering in the strain from a uterine prolapse—part of her uterus hung from her rear end like a wad of bubblegum as big as a fist. The woman was getting her ready for a Cesarean section.

"If you would just hold her. I'll get my clipper."

He put his hands on the woolly body and the woman picked up an electric clipper from a cart beside the table, plugged it into an extension cord in a retractable reel that hung from the ceiling, and flipped the switch. It came on with a snap, its gentle-buzzing hum reminding him of a barbershop. The comb was two inches wide, with many tiny teeth. The sheep lay silent and still.

"Donna Becker," Stan said, reading the nametag on her lab coat. "Are you any relation to Mike?"

"None whatsoever." Donna was a vet tech, as she was called, one of Dr. Kelly's assistants. She shaved the ewe's belly close to the skin and laid a handful of wool on the table. "When was she due?" she asked.

"The middle of February. She's a month early. Do you think the lambs will survive?"

"It's possible. Have you been feeding her well?"

"She's not mine, but I know she gets grain and oats hay every day."

"It just depends." She placed more wool on the table.

"On what?" he said, thinking, Not another one.

"On how well developed the lambs are."

*I wonder if this is the wise thing to do?* That question had nagged him all the way from Chuck's farm to the clinic. He had offered to pay for the surgery, but Chuck doubted whether it would do any good. The operation cost eighty dollars and there was no guarantee that either the sheep or her offspring would survive. The ewe was Chuck's "best producer," as Chuck had said, but he thought he should slaughter her.

Love is costly, Stan thought.

He used to help his dad deliver calves by Cesarean, but couldn't recall ever doing the same for a sheep. Yet he couldn't stand to see the ewe suffer or bear the thought of her young dying. His father-in-law, it seemed, had had similar feelings for Rose. Stan persuaded Chuck not to think of taking the ewe's life.

"Do you do many C sections on sheep?" Stan said.

"Not many. Most farmers think it's too costly. But don't worry, Dr. Kelly is specially trained to do sheep. He'll be in in a moment." She finished shaving the ewe, turned off and unplugged the clipper, and lay it down on the cart. The sheep took a breath, then heaved a great sigh.

The image of a lamb sleeping, its life slipping away inside the warm womb, evoked inexpressible feelings in Stan for his daughter.

"Do we have to tie her down?"

"No, I don't think so," Donna said. "We'll give her a local anesthetic. I think we can hold her. And you're lying so nice and quiet, aren't you, little mother?" She said this with tenderness, her face right up to the face of the sheep, as if to a child.

"Maa!" the ewe replied.

Doc Kelly's clinic was on the Heart River near Mandan, its buildings rough-cut siding stained dark brown, wood shingles on the roofs, with porches supported by round posts. Western porticos, replicas of hitching posts, the driveway and parking lot paved with scoria, burnt-orange—a lovely arrangement half-hidden among the trees of the valley, in the snow.

Here is a place, Stan felt, when he saw it, where creatures that cannot give words to their suffering are cared for. And spoken to, as Donna had spoken, in love.

"Mr. Thorlofson," Dr. Kelly said. He came up with eager strides and held out his hand.

"Dr. Kelly," Stan said.

"I didn't know you had sheep."

"I don't. Not yet anyway. This belongs to a farmer down my way named Chuck Ream."

"I know him." Doc turned toward Donna, who was arranging surgical tools on a towel she had spread on the cart. "Are we ready?"

"Not quite."

Doc turned back to Stan. "I was sorry to hear about your trouble with Owen Yuler."

"The trouble wasn't primarily with Owen." Or was it, he wondered. "Anyway, it's over. Not for you, though."

"No, I still go down there. Things are much more relaxed now that Lloyd is the owner."

"Do you know why Owen left?"

"No, I can't say I do. But from what I can gather, there were problems in the family. It's probably best not to say anything more."

Stan was about to ask, With Claire? But instead he said, "Did you ever find your missing steer?"

"Yes I did. The yardmen miscounted." He had to turn to check Stan's face on this, as if he needed Stan to know he was in the right.

"We're ready now," Donna said, taking up a position next to the table, behind the sheep, opposite Doc. She wrapped an arm around the ewe's neck, and slid the other down along one of its front legs.

Dr. Kelly picked up a plastic syringe filled with clear liquid, an anesthetic, and slipped the needle under the skin near the top of shaved hide. The ewe struggled a moment, Donna maintaining her hold, and Doc injected a measured dose beneath the skin, subcutaneously as it was called. Sub-Q, as dad would say, Stan thought.

Doc removed the needle and rubbed the soft bulge raised by the drug. He repeated the injection several times down the taut belly, numbing a vertical band of flesh where an incision would be made.

Stan used to be entrusted with this procedure in prepping a cow. His dad would also give a cow an injection between vertebrae at the base of the spine, a spinal that further deadened the nervous system.

Doc lay the syringe down, and picked up a scalpel.

The gentle incision parted only the skin—not the abdominal lining. A soft oval opened wider with each downward dab of Doc's scalpel, then he slipped two fingers of his free hand under the sides of the incision and, holding the skin toward him, parted it to a length of several inches. The oval's edges glistened deep red, tiny rivulets flowing down to a confluence of blood, there absorbed and halted by shaven wool, then by a square of medical gauze Doc pressed in place. He made a similar cut through the abdominal lining, an opening into the dark hollow of her abdomen.

The cream yellow of the wool, the pink skin's blood red edges, the pink-and-blue tinted gray-white tissue of the lining, the white gauze stained like a Japanese flag— the colors of surgery were nauseating to Stan, in a way that Sartre's ruminations weren't, combined as they were with odors of clipper oil, rubbing alcohol, wool, and the open, exuding stomach cavity of a sheep.

He usually felt light-headed giving blood, and once fainted forward into the arms of a nurse. Not much of a surgeon. Okay, love alone wasn't enough, he thought.

The tricky part of the procedure, Stan knew, was making the incision in the womb.

His dad would lay a scalpel flat in his left hand, the blade toward his fingertips, grip it with a thumb, then slip his hand into a cow's organed interior, right up to his shoulder, and make the cut in the thick uterine muscle, blind. Blind! His dad would struggle, his face up close to the cow, as if listening—

Doc Kelly removed a bloodied hand from the ewe's side, and laid the scalpel on the cart, then reached in a second time and moments later drew out the long, slender rear legs, and glistening body, then the head and front legs of a lamb, wet with amniotic fluid. "That's one."

"There are two?" Stan said, moistening his lips. He felt a pressure of tears.

"Uh huh."

"A ewe, Doc?" Donna asked of the newborn.

"Yup, about eight pounds, I'd say."

Twice what Rose weighed, Stan thought.

Doc wiped the lamb's nose free of mucous, stuck a finger in its mouth and extracted more, then laid it on the table near the ewe's head. Donna reached over to steady the lamb. The ewe raised her head, sniffed at her offspring, then started to lick her clean. The lamb lifted a wobbling head, blinked, then lay down again. Its long tail shook—its whole body was trembling—but it didn't make a sound.

Doc delivered another ewe lamb the same size.

"Twin girls!" Stan said when Doc held it up. "I mean females."

"They'll have a better chance of survival," Doc said. He handed the second lamb over to Donna who received it into a towel. "Their lungs are usually better developed than the lungs of premature males." This is what the doctor had said about Rose, Stan recalled. In brisk strokes Donna began rubbing the lamb dry.

Stan had done the same for newborn calves, rubbing slick hair into tufts using used overalls. He would stick a piece of straw up a calf's nose, trying to make it sneeze, and the calf would snort, jerk its head away, kicking its legs, and often utter a cry. The cow, standing in a restraining chute, neck through a gate, with an incision in her side, exhibiting more patience than Stan could ever muster, would turn her head in her calf's direction and answer—her first sound since surgery began.

The blanketed lamb in Donna's arm muttered, "uh uh," then bleated sharply. "Your lungs sound just fine," Donna said.

Donna warmed frozen colostrum (purchased from local sheep farmers, Stan learned), fed the lambs from a baby bottle, then placed them in a cardboard box. The colostrum, or first milk, was rich in antibodies and proteins and protected lambs from diseases in their first weeks. "I suppose Mr. Ream would have milk replacer," she said.

"I suppose he would," Stan answered.

Doc had reached in a third time and brought the uterus out; it hung over the ewe's sunken belly as if deflated. The ewe heaved another deep sigh, as if reading Stan's mind.

Doc's clean incision revealed the womb's inner walls and numerous nodes that secured the placenta, which Doc detached and removed. Stan always likened the nodes to meatballs—a comparison that arrived as soon he saw them and made him gag if he dwelt on it.

He swallowed hard.

Doc spread a handful of antibiotic powder in the opened organ, then located a bright stainless-steel suturing needle, crescent-curved, already threaded, and clamped in a forceps.

Stan's assistance had been required to hold the sides of the incision together on a cow, as one might do in starting a zipper, and his dad would sew, or suture, the womb shut in one long, continuous stitch. His dad would ease the uterus back in, suture the tissue lining the abdomen, and then sew up the skin.

The job often took two hours.

Doc gently washed the prolapsed part of the uterus, dusted it with the powder, pushed it back in, and sewed the opening shut. "You should remove these stitches in a few days," he told Stan. Doc administered some pills with a balling gun inserted at the back of the sheep's throat, then several shots. After washing his hands, he helped Stan load the ewe into the back of his pickup, which was bedded with straw.

"Donna will take care of the rest," Doc Kelly said. "Everything went as it should. I'm due out in the country."

Stop by any time. We have a complete line of products for sheep."

"I'll do that," Stan said. "And thank you."

"Give my regards to your dad!" the vet said. He put on a coat, a cap and his gloves, and strode out the door.

STAN GAVE DONNA his address and phone number in the clinic's office. She sat at a desk, typed on a computer, and printed out an invoice. "That will be eighty dollars," she said.

"How do you like your new computer system?" Stan asked, handing over a check.

"I think it's great."

Stan set the box with the lambs on the floor of the cab of his pickup, next to the heater vents, so they would stay warm. They didn't make a sound the whole way home. Stan called Chuck on the phone and told him the news.

"Do you have some place to keep them? And the ewe?" Chuck said. "You paid for the surgery. I want you to have them. I'll bring over some hay. And milk replacer—I don't suppose you have any of that. Did I miss anything?"

Love is plainly not enough, Stan thought, unless love comprehends everything else, down to hay and milk. Without love, he concluded, gates and doors slam shut.

"Not a thing," Stan told him.

CHUCK STARTED LAMBING on Valentine's Day, and that day Stan started carrying lambs into their house in Lark—bum lambs or bottle lambs, as they were called. Most were runts, often a twin, or the tail end of a set of triplets, too weak to work at getting a full share of their mother's milk. One was orphaned, its mother dead of a prolapse.

They bought the lambs from Chuck for twelve dollars apiece, and by mid-March they had eight, counting the two earlier premature lambs. Taking in bottle lambs was a way to start building a flock of their own.

Each lamb had individual markings, as all animals do, and something approaching individual character, which Stan began to perceive after several weeks. Each one became dear to them, and each had a rough beginning, Stan thought, as Rose had had.

They boarded the lambs in the basement, where Stan's office had been, in two sunlit pens, four feet square, four lambs to a pen. He constructed a wooden, slatted floor for each pen out of two-by-twos spaced three-quarters of an inch apart; this allowed waste to fall through. While the lambs were on fluids, their manure was like paste.

They fed them from baby bottles—four ounces of milk replacer, made from a powder—five times a day around the clock. The milk replacer was medicated and Stan wished they had goat milk too.

The lambs sucked hard, and butted at the nipples with a force that could raise even ewes off the ground. Dale would fumble the bottle he was holding to a lamb, and then whine. Vernon and Lee would hold on tight with both hands. Stan learned to feed four at a time, two bottles in each hand.

He also gave them alfalfa, which they used mostly to bed down on, all four huddling together for warmth. The basement was forty-five degrees on the average.

He let the lambs loose for exercise each day. They ran in circles around the furnace in the middle of the basement, following the boys' lead, kicking their hind legs as they ran, then halted and sniffed at the furnace, the legs of the wood stove, a bale of alfalfa, and then one another. They nibbled on wood, on Lee (who liked it; it tickled), on

Dale (who backed off from their noses in his face), on a torn spot in Stan's jeans. He often felt surrounded.

They also made puddles on the floor that dried to small, chalky rings. The cool temperature of the basement kept the smell down.

One day Stan heard whimpering when he walked past the door to the basement, which was open a crack. He paused and listened, then swung it wider and went down the steps. The lambs were standing on alfalfa in their pens with their noses in the hay.

Lee was kneeling on the concrete floor with a lamb lying across his lap, crying. He held a pale blue plastic baby bottle in one hand. "She's the littlest one. Why do they have to be so mean?"

"Who's so mean?" Stan said, crouching beside his son. The pale lamb on Lee's lap blinked. Then he noticed something. "What's wrong with her ears?"

"They were chewing on them," Lee said. "The other lambs were chewing on her ears. She was down on her side and couldn't get up."

"I didn't know they chewed on one another."

"Neither did I. They're so cute."

"I suppose we should put something on her ears, iodine or something."

"I sprayed them with stuff mom uses for sunburn."

"Isn't this 'Baby'?" Stan asked.

"Uh huh."

"Let's make her a separate place where she can be by herself, okay?"

"I already fixed up a cardboard box in the corner. I got a blanket, and some hay, and fed her this bottle, and I prayed."

"It looks like you've done all you can then. Is there anything I can do for you?"

"I don't know," Lee said. "I just want to hold her."

"I know how you feel. It was hard for your mom to leave Rose when she had to stay in the hospital and it was time for Mom to come home. It was hard for me to put Rose back in her bassinet and then leave. Grandpa Henry came to see Rose almost every day. Are you sure there isn't something I can do for you?"

"Could you bring me my jacket?"

"You're cold?"

"It's chilly down here."

"How about if I bring you your jacket, and then make a fire in the stove."

"That'd be good," Lee said, perking up.

"Okay," Stan said, rising. "Grandpa T would be proud of you."

"That's what I want to be when I grow up."

"A grandpa?" Stan said.

The lamb raised her head from Lee's lap, then laid it back down.

"That too," Lee said. "But first I want to be a veterinarian."

"HONEY," GRACE SAID in a hushed voice.

He turned and saw her standing in front of the window that had reflected her image on that dark morning when she went into labor with Rose. Grace put a finger to her lips, signaling silence, then pointed into the room.

He turned at the moment when Rose, with a two-handed grasp on a cushion of the couch, pulled herself up on her own for the first time. Rose turned her small face toward him, and her streaked blond hair, the glint in her chocolate-brown eyes, he saw—

She was an image of Grace.

THEY KEPT TRACK of the lambs' progress by marking a calendar and, after six weeks, moved them and their pens to a garage where they kept the ewe. The basement was warming up; the season was changing. The lambs weighed twice what they did at birth and needed more room to run.

Stan and the boys now gave them eight ounces of milk replacer three times a day, then weaned them.

The days grew warmer and longer toward May.

In the first week of May, they let the sheep into the creek pasture they had fenced the fall before. The lambs ran and jumped up in the air, bucking and kicking their hind legs. The lamb named "Baby" had fully recovered.

MORNING, MAY 23rd, Rose's first birthday.

"The experts are replaced, one after another—"

Stan was thinking out loud, and speaking his thoughts to Grace who, he thought, was behind him. "As kings are displaced." He gazed out the door of their house at a sky filled with clouds, receding in rows so regular they seemed to represent regiments.

The roads were beginning to dry out under the strong winds, becoming firm again. The soil in their region was like soup when it was saturated—*gumbo* it was called locally—and hard as stone when was it dry. Their vehicles were sheathed in the stuff, even the windshields smeared in arcs by the wipers, needing to be washed.

Stan turned into the room and sighed. "And I owe Mike money."

Rose took several unsteady steps over the carpet, standing upright, maneuvering among toys at her feet on the living-room floor.

"There's no answer," Grace said from the kitchen, placing the telephone receiver into its cradle. She walked into the living room. "It could mean they're coming."

"Or they're not. Maybe Henry just didn't hear the phone."

"That's possible, but it might also mean they're both coming. You should remember to trust."

The door flung open and Lee stuck his head in. "Somebody's driving up!"

"Grandpa and grandma?" Grace asked.

"I think it's Uncle Jim," Lee answered.

"Uncle Jim? He's early," Grace said. "I wonder why."

Stan said turned to his son. "Come in, or go out. The wind will catch the door."

Lee stepped in and latched the door behind him. Rose tottered across the carpeted floor to him, and Lee lifted her onto a hip. As his mother would hold her, Stan thought.

From the door Stan watched as Jim was led away from his mud-spattered pickup, and the house, by Vernon and Dale, each holding a hand. The merry-go-round, Stan thought. He saw sheep grazing near it in grass lush and deep green. Jim's baseball cap blew off, and Dale ran and retrieved it. "Something must be up."

"You want to go see Uncle Jim?" Lee said to Rose.

"Now don't run with her," Grace said.

"I won't."

"It's muddy besides," Stan told him. "You wouldn't want to slip."

"She's not dressed for the outdoors," Grace said. "Let me get her hooded sweatshirt."

Lee turned his face to his sister, and spoke into her ear. "Let's go see him, okay? And tell him you're one."

"When your mom sees the road, she might just turn right around and go home," Stan said, speaking to Grace.

"Stan, stop it. She wouldn't do that," Grace said. "Her granddaughter's first birthday?"

ROSE WAS READY. Stan followed the others out the door and down the steps. A dry crust over the wet ground, where he had fallen on a dusty day, crunched underfoot, releasing a sense in him of the earth hanging above a watery abyss, depending from heaven, and being lowered from there as it would be again—a new heaven and earth.

Suddenly Rose started to gag.

"The wind's taking her breath away," Grace said. "She'll be all right once we get to the others."

Jim, Vernon, and Dale stood near a wide woven-wire gate that closed off an opening to the former Lark city park—still surrounded by bushes, mostly lilacs, after these many years.

Blossoms were now in bloom, waving in tufted clumps on the stems.

Sheepfold of lilacs, Stan thought. Poor Jim and his allergies. But shelter for Rose.

When they caught up with Jim and the boys, lambs were sticking their heads through squares in the gate.

"They still think we're going to give them their bottles," Vernon told Jim. "But we don't any more."

"You've weaned them," Jim asked, turning to Stan.

"Yes. Welcome to Lark," Stan said.

"We didn't expect to see you this soon," Grace said, and gave Jim a hug. "But it's wonderful to see you,"

"And to be seen." Jim's sunglasses reflected the east morning light.

"Uncle Jim, it's Rose's birthday today," Lee said, turning to the sister riding his hip. "She's one year old."

"Happy birthday, Rose," Jim said. "May I hold her?"

Lee brought her to him, and Jim held her up near his chest. Rose grabbed a bow of Jim's sunglasses, but Jim pulled her fingers loose, and held her hand down.

"It seems strange to me," Stan said. "If she had been born when she was due, on July 4th, she would be only about ten-and-a-half months old today. Yet here she is a year old. She ought to be younger!"

"We have been blessed," Grace said.

Jim placed a hand on Rose's hooded head, and said, "May the LORD bless and keep you, and make His face to shine upon you, and be gracious unto you. May He lift up His countenance upon you, and give you His peace." He spoke face to face, as if exhaling over her.

"I've always loved those words," Grace said.

"Uncle Jim," Vernon said. "Look at our lambs."

Jim handed Rose over to Lee.

Near the gate, Vernon and Dale pulled up fistfuls of grass and held them out to the lambs, who nibbled at them, wrinkling the skin of their noses. Rose pointed to them. Vernon held his hand higher and a lamb lifted its chin to reach up for it.

"Look at his chin," Vernon said.

"It's green!" Lee said. "It's a grass stain."

"A little green beard," Dale said.

"A little goatee," Stan said.

"Those two are big," Jim said, pointing to the twins.

"Those are the preemies," Vernon said. "But, boy, did they grow!"

"Rose has grown," Grace said. "She's begun to pull herself up and walk."

"That's their mother over there by the merry-go-round," Stan said. "At the clinic, they clipped the wool off her side before surgery. You see? It'll be time to shear the rest of her soon. Wool prices are higher than last year, but not much. Thirty cents a pound. I'll take her to Chuck's and I may even give shearing a try, if I can take the strain."

"She couldn't nurse the twins," Grace said. "So we fed them, as we fed the others, from bottles. They came too early, like Rose."

"So did I, to tell you the truth," Jim said. "I forgot about Mountain Time."

"Then you can live a small part of your life over again," Grace said.

And lose it on your way back, Stan almost added, but didn't want to be either exact or negative any more, not on this day.

"It gives me an extra hour with you," Jim pointed out. "I'm afraid I can't stay."

"You can't stay?" Vernon said, disappointed by his tone and look. "We're going to put on a play taken from one by Shakespeare for everybody, and for Grandpa, if he comes."

"No, I'm afraid not. How about a rain check?"

Dale ran up. "May we take Rose to the merry-go-round?"

"Sure," Stan said. "Let me get the gate for you. I don't want you climbing over it." Which is what they did.

"I can get it," Vernon said.

"Dale is speaking more clearly," Jim said to Grace.

"What a difference a year can make!" she said.

Vernon opened the gate just enough for Dale to squeeze through. The lambs gathered around him as he entered, jumping up, butting at his pant legs. Dale took off on a run, all of them chasing after him. Vernon opened the gate for Lee and his sister. "Happy birthday," Vernon said to Rose, as she went past, then he closed the gate, and ran ahead of Lee to the merry-go-round.

"How long can you stay then?" Grace asked Jim.

"A couple hours. Mike called, and I promised to meet him at the ranch. He's planning to sell the ranch, the hog farm, and all his stores."

"He is?" Grace said. "Why's he doing that?"

"And you're helping him through it," Stan said, shaking his head. "Poor—and patient—Jim Fluck."

"He's been taking a beating in the local press ever since he fired the one deputy and the other resigned," Jim said. "The papers reported he was taking trips to Japan at the state's expense."

"Mike said he was on business," Stan interrupted. "*Whose* business was the question."

"Then they reported he had granted state funds to a company he had personal investments in," Jim said.

"Do you believe these reports?" Grace asked.

"All I know," Stan said, "is that when his term ends, they'll appoint somebody else to take over. And what good will that do? They come and they go. It seems only the earth abides forever, doesn't it?"

"Mike is thinking of leaving for good," Jim said. "And moving to Texas, to Houston."

"Maybe Candy will be happier," Grace said.

Mike and Candy, Owen and Claire, all gone, Stan thought, and here we are, settled at last in our native state— an undeserved blessing.

"And you—you're settling here," Jim announced, as if clairvoyant.

"We've upped the population from five to six in just a year's time," Stan said. "Lark is one of the fastest growing towns in North Dakota, percentage-wise."

"And a big garden to match," Jim noted.

"It's roughly sixty feet square," Grace said. "Not sixty square feet, as Stan says when he gets the dimensions mixed up."

"We've been planted here, I believe," Stan said. "Farming is hard to get into. It's hard to find land. It's all in the hands of families that have lived here for years. That's good. That's the way it should be. But I think if we seek the Lord's blessing, our time will come."

"And Butech?"

"Ah, it was sold on the block that day, I've come to feel," he said, glancing at Grace.

"No it wasn't," she said.

"I've tried selling hardware and writing software. The public schools around here all have Apple computers, but the businesses and homes all own IBMs. People don't want to take their computers to a central location where I can give classes, and I don't want to move mine either. So what do you do? I'm trying to put together a lab, but it's already obsolete. I am. Butech is history."

"And the future is sheep," Jim said.

"Yeah, and coyotes."

"A different kind of coyote," Jim said.

"I had a professor once, who said that programs 'ate' data. I suppose I could keep my data on sheep in Coyote, but I wouldn't want coyotes to eat them."

"You guys!" Grace said, then said to Stan. "Does Jim know that Chuck has been talking about taking you on as a partner?"

"Really?" Jim said.

"He and his wife, Evelyn," Stan said. "Their children have grown up and left the farm. He's mentioned this to me several times. But I don't know. I could get in over my head again. His sheep are old; his equipment's run down. With no son or daughter to take over, why keep the place up? Just look at Lark."

Nobody said anything for a moment, as if this remark had hit home harder than Stan had intended. Jim was unmarried, and had no children. Stan stared at the ground, ashamed.

"Chuck and Evelyn are coming for supper," Grace said to Jim. "But you have to go."

"I'm sorry," Jim said then added, "Oh before I forget. I stopped at your mailbox and brought up the mail. It's in the pickup. Let me go get it. There's a package for Rose, and one for you, Stan."

His mother addressed the package addressed to Rose. She had written inside a card: *For Rose. May you bloom, honey. Love, Sig & May.* "Red heart-shaped sunglasses," Grace said, opening the package. "And a little plastic coronet." Grace blew on the instrument, sounding a reedy note.

"For her eyes and lungs, and her heart," Stan said.

"Your mother," Grace said.

The package for Stan was in his dad's hand. The return address was the vet clinic's. Stan found a book inside, thinking, He gave me a book. "*Animal Health,*" he read aloud, showing the cover to Grace. He opened the cover. "He's written something on the inside—*Given to Stanley Thorlofson, May, 1991, by Sigurdur Thorlofson, originally given to Sig by Dr. Bill Vance, North Dakota State Veterinarian.*"

Stan blinked back tears, then drew a deep breath, and let it out slowly. His dad's handwriting, nearly illegible to others, never looked so dear to him.

"Thank you for bringing it, Jim," Grace said.

"It was just in your mailbox."

"Thank you for delivering it, all the same."

"I brought a present for Rose," Jim said. He went to the rear of the pickup, and let down the tailgate.

Stan glanced over the side of the box. I knew it, he said, when he saw. Jim hopped into the box.

"Grace," Stan said. "What would a lumberman, a carpenter's son, bring a country girl on her first birthday?"

Jim, stooping over, waited for her response.

She thought for a moment, then answered, "A rocking horse!"

"Of course!" Jim said. He lifted the wooden figure, and he handed it over the side of the pickup to Stan. "Dad made it. It's a gift from both of us."

"It's beautiful!" Grace said, caressing the wood.

"It sure is. What is this?" Stan said, running a hand over the grain of the saddle seat.

"Hackberry," Jim said. "It grows along the Red River—your country, Stan."

"I've never seen it before."

"Dad knows a fellow from Fargo who cuts it and cures it the old way," Jim said. He jumped onto the ground and closed up the tailgate.

"The grain—the highlights in it are a lot like Rose's streaked hair!" Stan said.

"It's perfect," Grace said. "Thank you, and tell your dad thank you. She'll love it." She clasped Jim's arm to her cheek.

"So will the boys," Stan said. "Though I don't think the bigger boys should ride it."

"No," Grace said. "Maybe Dale."

"One more thing," Jim said, opening the door to his pickup. "I brought these. One for each of them." He turned and brought out three felt cowboy hats in three different colors.

"Oh, Jim, they'll be thrilled," Grace said, taking the hats from him. "Lee will sleep in his."

"What do you think?" Jim said, placing a hand on his own cap. "In this wind?"

"Absolutely!" Stan said.

"WHY DOESN'T EVERYBODY GET ON, and I'll push," Jim said.

"Are you sure?" Stan said.

"Sure I'm sure."

"Did you see how we painted the seats," Vernon said, at his throat the wooden bead of the cowboy hat's chin strings, the red hat itself behind his large head. Climbing over the top of the handlebars, he pointed the seats out to Jim.

"Dad calls it frosty green yellow," Dale told Jim, looking up from under a hat his head swam in, down over his eyebrows.

"I like the color," Jim said, motioning to Stan with his eyes to get a load of his son, then climbed over the handlebars, as Vernon had, into the middle of the merry-go-round. "You boys did a good job."

"Spread out," Stan said. "So we can balance this thing." Grace slid onto a seat; he sat on the other side to complement her, with his dad's gift of the book in his hand. I'll ride one-handed like Dale, he thought.

Lee sat with Rose on his lap, halfway between his father and mother, the strings of the white cowboy hat so tight his cheeks stood out. Vernon and Dale sat beside each other, opposite Lee.

Jim set the merry-go-round in motion, slowly at first, then with a screech. "That center post sure needs some oil," Stan said.

"Do you have a good hold on Rose?" Grace called to Lee.

Yes, he said he did. "Four stiff standers, four dilly danders," he recited in time to the ride's rocking rhythm.

Stan gazed at Jim, the carpenter's son, and felt his vision return to centripetal focus—Jim, clothed in a sky-blue jacket, embroidered with golden thread, dressed in the gold blue of the sky, christened with water. Let's spin and fly out to the hem of it all, he thought, feeling the centrifugal force set in motion by a wonderful friend.

Then he thought—the family has begun to revolve around *him*. He envisioned a common laborer, a hired man, a carpenter when somebody would need a kitchen redone, a plumber, an electrician's helper, a farmer, a computer consultant—brothers in unity, wrapped into one.

"Faster, faster," Dale cried, leaning way back off the seat, holding on with one hand. His hat flew off.

See, what did I tell you, Stan thought.

"Yahoo," Vernon yelled, copying Dale.

"It's fast enough," Stan said, feeling warmth where his legs met.

Him, he thought, a shepherd, a brother, a father, a husband, a son attending to the needs of their flock; and the needs of his sons and his daughter; and of his wife who, Stan hoped, would give birth to yet another child, and raise the population of their village to seven.

JIM extricated himself from the skeletal structure, panting loud. A gust of wind tore through the shelter of the bushes with invisible power, and swiftly passed. Stan glanced at his daughter in his son's arms, then took a deep breath.

"May we take Jim to the creek?" Lee asked. "And bring Rose along with?"

"Yes you may," Stan said.

"I know how a minnow trap works," Vernon told Jim. "How they get in, and why they can't get out again."

"Unless somebody reaches in and pulls them out," Dale added, wearing his cowboy hat again, unconscious, Stan thought, of how the remark applied directly to him. By a trick of hypocrisy, Stan almost let go the thought that it applied directly to *him*. To them both. To us all. How long it takes to reach a conclusion!

Dale, Stan thought. He's a deep mystery, that kid.

Lee took the sunglasses from his mother and put them on. "Now I look like Jim," he said, shielding the glasses from his sister's grasp, as Jim had done.

"You're right," Stan said. "You both see everything through eyes of love."

"Honey," Grace said, "what a sweet thing to say."

Rose began arching her back in Lee's arms. "She's fussing," Grace said, taking the girl from Lee. He asked for the plastic coronet, and Grace handed it to him. "She still wants to nurse, but I've weaned her, too!" Grace said.

"Mom has two dilly danders," Dale said. "Like a sheep."

Grace glanced at Jim, then at her husband. "See what you started."

"I started?" Stan shook his head, and wagged a finger at Dale. "Honor your father *and mother*."

"A wiglet," Dale informed Jim.

"You remind me to trust," Stan told his son, pulling the cowboy hat down over his eyes.

"Grandpa's car!" Lee suddenly shouted, pointing toward a break in the bushes. "I saw it, I saw it drive past!" Lee ran toward the sheep gate. Vernon ran after him. Dale raced after his brothers.

Lee reached the gate and waited for Vernon, who opened it a ways, allowing Lee and Dale to go through, then shut it behind. Vernon, their firstborn, was learning to serve, Stan thought, and it was heartening to see.

"Don't you run out on the driveway," he called after them.

He was about to call a second time, when a car slowly came into view through the squares of woven-wire of the sheep gate. It was Henry's all right, he saw, its metallic-blue glinting in the sunlight, with mud thrown outside its wheelwells onto the fenders on tangents. There were two figures inside the car. The driver was wearing a hat.

When Grace, carrying Rose on her hip, and he reached the sheep gate, Stan glanced back and saw Jim withdraw to the merry-go-round, as if spent, lambs gathering at his feet.

"Are you are right?" Stan called to him.

"I'll catch my breath," Jim said, his sunglasses sparkling. "Look to your family."

The boys lined up along the driveway from oldest to youngest. The car slowed, then stopped beside them.

Vernon bowed in a manner of a Shakespearean prince, flourishing his cowboy hat. Henry opened his window and said hello to his grandsons. Emma waved.

Lee heralded their arrival on the toy coronet like a cavalryman sounding reveille. Henry held onto his hat, and sounded the car horn.

And Dale said, loud enough for everybody to hear, "Honor your grandpa and grandma," his body straight as a fence post, his voice clear as a lark.

It was indication to Stan of what he was beginning to hear across the countryside that season from the throats of robins and meadowlarks, a song carrying spring's tongue to the newborn, plants and animals alike, and to reborn generations of children and grandchildren, as yet unheard from.

Dale's blue hat blew off in the wind a second time, flipping across the road, bumping down. He scurried after it, and caught it on the run, as it held in the grass.

Jim saw a still moment framed by lilacs, purple and white, the sky above, the earth at their feet, the Thorlofson household held between in their unity and separateness.

And then in his recent manner of trying to add levity to the moment, Henry called out, "Anybody home?"